The Amazing Quest of Doctor Syn

Black Curtain Press
PO Box 632
Floyd VA 24091

ISBN 10: 1-61720-977-5
ISBN 13: 978-1-61720-977-2

First Edition
10 9 8 7 6 5 4 3 2 1

The Amazing Quest of Doctor Syn

Russell Thorndyke

With gratitude to George Arliss
Who so brilliantly brought Doctor Syn to life on the screen

Chapter 1. Doctor Syn deals with an Excise Officer

During a midsummer night in the year of Grace 1780, Romney Marsh lay wreathed in a sea-mist which hung in thick walls over the dykes and floated in wispy shapes across the broad fields which they divided. Flocks of sheep huddled in the centre of these many meadows, as though avoiding the broad white ribbons of fog which hid the bulrushed waters.

Had any traveller been crossing the treacherous marshes he could not have failed to notice that the animals were in dread of something that moved under cover of the dyke-water fog.

But there was no traveller crossing the Marsh that night, for it had been whispered behind the barred doors of every isolated cottage that the sinister Scarecrow and his Night-riders were out, and it was not healthy for a lone wayfarer to fall in with that crew, desperate men all, with the shadow of the gallows ever before them. It was the new hands who feared the law most, though their elders told them that the Scarecrow was infallible, and that so long as they obeyed orders the rawest recruits need have no fear of the revenue men.

The Scarecrow ruled his men well. For years he had terrorized the level lands reclaimed from the sea, which stretch from Sandgate to the Sussex border. His organization stretched farther, for his agents worked the smuggled goods to London, which was linked to the coast by a long chain of convenient 'hides', and up and down the road to the capital his orders were carried secretly. Such followers as might have been tempted to turn King's evidence against him did no such foolish thing, for he saw to it that they never lacked money in their purses, and they knew very well that their leader could deal with treachery in a surer manner even than the law and its scaffold. Besides this, it had been proved that his spy system was most competent. Even the mail coaches were impressed into his service, and the tunes that were wound on the guards' horns sounded his warning messages, so that a farmer awaiting letters or packages at the door of a coaching inn would know before the vehicle came into sight what was happening to the free-traders both up and down the roads.

Very often, when he received his goods from the guard or was taking a drink with the driver, it would be whispered in his ear that he was to place three cows and his white horse, or two bullocks and his bay horse, in such and such a field, which carried the news across the valley that all was safe to proceed, or that the revenue men were out up yonder and the goods must remain in hiding.

Then the woodlump was not disturbed till another signal was passed for their hide to be moved.

Who was the Scarecrow? There were only two men who knew, and they would have gone to the scaffold rather than betray their leader's identity. One of these men was Jimmie Bone the highwayman, who, by reason of his daring riding and a similarity in height, was able to impersonate his chief when it became necessary for the Scarecrow to be in two places at once.

The other man who knew who it was beneath the Scarecrow's hideous mask and ragged cloak, was Mipps, the sexton of Dymchurch-under-the-Wall, which was the principal village beneath the old Roman sea-wall. This stalwart little fighting rat of a man had served his master aboard a pirate ship when the Scarecrow had been known on the high seas as Captain Clegg. The best part of his life he had given to his service, and as Hellspite he rode second in command of the Night-riders on Romney Marsh. He also served him as general parochial factotum when his versatile master was ministering as Vicar of Dymchurch and Dean of the Peculiars, and it was he who discovered that George Plattman, Excise Officer, thought a good deal, suspected too much and then, ignoring constant warnings, became daring; so daring, indeed, that the Scarecrow was forced to put an end to him.

Now there was a field, and one field only, which boasted a hummock on Romney Marsh, and on this particular night, just as the watchman made his rounds in Dymchurch, crying out, 'One o'clock, and a starry night, with a seamist blowing and All's Well,' the sheep crept closer to this hummock bleating with terror.

Who was it they feared? Just what they had often seen in the dark hours and could not understand. Wild mounted men who would suddenly squeal and howl and gallop from the ribbons of mist. The Scarecrow's Night-riders. The beings who frightened folk from the Marsh. Suddenly the huddled, bleating sheep began to scamper, scattering here and there in panic, as from every side of the field's mist walls the weird horsemen appeared.

The horses they rode were wild and vigorous, and their faces shone with a phosphorescent light. The riders' faces were as uncanny, for they wore grinning masks that glowed in the darkness. The clothes they disguised themselves in were wild black rages that streamed behind them as they galloped to the hummock.

A terrible figure, the Scarecrow, as he cried out, 'Whoa Gehenna!' Gehenna roared, kicked the air with his forelegs, and then came to rest with a screaming neigh that rang across the Marsh.

'Messengers report,' cried the Scarecrow. 'Curlew!' Immediately, from the front rank of the massed circle of horsemen, one rode forward, holding his pistol high above his head and crying out 'Curlew!'

When he reached the base of the hummock, he croaked out, 'Orders carried out, Scarecrow. All's Well!'

'Falcon!' ordered the Scarecrow.

Another horseman took Curlew's place, the forelegs of his wild horse resting against the steep sides of the hummock beneath the towering Scarecrow.

With his pistols held high, he too croaked out in the voice of a carrion bird, 'Orders carried out, Scarecrow. All's Well!' Five of the fifty took part in this ritual—Curlew, Falcon, Owl, Raven, Eagle.

And then the Scarecrow cried, 'Vulture!' There was a hesitation before this messenger rode forward. He seemed to have some difficulty with his horse, and did not show the same precision as the others. It seemed that he was not used to riding with his pistol held high above his head. When he reached the hummock, however, he answered boldly, 'Vulture. Orders carried out, Scarecrow. All's Well!'

'All is not well,' replied the Scarecrow, in a hard voice. 'You are not Vulture, though you wear his mask. You are George Plattman, excise officer, and a spy.'

'Fulfilling his duty, Master Scarecrow,' called back the other in as sharp a voice. Then down came his right arm, and his pistol flashed point blank at the figure above him.

The Scarecrow did not move. Only his black horse uttered a scream as his nostrils sniffed the powder.

As the fifty horsemen silently covered him with their pistols, the desperate excise officer realized that his pistol must have been tampered with, for the Scarecrow had taken no hurt. The alert little Hellspite had ridden beside him most of the way, and he remembered that he had been jostled twice when crossing one of the dykes. Mipps knew a trick or two, which the excise officer should have been more careful not to have had played upon him. Then the Scarecrow spoke again.

'The ball has not yet been cast that can penetrate the Scarecrow's heart. Nor will it be. But it is well for us that you cannot boast the same. You have been warned repeatedly to lay off our tracks. Had you caught us, the authorities would have sent us to our deaths. Now we catch you, and we are forced to send you to yours.' Out came two pistols from his holsters, and both barrels flashed. Without a groan the government spy slid from his saddle. Immediately Hellspite closed in on the riderless horse and seized its bridle. Then, leaning down over the still man on the ground, he fired his pistol into the corpse, saying, 'All are in this with the Scarecrow.' One by one the fifty horsemen walked their horses past the murdered man, and as each passed, he fired his pistol into the corpse as Hellspite had done.

The last two to fire dismounted and lifted the body. They were about to throw it across the saddle of the riderless horse when the Scarecrow, who had thrust his pistols back into his holsters, interrupted them. 'No! In front of me! Gehenna can carry us both. It will be quicker, and Hellspite can lead the spare horse.' The body was carried up the hummock, lifted to the great black horse of the Scarecrow, and doubled over, arms and legs hanging on each side in front of the grim rider, who cried out, 'And now, my merry lads, follow me to the Kent Ditch. The body must be found across the Sussex border.' Waving his hand, he turned his horse, and, steadying the corpse before him as he rode down the hummock, he dug in his heels and with a wild yell dashed for the curtain of mist and leapt the hidden dyke. After him went his fifty horsemen, and not till they had all disappeared did the frightened sheep huddle back around the deserted hummock.

Meanwhile in stables far and near upon the Marshes and up in the hills of Lympne and Aldington, tired pack-ponies were being rubbed down after their exertion of carrying brandy barrels from the sea to hiding. From the stables to the houses the others carried the news that the Scarecrow had accomplished another successful 'run'.

And what of the Scarecrow after he had tumbled the corpse on to the Sussex bank of the boundary ditch? Why, back to Romney Marsh he galloped at the head of his Night-riders, after Hellspite had lashed the riderless horse in a mad stampede towards Rye, where it was found wandering by a coastguard at dawn.

Just before the first streaks of dawn had appeared over the sea, an old hag of a woman named Mother Handaway, who lived in a tumble-down cottage surrounded by dyke water in the middle of

Romney Marsh, was busily brewing a queer concoction in a cauldron that hung over a mud-clod fire. She was reputed on the Marsh to be a witch who had dealings with the devil. Certainly she herself thought she had, but the devil whom she faithfully served was none other than the Scarecrow who rode at the head of the Romney Marsh smugglers.

Having disbanded his followers outside the old village of Brooklands, the Scarecrow, now accompanied only by Hellspite, rode fast towards Mother Handaway's.

The old woman, hearing the riders approach, opened the cottage door and saw the two horsemen jump the dyke. As they swept by the cottage, she knelt on the threshold, covering her face with her claw-like fingers, and muttering, 'Welcome, Masters.' The two riders pulled up in front of a dilapidated cowbarn. Behind this was a deep dry dyke with great piles of dried bulrushes stacked up against its side. Riding their horses down into this ditch, they were immediately hidden from the level of the Marsh, even though they were still mounted. Then Hellspite slid from his horse's back, and, pulling at a section of the bulrush stack, he swung open a door so covered with rushes that it would have been unnoticed to anyone not in the secret. Above it grew the rich marsh grass, but the open door revealed a stone-built underground stable. The Scarecrow, bending low to his horse's neck, rode through it, followed by his companion leading his horse. The little man let his animal walk to its own stall, while he closed the door behind them.

Had an observer watched the uncanny pair enter the stable, he would have been astonished. But had he waited some twenty minutes while the two spirited animals were groomed, watered and fed, he would have been even more astounded at the metamorphosis of the two riders when they came out again leading a fat little white pony and a donkey. Once more the door was closed, and no one would have believed in its existence. Nobody was near, however, but Mother Handaway, who knew very well the miraculous ways of her master the devil, who ruled the Marsh at night; so often had she seen him enter the stable after a ride in the hideous mask which struck fear to all who beheld it, and then emerge in no less a disguise than that of Doctor Syn, the respected and dearly loved Vicar of Dymchurch. Similarly his companion, who had entered as the devilish Hellspite, would reappear in the guise of the quizzical sexton and undertaker, Mr. Mipps.

Mother Handaway knew, however, that both these disguises hid the same creatures—the devil himself and his attendant spirit. Before mounting the ample back of his pony, the figure of Doctor Syn towered over her and cautioned her to be faithful to his service. When she muttered, 'Yes, Master,' he dropped a bag of guineas on the ground in front of her, then rode away at a slow jog-trot for the nearest dyke bridge, for the pony was not able to leap the water like Gehenna. He was followed by the sexton astride the churchyard donkey.

Mr. Mipps had his own method of riding this animal, which on orthodox occasions pulled the stone roller over the Vicarage lawns, or nibbled the grass between the graves in the churchyard. The rider sat far back on the animal's rump, and with both hands steered the reins like the ropes of a rudder. A comical figure, Mr. Mipps, but more comical than ever when aboard the churchyard donkey in the wake of his master.

Not until both riders were over the bridge and had turned on to the winding marsh road did the claw-like fingers of Mother Handaway grasp the devil's payment, which she carried into her hovel, where she counted the contents of the bag with greed and then concealed it with many other bags within the straw mattress of her bed. She told herself that she was rich, for her dread master had kept his bargain by paying well, and would continue to do so while she kept her promise to keep her mouth shut about his night visitations. She was never to describe him to the revenue men. She never had. But she had played the spy for him, and had given him information against George Plattman, for which she had received three extra guineas. No, she would never betray so generous a master, and if it pleased him, as the day broke, to disappear in the likeness of the Dymchurch parson, that was no affair of hers.

Half an hour later the white pony and comical donkey were stabled at the vicarage, and a new day was brightening the sky. 'A good night's work, Mister Mipps,' said the genial vicar, as he parted from the sexton at the vicarage door.

'Get along now and snatch what sleep you can.'

'Aye, aye, sir,' returned Mipps, and he trotted off through the deserted village street to his coffin shop on the edge of the Marsh. He shut the door of his work-shed, lit a tallow dip and placed it on the floor beneath a ship's hammock, into which he swung himself with an old sailor's agility. He pulled off his coat, and spread it on his lap. Then, as he took off his shoes, he began talking aloud to a large spider which had run out to look at him from a hole in the rafter which supported the hammock.

'Sorry to disturb you, Horace,' he chuckled, as he puffed tobacco smoke from his short clay pipe in the direction of the insect. 'I shall not be swinging like this from your rafter tomorrow night, because as you know I like best of all to sleep in a coffin, and by then I shall have knocked one up. Nice big coffin for the revenue man. Yes, Horace. He's gone. Dead! Quite dead! Too bad! They'll find him riddled with lead in the Kent Ditch; Sussex side, of course. Things like that don't happen in Kent. "Naughty Sussex smugglers", they'll say, and they'll bring him to me to knock up solid. Like to come to the funeral, Horace? Swell affair! Gallant officer dies in execution of his duty. Everyone in tears.

You'd have to be in 'em too, Horace. You'd be able to crawl down into the grave and take a last look. I'll see no one steps on you. Well, make up your mind, and let me know. Good night, or rather, good morning.' Mipps flung one shoe over the rafter, just to give Horace a fright; the other he dropped with accuracy on the flame of the tallow dip, and as the day began to shine through the closed shutters, Mipps closed his eyes and pulled hard at his red-hot pipe.

Doctor Syn was not in the habit of keeping a tame spider to converse with, but before reaching his bed he had a conversation nevertheless, for Mrs. Fowey, his capable old housekeeper, always rose with the dawn, and on this morning she met the vicar as he was climbing the stairs.

'Been out across the Marsh,' he explained. 'That poor old Mother Handaway has had a recurrence of her ailment. Mr. Mipps brought me the news of her sad condition last night after you had retired to your quarters. I took her out some nourishment and conversed with her upon the scriptures during the night.'

'And a lot of good that did her, I'll be bound,' replied the housekeeper acidly. 'She's a dirty old pickle-pot of witchcraft, with her cauldron asimmering and them cats.'

'Come now, Mrs. Fowey,' reproved the doctor kindly. 'You must please remember that she is one of my flock. A poor old mad thing, no doubt, and not so brisk and young as yourself. So you can afford to be charitable.' Mrs. Fowey, well pacified with this compliment, replied, 'Aye, sir, and if the poor body is haunted by the devil, your visits must drive him away, for we all knows that you are an angel in disguise.'

'Nonsense!' returned Doctor Syn, with such conviction that the old housekeeper said to herself, 'And the dear good gentleman really believes it is nonsense.'

Doctor Syn knew very well that it was nonsense; and, asking that a dish of chocolate should be brought to him at eight o'clock, he climbed the remaining stairs to bed.

After changing his clerical clothes for nightshirt and cap, he sat for some minutes in the great four-poster bed, with hands clasped round his drawn-up knees. He was thinking of the possible difficulties that might confront him when the body of the murdered exciseman was discovered. As the Dymchurch officer, he would be brought to the Court House. The twelve good men and true who would sit at the inquest would all be Scarecrow's men; and the good squire, Sir Antony Cobtree, in a well-chosen speech, would see to it that his parishioners were kept free from any suspicion of having had a hand in foul play. It would be laid against the Sussex smugglers, and he himself as vicar would pray that Heaven would avenge the brave officer who had fallen at the hands of such wicked men. Doctor Syn wasted not a second in regrets. He had fought out the question days before and had come to the conclusion that in order to save his followers the officer must be sacrificed. The fellow had been warned repeatedly to keep clear of the Marsh at night, and to turn the other way, if during his watch upon the sea-wall he should happen to see suspiciouslooking vessels heading for the bay. No, the excise officer had had to die, and he was now dead. He had sealed his fate when he had discovered that old Mother Handaway was in some way connected with the Scarecrow. Many a night he had been seen crawling along under the protection of the deep dyke banks. Once he had waded through the water and for an hour had watched the cow-barn, behind which the hidden stable lay. The Scarecrow's spies had duly reported this to Sexton Mipps, who immediately informed his master. The very next day the excise officer had visited the old witch, told her of his suspicions and commanded her help in the name of the law.

'Unless you wish to find yourself up for trial,' he had threatened, 'you will inform me when the next "run" is to take place. I should not be surprised to learn that this is the devil's tiring-house. If so it will be easy for you to provide me with one of his uniforms. These Night-riders do not frighten me. They are flesh and blood beneath their masks and cloaks, and it is their business to protect the pack-ponies, by frightening unwanted folk from the Marsh. Well, I intend to ride with them and see for myself. I will provide a horse, and you my rags, and then I shall meet the Scarecrow face to face. So get me information.' The terrified old woman sought the advice of Doctor Syn, and he advised her to do just what the good officer asked. So the officer had ridden with the Scarecrow's men, who were one and all commanded to address him as Vulture, and the adventure had resulted in a corpse lying on the Sussex side of the

Kent ditch.

'Well, God rest his soul,' though Doctor Syn, as his hand felt for a brandy bottle hidden behind the books by his bedside. Favourite books these, which the housekeeper was enjoined never to touch. As he tilted the good liquor down his throat and pictured the exciseman looking up at the sky with glazed eyes, he began to hum the song he had written before as a chantey, when as Captain Clegg he had sailed a pirate ship.

Oh, here's to the feet what have walked the plank, Yo-ho for the dead man's throttle!

On the other side of the village Mipps still smoked with his eyes shut. He felt in a happy mood and was not at all exercised in mind as to possible dangers. He trusted his master to cope with any difficulties that might arise.

Neither had he any creepy feelings that Horace might crawl along the rafter and drop down on him. He never slept with his mouth open, but with teeth clenched about the short stem of his pipe, and when he snored he did so through his long thin nose.

In all probability Horace thought that the little sexton was more creepy than himself. Swinging himself to sleep in that hammock Mipps no doubt looked to Horace like the most enormous spider in a web, and the glow from the pipe an evil eye.

But Mipps was not thinking of Horace. He was thinking of the coffin which he would be called upon to make for the remains of the man they had murdered. It would command a good price. A hero of the law would be buried well. So he swung himself backwards and forwards, and then from side to side; and while the tobacco still burned in his pipe, he sang the song of his profession:

We're the undertakers undertaken to provide
The elongated coffin with your fitting shell inside.
For be you the gentility or rank you in the poor,
You all has to pass through the coffin-shop door.
Now the doctor tells the parish clerk a case has gone astray,
The parish clerk informs the shop just in a business way.
The sexton is bespoken, and he grasps his dirty spade:
But ere he's shoulder-high-below, we've got the coffin made.
For we're the undertakers, and we takes the doctor's case,
And cases it in coffin wood, with very little space.
You cynics call us squalid, but we knocks you all up solid.
You all has to pass through the coffin-shop door.

After singing this song once, Mr. Mipps hummed it through
again, and then gave himself a further 'encore'. But in the middle
of the first verse, this time, his voice gave way to a long nasal
snore. The sexton was asleep. Horace the spider crawled nearer.

Chapter 2. Doctor Syn and a stranger in Dymchurch

On a hot summer's afternoon of the day following the inquest held to inquire into the death of the exciseman, Mr. Mipps, sexton of Dymchurch, was digging a suitable grave. As undertaker to Romney Marsh, he had finished a suitable coffin that very morning, and the corpse was already screwed down awaiting burial.

Despite the heat and the hard work, Mipps was enjoying himself. The whole affair had worked itself out very nicely. Without question, the guilt had been fastened upon certain Sussex persons unknown, who were concerned in the nefarious pursuit of smuggling.

After stating how thankful he was that no suspicion could fall upon his own beloved village, the squire of Dymchurch shook his head sadly and said, 'Very reprehensible.' Mr. Mipps allowed himself the privilege of muttering 'Horrible!' quite audibly, and then added with a touch of burning zeal, 'Sussex didn't ought to allow such things.'

'May such transgressors be forgiven in the Later Day,' breathed Doctor Syn in solemn charity. He then expatiated upon the virtues, the manly virtues, of the deceased officer who had fallen so nobly in the exercise of his duty.

Recalling all this in his toil, Mipps worked cheerfully, for it meant not only money in his purse, but the end of one who could now make no more trouble.

He worked harder when he realized that one foot deeper would be sufficient, and that he could then cool himself in the Ship Inn by pouring good spirits down his parched throat. He worked harder still when he heard the voice of Doctor Syn humming a hymn as he strolled from the vicarage garden into the churchyard.

'Ah, Mister Mipps! Hot work I fear.' Mipps looked up from the grave at the tall thin parson above him, and nodded. 'Might have been hotter, sir,' he said with a wink. 'In matters of death, I says, one's better than lots!' Doctor Syn returned the nod sadly without the suspicion of a wink. 'It is expedient that one should die for the people. A scapegoat, eh?'

'Quite right, sir,' answered Mipps. 'Them elders of the people in the scriptures knew a trick or two, same as them Sussex smugglers do, by killing one to save the many.'

Doctor Syn placed his right foot upon the sexton's barrow, and, with his elbow on his knee, leant forward and peered into the grave. 'Sussex smugglers may sound well enough to a Dymchurch jury, Mipps,' he said, 'but I am thinking that the authorities elsewhere may suspect a closer connection with the Romney Marsh. In any case they will be expecting a quiet time. The death of an officer of the Crown is serious, and the smugglers of both counties will wait till this outrage is forgotten. That is what the authorities will be thinking, Mipps.' Doctor Syn dropped his voice to a whisper, and added, 'But the Scarecrow is not to be intimidated even though his followers may be. Pass the word at once that nothing is to be changed till after tomorrow, and then, well, perhaps a little rest would be healthy. I am now going to take a stroll upon the sea-wall, and then I hope the parish will leave me in peace for an hour or so, as I intend to pen a sermon for next Sunday morning.'

To Mipps this innocent sentence meant that the vicar would be alone in his study and ready to receive him, should he have anything urgent to report.

Mipps watched the vicar stride away towards the sea-wall, with his Bible in one hand and his brass telescope under his arm, and he told himself that his old master was still as cool a customer as he had ever been during the long years they had worked together. Then, finishing off the grave to his satisfaction, he climbed out of it, pulled on his coat and set out for the Ship Inn across the road.

He knew that the tap-room would be full by now, for it was just about the time which the Scarecrow had arranged for word to be passed, and it was Mipps who was responsible for the passing. The front of the Ship Inn faced the sea-wall and was built in a plain but stately style. The back, however, was homely, with innumerable little outbuildings, servants' cottages, stables and sheds. Whereas most of the patrons of the tap-room used the back entrance, Mr. Mipps preferred the front, for he liked to take a look at the sea-wall standing up against the sky across the broad field. It was there that the coastguards walked and swept the Channel fairway with their spy-glasses, and as often as not they would see the good vicar sweeping it too with his telescope, or Mipps peering out from under the shelter of his hand.

Mipps would explain to them that he watched the sea because he had spent his life upon it, whereas they watched it, so he would tell the coastguards, merely in the way of their duty. 'And a very good duty too,' he would say, 'looking after us so pleasant and

keeping our nice coast clear of smugglers and such bad things.'
The coastguards on their part were never quite sure about Mipps;
for although he took their position very seriously, and showed an
interest in their work, they were sometimes a little suspicious that
he was laughing at them.

That smuggling went on upon the Marsh they were well aware,
for the Scarecrow and his fearsome Night-riders had been seen by
many in the dead of night, so that the winding paths that zigzagged
along the dykes were avoided by those who were cautious. A
cracked skull remembers little; a dead man in a dyke, nothing.

In front of the inn, Sir Antony Cobtree, astride a magnificent
bay, was drinking ale from a pint tankard. As Mipps approached
the squire was talking to an ostler, but, seeing Mipps, he broke off
to ask him heartily what he would take, 'For I saw you digging
away over yonder, and in such heat it must be thirsty work.'

'Thankee kindly, sir,' replied Mipps respectfully. 'Rum.' The
ostler ran off to fetch it. Mipps did not tell the squire that digging
a grave was such thirsty work that he always carried a bottle of
rum into it, or that the bottle was now empty but would soon by
replenished. He just hoped that the squire would not see the shape
of it in the set of his capacious tailpocket.

'A very grievous thing, Mr. Mipps,' said the squire, 'this death of
poor George Plattman. A very sound officer! He played his part well,
but he did a foolish thing in riding so far by himself. He should
have taken his men with him.' Mipps shook his head. 'No, sir,' he
replied. 'If you will pardon the contradiction. But that would never
have been George Plattman's way. He would have thought of our
safety first, sir, as he did, and left his men to protect us here where
they belong.'

'The Government should see that their officers are not so
shorthanded,' said the squire.

'Aye, aye, sir,' agreed Mipps. 'They ought to have lots and lots
more men, especially for patrolling on the Sussex border. Plattman
often told me that it was there that the mischief went on. A very
strong gang of desperate fellows from Rye, he thought, and he
ought to have known. His only fault, if I may say so, was being just
a bit too zealous to duty, what wasn't his duty at all. He should
have been content to hide here where he was safe, instead of
poking his nose into the doings of the next county. Very sad
though, sir! He was very much liked too, sir. How he would have
enjoyed the coffin I've made for him! I wish he could have seen it.
He'd have scored me up a rum or two for all the trouble I've took.'

The ostler brought out the rum, and took the squire's empty tankard. 'Your Honour's health,' said Mipps, and tossed it down. A noggin of rum was nothing to him; he preferred to drink from the bottle. So he was relieved when the squire said, 'Thankee, Mr. Mipps,' and turned his horse towards the Court House stables.

Mipps stood touching his forelock till the squire had ridden round the corner, and then he swaggered through the door, crossed the inn hall and so into the tap-room.

Now Mipps was perhaps the best-known man upon the Marsh, especially amongst those of his own class. The gentry treated him with deference above his station, by reason of a quizzical something about him which they failed to understand. They put him down as 'quite a character' and allowed him to give his opinions. He invariably got the truth out of people too, for when he asked a question he conveyed by a guarded reserve that, since he knew the correct answer, the other had best tell the whole truth and nothing but the truth. The vicar's high opinion of him went a long way to ensure his popularity, but even those who thought him comical admitted that there was a 'something about him'. A mysterious man! His own class understood him better, and would answer him with a wink, for they knew his language, and to know that was to understand the Scarecrow's orders, which, if obeyed, meant money in their pockets, but if disregarded, quick disaster.

Mipps had a system of wrapping up his master's orders in the simplest sentences, readily received by those in the know. A movement of the hand; higher or lower inflections of the voice; suddenly speaking vaguely with his eyes shut; the movement of his pipe from one side of his mouth to the other; these and a hundred other tricks stressed the important words of the sentence, and were easier to translate by those concerned than the learning of the alphabet.

So now when he entered the tap-room, the noisy welcome with which he was received very quickly died down into silence, so that he would be free to convey something to their advantage.

'A very nice warm day,' he said, 'and although the wiseacres predict a sudden change, I says THERE WILL BE NO CHANGE. Anyhow I says there'll be NO CHANGE TOMORROW.' He then turned to the landlady and nodded, 'Thankee, Mrs. Waggetts, rum if you please, ma'am.' she had it ready for him and he raised his glass saying, 'I drinks to the memory of the poor brave man whose grave I have just dug. This will be a serious business for some scoundrels. And if the weather breaks and we gets wet just now, you farmers will be having a serious time too with your crops. A QUIET TURN FOR A SPELL.' This innocent speech, being translated by the outward signs of the sexton's gestures, was as plain in its meaning to those who waited for it as it had been to Mipps when Doctor Syn had spoken to him by the grave, saying that although the murder was a serious matter, and the authorities would expect a quiet time from the smugglers, who would lie low for a while, the Scarecrow would not alter his plans for the run the next night, but that afterwards the business would be given a quiet turn for a spell. After any message had been thus delivered from the Scarecrow, it was customary for the whole assembly to break out into lively conversation and loud laughter, so that any important whisperings in explanation could not be noticed by a possible spy.

It was during this usual din, following the sexton's speech, that the mail coach rumbled up in front of the 'Ship' to deposit the letters for the village. It also deposited a traveller and his valises, who, never having visited Romney Marsh in his life, went to some pains in order to assure himself that there was no mistake about his destination.

'Do you mean to tell me that this is the place I am seeking?' he asked the guard, who, not used to having his word called in question, replied curtly, 'This is Dymchurch, sir, as I told you.'

'But it was Dymchurch-under-the-Wall for which I booked by seat,' retorted the passenger.

The guard was about to answer irritably, but, seeing the little fat gentleman blinking about him like a bewildered owl, he had a suspicion that he was not quite all right in the head, and should be humoured.

'Dymchurch-under-the-Wall is right, sir. This is the "Ship" o' Dymchurch, and that there thing yonder—that grassy bank hiding the sea—is the Wall. And if that there wall was to break, this village would be Dymchurch-under-the-Sea instead of under-the-Wall.'

'And a very neat way of putting it,' thought the guard.

The pompous little passenger, who had followed the direction of the guard's pointing finger, seemed still a bit doubtful. 'And you call that grass bank a seawall, do you?' he asked with a supercilious sniff. 'Now, where I come from—' This was too much for the guard, who cut in with, 'You wouldn't find such a good sea barrier as that. From the time of the Romans it has stood good friend to the Marshmen, and the sheep have nibbled its rich side from them days to these.'

'I dare say it's a good enough bank in its way—' argued the

other.

Again he was interrupted. 'I tell you, sir, it's a wall. There's masonry enough on it sea side to warrant the name. Great fat boulders almost as big as your—' he was about to say 'belly', but thought the better of it and added 'you'.

The passenger frowned and gave a tug to his waistcoat. Then, turning from the distant sea-wall, he looked at the inn and frowned at that. 'Is this the best inn the village can boast?'

'It's the largest of the three, anyhow,' explained the guard. 'And since the Lords of the Level house their great china punch-bowl in her dining-room, I suppose it would be termed the best. Two other good ones though, sir.'

'Bring in my baggage then,' ordered the passenger, 'and I'll be taking a glass of something while I have a look.' Having made up his mind to enter the inn, the stranger seemed to shed his doubts though not his displeasure, and as he strutted into the hall and looked about him, the guard said to the driver, 'Thought he was an owl till now, but he's more like a pouter-pigeon. Well, he ain't my fancy, and I doubt that I shall earn the price of a drink for all the trouble I've took on the way down to interest him. He's close he is, and I should think he's down here on no good.'

'Pass that warning on to Mister Mipps,' answered the driver, 'and then all his no good won't do no harm. The little sexton's bound to be within, and he'll soon find out if the stranger is here to nose about under the wall.' Meanwhile the stranger in question, finding no one in the hall and seeing no one in the large dining-room, resolved to enter the tap-room, from which he heard shouts of laughter and high-pitched conversation. As he pushed open the door, the top of which was panelled with bottle glass, all he could see was a vast cloud of tobacco smoke. Although at first he could only see vague forms in the crowd, the draught from the door in which he stood cleared the smoke from him, and he was conscious that everyone was taking sudden and silent stock of him. Every voice had been cut off. Instead of the chattering babble and uproarious laughter, this resentful hush at his entrance made our traveller selfconscious. He knew that the silence was not meant for respect. As the smoke cleared further he saw that every settle, bench, chair, stool, and even tables, were occupied with sitting men who stared at him sullenly. His appearance had arrested their very movement. He saw some with their tankards half-way to their mouths, and he noticed four men who had been playing dice round a table, and he whose turn it was to cast still held the dice-box in his hand and was half-heartedly shaking it in mid-air, but with all his concentration was watching as the rest. Over the dice-box he fixed the stranger with a gimlet eye; then he pointed to the bar on the traveller's left.

As the stranger stared back at him haughtily, the man with the dice-box approached him, and in silence led him to the bar. 'Missus Waggetts,' he said in a hoarse whisper, and then by way of explanation added, 'landlady of the "Ship".' He then turned to Mrs. Waggetts and with a gesture of introduction said, 'Mrs. Waggetts—a stranger. Nice gentleman named—?' Here he looked for the gentleman to give his name, but failing to get any reply, added, 'From?' Again he was disappointed, and it was obvious to the rest that although the stranger had accompanied his guide to the bar, he did not intend to be communicative.

Staring hard at his self-elected guide, the stranger saw a little man with thin wiry limbs, sharp-eyed, and with a long pointed nose that reminded him of a ferret. Despite his somewhat rusty black suit, which gave him a sombre dignity, there was a jauntiness about him, which he was unable to hide, and which smacked of the sea. His tarred queue, which stuck straight out from beneath his three-cornered hat, encouraged this nautical appearance. This curious individual, not being able to make the strange gentleman communicative, and knowing well that the eyes of the tap-room were upon him and expecting results, began a new attack, by being communicative himself.

Pointing to himself, and fixing the stranger with his sharp eyes, he said, 'Me? Mister Mipps. Sexton! Clerk! Undertaker! Verger! General Store-keeper! Carpenter! Blacksmith! And what's more, right-hand man in all matters spiritual and otherwise to the vicar. And now, sir. Just off the Mail Coach, I take it? And here's Edward the guard come in for his usual, I see.' With a 'How do, all?' the guard approached the stranger. 'Your baggage is all put together, sir.'

'Where?' asked the gentleman.

'Mrs. Waggetts, the strange gentleman can speak,' said Mipps in an audible whisper.

'Hall in the 'all,' explained the guard.

'And we'll be hall and hall the better for a drink,' said Mipps, imitating the guard's speech with a wink to the stranger. 'You'll excuse Edward, sir. Very casual with his aitches. Not so me. Have to come in first with the Amens you see, and the vicar is very particular.'

'Queer sort of parish clerk, I must say,' said the stranger. 'You look to me far more fitted to the lower deck of a ship, than to the lower deck of a threedecker.'

'Funny you should say that!' replied Mipps, looking pleased. 'Was a sailor most of my life. Captured by pirates I was too, and pressed to become their carpenter. But the Lord delivered me from the jaws of the lions and once more I became a carpenter on one of His Blessed Majesty's ships o' war. But belay there, Mipps, for you're keeping the gentleman from his drink. Now sir!' Rattling the dice, he threw a four and a three upon the bar, swept the dice back and handed the box to the guard.

Edward threw a five and a three.

'And last, but I hopes not least, hand it to the gentleman, Edward,' ordered Mipps.

The stranger felt that he could do nothing else but throw, and out rattled a double six.

'Now I never did!' said Mipps with a sigh. 'Them dice ought to have better manners towards a stranger. The honours are yours, sir. On Romney Marsh a double six means "doubles" all round. Ill luck indeed, sir!' Though he failed to see the justice of this Mr. Mipps and his dice-box, the gentleman produced a guinea from his pocket, threw it on the counter and nodded to the landlady.

'Give them whatever they take, my good woman,' he said, allowing a smile to creep into his face for the first time. 'A traveller must abide by the customs he encounters, although I doubt the justice and truth of this one, Mister Mipps.'

'Everyone's entitled to his own opinion, sir, and no offence took,' answered Mipps generously. 'And the best of health to you, sir.' He drank off the double rum which Mrs. Waggetts had supplied to him before the rest, and pushed it back to make room for the glass of sherry which the gentleman had ordered for himself. He knew that the landlady would fill it up again when the gentleman's back was turned.

The stranger looked round the room, and holding up his glass in salute, said, 'I fear I have interrupted your merriment. Please take your drinks and continue your talking. This silence is disconcerting to me, and makes me think that I may not be welcome.' 'As to that, sir,' put in Mipps, 'we can hardly tell, not knowing who or what you are. You may be one of them Parliament troublers for all we know.'

'And what trouble do you suppose I could cause down here?' asked the stranger.

'That's right, sir, you couldn't,' said Mipps in a tone of relief. 'We're independent on the Marsh. Our own laws, sir, from the time of William the Third. Dymchurch has its own Court House, sir, and whatever you do don't go stealing sheep, 'cos our squire can hang you for that out of hand. In the sheep trade, sir? Ah, there's good wool here, second to none.' Ignoring the inquisitive sexton once more, the stranger turned to the landlady and asked, 'Is there a smaller inn than this? I do not yet know how long I shall be staying, but I like quiet, and it seems that your good house here is too busy for my liking.'

'Meg Clouder of the "City of London" has a spare room,' said Mrs. Waggetts. 'She might accommodate you, sir, to your liking.' The stranger made a note of the name in his pocket-book, and asked, 'Is she married?'

'Been widowed twice, poor girl,' explained the landlady. 'But she takes the name of her first husband, who was a good man, and not that of her second, who was so bad that God struck him down. She's a good young person and a good cook too, and I would never grudge her custom. Mr. Mipps will, I am sure, run round your baggage on his burrow. If she cannot take you in, I can show you my quietest room upstairs, for fault of nothing better.'

'That is kind. I will see it now to save time,' said the stranger, finishing his wine and picking up his change.

There was silence as he followed the landlady from the tap-room, but no sooner had the door closed upon them than a general babble of speculation broke out, which was quickly silenced by Mipps jumping to the middle of the room and addressing the assembly in a hoarse whisper.

'Now then. Orders, gentlemen. Who is he? As close as a hermit crab, and that's all we knows. Now you, Edward. You've seen him on the coach. Did he book from London?' Edward nodded.

'And what did you make of him on the way down, Edward?''' 'Same as you. Hermit crab.'

'There you are then,' replied Mipps emphatically. 'No good, I'll be bound.

Bow Street Runner most like.' But at this Edward shook his head. 'No! I knows all them Runners.'

'Well then, he may be something worse,' said Mipps, 'and till we knows what, he'd best be lodged here so that we can keep an eye on him handy-like.

We'll make it up to Meg Clouder, but Mrs. Waggetts should never have suggested such a thing. I kept frowning at her too. But we can stop him from going there. Off with you now, all of you, to the "City of London". Fill Meg's bar, and when I fetches him alongside see that none of you stops talking. Make a hell's din. You, Murrain, tell 'em that your sheep has the best wool on the Marsh, and if that don't start 'em all shouting I'll be surprised. Be noisier than what you was here when he come in first. He won't stop there, and I'll then take him along to the "Ocean" by the road, and when we've gone, you all skip out by the sea door and run along to the "Ocean" tap under cover of the seawall, and see that you're making more noise there. Then he'll make the best of it and come back here and we'll soon find what he's after.'

'Smugglers, no doubt,' said Farmer Murrain.

Mipps nodded. 'That's my opinion. He's got "lawyer" writ all over him.

And I don't like his accent. It's kind of queer. Now, where have I heard it before?'

'It's the lingo of Wales,' explained Murrain. 'My wife was Welsh, a Jones, and her brother talks just the way of this man.'

'That's it,' said Mipps. 'It's your wife. Knew I'd heard someone who pops up at the end of a sentence. Well, we'll take it then he's a Welshman, and that's something, and it'll take more than a Welshman to find smugglers on Romney Marsh.'

'He's seen the Government reward for the Scarecrow's capture, more like,' argued another, 'and he thinks it worth while trying his hand at it. Well, we don't know nothing about the Scarecrow, nor smuggling neither, so he won't get no help from us.'

'P'raps he's after looking into the death of poor George Plattman,' said Mipps. 'But no. He'd have gone to Sussex then. Unless he thinks the murderers would be sort of compelled to attend the funeral. He may be Plattman's lawyer.'

'Whatever he be you'll measure him up with that coffin rule of yours,' laughed Murrain.

'Aye, we'll know his secrets before night,' agreed Mipps, 'and now off with you from the back door and I'll be waiting with his baggage at the front.' By the time the stranger had returned to the hall after his inspection, Mipps was piling up the baggage outside the inn. There was a delay while the sexton went for the barrow which was in the churchyard shed, and this gave the villagers ample time to reach the other inn unseen by the stranger.

'Then if Mrs. Clouder's is not to my liking I will return here,' he said.

Mipps bestowed a secret wink on the landlady and set off with the barrow, followed by the stranger.

Three times during the walk through the village Mipps contrived to upset the baggage. This occasioned enough delay to satisfy Mipps that his cronies were at their post.

When he set down his barrow at last, it was the back door of the 'City of London' which he chose, for the door of the tap-room opened upon the street while the front door and bar parlour were facing the sea on a higher level of the wall, and Mipps knew that his friends could creep up the stairs and out of the front door to reach the sands, which would take them along to the Ocean Inn without being seen.

'Here we are, sir,' said Mipps. 'I'll come in with you and tell Meg who you are. What name was it?'

'I'll go alone,' replied the stranger. 'You remain here and keep an eye on my baggage.'

'No one won't touch it,' retorted Mipps. 'This 'ere village is the honestest in Kent.'

'For all that,' replied the other, 'you will kindly stay and watch it.'

'Well, be as brisk as you can, sir,' said Mipps. 'I happens to be particular busy today.'

'I have seen no sign of it,' replied the stranger drily. 'Unless you call tilting drink down your throat being busy.'

'I calls being busy having to get ready for a funeral tomorrow,' explained Mipps gravely. 'Got to bury the excise officer what was murdered by Sussex smugglers.' The stranger looked grave, as he repeated the two words, 'murder', 'smugglers'.

'Not here,' added Mipps. 'Sussex. But he was our very own good officer, so is to be buried here.' At the tap-room door, the stranger turned to Mipps and said, 'This sounds a noisier inn than the last.'

'Oh, Meg does a good enough trade,' remarked Mipps casually.

The stranger, with another 'Stay here', entered the 'City of London'. In a few seconds he was out again. 'The Tower of Babel would be quiet to it. Is there no other inn?'

'The old "Ocean" at the further end of the village,' replied Mipps.

'Take me there,' ordered the stranger. 'And since you are so busy, look lively.' Mipps had taken the precaution of removing the valises from the barrow to the pathway during the few seconds that the stranger had been out of sight. He now busied himself with restacking them on to the barrow. He could plainly hear the crowd of villagers mounting the stairs in order to leave by the front door. He tried to detain the stranger, but unfortunately that gentleman had impatiently walked to the corner of the inn, and looked up an alleyway of steps which separated the 'City of London' from the next cottages. These steps were the means of a short-cut up to the sea-wall, and the stranger was able to see the whole crowd go by at the run.

'The rest of the village seem busy too,' he remarked drily.

'Aye, they would be just now,' explained Mipps. 'The tide will be just right for the fishing boats. Most of the village is concerned with fish. Well, we shall find the "Ocean" quiet, I expect.'

'I hope so,' snapped the stranger.

Once more Mipps waited outside with the baggage when they reached the Ocean Inn. Here, however, it seemed that the crowd was greater than ever, and Mipps began to congratulate himself upon his clever ruse. He was to find that the stranger was no less clever. At all events he proved that he had sharp eyes and could put two and two together.

'We will return to the Ship Inn,' said the stranger rejoining Mipps. 'I will stay there. It is strange to me why these villagers go from inn to inn before us. It seems they are desirous of crowding me out. I believe them to be the same crowd, for I recognized the fellow with a sack over his shoulders in each bar, and there were certainly half a dozen others who drank with me at the "Ship".

If they are bent upon spying in order to find out my business, they will find it none so easy.'

'Spying?' repeated Mipps with scorn. 'And why do you suppose they should do that? If a man thinks he's being spied upon, he should keep it to himself, for it shows he has some good reason for thinking so. I mean to say, sir, that a spy don't like being spied. I don't know what is on your conscience, that keeps you so close with your name and business, but just because some of the lads can shift quick from tavern to tavern there's no call for the word "spy". They likes to give custom all round. It's a busy village, and we has to step lively even in our drinkings, and if they likes to go from inn to inn in the way of fairness to all, I don't see anything suspicious in that. Well, it's back to the "Ship", is it?'

The other nodded and started off at a brisker walk. Mipps trotted after him, and went on talking.

'You'll find it more comfortable there, sir. Mrs. Waggetts keeps a good table. But don't be too free with your "my good ma'ams" or London Town oglings 'cos the poor woman is very much in love with here husband what lies in the churchyard.'

'She will not suffer from my attentions, I assure you,' replied the stranger.

'Glad to hear you say so, sir,' said Mipps. 'She's a lone widow, and if she's a bit free with me, it's because I was a good friend of her old man's and knocked him up solid with my own hands. Lovely bit of wood I gave him, and the handles were best brass. I took 'em off, though, after the funeral, as it seemed a sin to bury 'em and they was not paid for, only lent.' They were passing the churchyard and Mipps pointed out the grave of the late Waggetts. The stranger asked, 'What is the name of your doctor here?'

'Pepper,' replied Mipps. 'Doctor Sennacherib Pepper. And if you wants a blood-letting, there's no better man. But he's the very spit of you, sir, in one respect. He's suspicious. You know, sir; fond of poking his nose about. He's got a bat in his belfry about smugglers, just as our poor dear late-lamented customs officer had. Smugglers over in Sussex, yes. But here, no! It was Doctor Pepper, now, who was the first hereabouts to swear that he had seen the Scarecrow, who is supposed to ride at the head of a wild gang of devils.

Nonsense, I say. Just cast your eye, sir, over that there marsh. Ain't it as innocent a piece of land as ever God made? And so it is, I says; but Pepper, he says, "Avoid the Marsh at night. It ain't healthy", he says.'

'A doctor goes out at nights, Mr. Mipps,' returned the stranger. 'No doubt he sees more than the rest of you. Now, I know a good deal more than most concerning smuggling. Perhaps the very innocent look of the landscape gives it an advantage.'

'My advice to you, sir, is to go and get blood-let from old Pepper,' snapped Mipps. 'You'd get on remarkable between you, sir.'

'An advantage,' replied the stranger, 'that I do not mean to take. I have no interest in Doctor Pepper, though there is another doctor whom I am most anxious to meet. Tell me, where does Doctor Syn practise? Ever heard of him?'

'Now don't go upsetting him with your tales of smuggling,' cried Mipps.

'He'd be very grieved to hear your suspicions. He practises from that there house beyond the Court House.'

'Is he the chief doctor here?' asked the stranger. 'Perhaps he and Pepper are partners?'

'Oh ah,' said Mipps with a wink. 'Old Pepper kills 'em and Doctor Syn reads the burial service over 'em. Doctor Syn is a curer of souls, sir. Doctor of Divinity, vicar here and my master. If you wants to see him, sir, you'd better tell me your business, me being his right-hand man, so to speak.'

'So Doctor Syn is a parson and lives there, eh?' said the stranger. 'Very well, then. You may deposit my baggage at the inn, and go then to this Doctor of Divinity and inform him that I have important business with him.'

'And what name shall I tell him and what nature of business?' asked Mipps.

'Since my name would convey nothing to him, why send it?' asked the other. 'As to my business, well, you can say that since I have travelled from the north of Wales to divulge it, it must obviously be of sufficient interest for him to grant me an interview. Now let me hear you convey that message.' Mipps closed his eyes and amused himself while annoying the other by repeating it like a school-child. 'Old gentleman who knows all about smuggling has come from the north of Wales to divulge a bit o' business. Will you have the time within the next few days to grant him an interview? He's staying at the "Ship".'

'No, no!' corrected the stranger. 'You will ask him to see me this very evening.'

'And no name, eh, sir?' asked Mipps. 'You'll be required to give your name at the Ship Inn. Our squire is very particular that he shall know who stays in the village. Especially strangers, like yourself.'

'I'll give my name at the proper time, and to the proper people,' returned the other sharply. 'You will now carry my baggage to my room, while I tell the landlady about supper. You will then go over and deliver my message to the vicar, thereby earning the double drink which I bestowed upon you.'

'What?' cried the disgruntled Mipps. 'Nothing more for pushing your baggage on a grand tour of the village?'

'You will remember,' said the stranger reprovingly, 'that I bestowed drinks upon the whole parish at your instigation.'

'It wasn't my insta-something,' retorted Mipps. 'It was the dice.' It was a very disgusted Mipps that carried the baggage up to the room, saying that if it was not for helping Mrs. Waggetts he would not do it at all. When he came down again the stranger was waiting for him in the hall, and Mipps was hailed with, 'Now then! Get along please!'

'I'm going along for my own convenience, and for the safety of the parish.

And at once,' said the sexton firmly. 'And let me tell you, sir, that we are not used to being ordered about on Romney Marsh. We are independent, sir, we are. But since both squire and vicar likes to know when suspicious strangers enter the village, I'll lay the information. Stranger with no name, who won't tell his business. Sounds queer.'

'As I told you, my business with the vicar is of the utmost import, and what perhaps will interest him is the fact that it may be very much to his advantage.'

'That will be for the reverend gentleman to decide when he hears it,' replied Mipps. 'So you stay here and I'll come back and tell you at what hour and on what day he can see you.' To the sexton's astonishment the stranger drew a crown piece from his pocket and, handing it to him, said almost pleadingly, 'I trust you will be able to arrange it for this evening, since the matter which concerns us both is pressing.' Mipps trotted off to the vicarage, and gave Doctor Syn a full account of the peculiar stranger.

After listening to a lengthy version of the gentleman's brusqueness and queer behaviour, Doctor Syn did not fall in with the sexton's suggestion that he should refuse the interview till he knew the cause. 'Well, my good Mipps, I confess I am curious, and at least he is not the only man I have met who refuses to give his correct name.'

'Ah yes,' nodded Mipps, 'but this is no gentleman of fortune like yourself and Jimmie Bone.' Syn put his long thin finger to his lips quietly. 'Hush, my good friend! We cannot be too careful.'

'Just what I'm pointing out to you, sir.'

'Oh, but I am going to be very careful, I assure you. I shall have you on hand, never fear. The stranger will sit there, so that I can get the evening light upon his face from that window. I shall receive him standing behind this highbacked chair, so that I can grasp my pistol from beneath that cushion, if need be. We have rope and gags in that cupboard, and if the gentleman is as you describe him, and no virile young giant, I think you and I can deal with him.

Your part will be to leave him in the hall while you announce him. You can walk on tiptoe, saying that I am preparing a sermon. As he enters he will find me letting you out through the garden door. At least so he will think. In reality you will be hidden behind the alcove curtains there behind his chair. It is better that we should hear his business before he tells it to anyone else. He may be here to ask awkward questions. Fetch him from the inn, and if I like the gentleman he shall sup with me here. But if we dislike him too much, Master Carpenter,' and Syn's face grew hard and grim, 'well, who knows? There may be another corpse found across the Kent ditch.' Before he finally dismissed his lieutenant, Doctor

Syn looked to the priming of two duelling pistols, one of which he gave to Mipps, while the other he laid carefully upon the flat top of the right ear-flap of his tall embroidered armchair. Over the weapon he carefully laid a cushion.

'You will cover him from the curtain, Mipps,' he ordered, 'and I can throw down this gun-trap if necessary. Quite like old times, Master Carpenter.'

'From the looks of the gentleman,' replied Mipps, 'I thinks it will be, and little danger to us. We can manage him.'

'Then go and fetch him,' said the vicar.

Mipps departed on his errand, and the vicar sat at his table and continued the penning of his sermon for the following Sunday morning, dismissing the coming interview entirely from his mind.

Chapter 3. Doctor Syn hears tell of a Tontine

A few minutes later Mipps opened the front door of the vicarage, and as he closed it gently behind the stranger, he whispered, 'Hush!'

'Why?' asked the stranger.

Again in a whisper the sexton answered. 'Because the vicar is writing a sermon, and when he's scratching away with his quill all about Hell-fire and God's mercy, he don't expect a mouse to squeak. I has to keep him in a good temper when he's sermonizing, 'cos then he does it nice and tells the congregation happy things about playing on harps and talking with angels.

Otherwise he just scares us with pits o' sulphur and the like. You sit down there on that there settle, and I'll creep over and have a look at how he's getting on.' The stranger sat down on the seat indicated, which was close to the front door, while Mipps crossed the hall slowly on tiptoe.

Mipps opened the study door very cautiously and peered round. The wink which he bestowed upon his vicar inside the room was not seen by the stranger, who only saw the sexton sidle round the door and close it again very quietly.

Presently the door opened again and the stranger saw the sexton beckoning him. As he crossed the hall slowly he heard the sexton called into the study by his master, and this gave him an opportunity to draw a pistol from his right side pocket and look at it. Having glanced at it somewhat fearfully, he drew back the trigger to full cock and very carefully put it back into his pocket. He then went to the open door and looked into the study. He heard a hearty voice saying, 'Thankee, Mister Sexton. Lock up the church safely. Oh, and empty the poorbox. I forgot to do so. And do not forget to bring me back my keys.' The stranger saw a tall elegant figure in black standing just outside the garden door and talking round the corner. With a wave of his hand Doctor Syn came back into his book-lined study and bowed to the little fat stranger. He knew at a glance that he had never clapped eyes on this soberly dressed, pompous, country-looking gentleman before, and for this he was relieved.

Doctor Syn had the talent of never forgetting a face, and at least this man had never met him in the past.

'Good evening, sir,' he said heartily. 'My excellent sexton, who has just gone to empty the poor-box and lock up the church for the night, tells me that you have but now arrived by the mail coach, and that your object in visiting such a remote part of the country is in order to have words with me. Let us hope they are pleasant ones, sir. He also tells me that you are Welsh and have journeyed from North Wales for this purpose.'

'I told him I had journeyed from North Wales certainly,' replied the other, 'but I did not mention that I was Welsh. How did he know that, now?'

'If as a parson I may be permitted to quote Holy Script, perhaps because "thy speech betrayeth thee".'

'I can speak the Welsh,' admitted the stranger, 'but I have been told that my English is, well, very English.'

'It is excellent,' said Doctor Syn. 'And if it were not for the fascinating tendency to the rising inflection at the end of each sentence, which is the idiosyncrasy of a Welshman speaking our vulgar tongue, I would say "English.
Very English".'

'You are Doctor Syn, of course?' asked the stranger.

'I am, sir, but you have the advantage of me.'

'I am David Davis Llewellyn Jones.'

'A Welshman certainly,' smiled Doctor Syn. 'And, of course, very proud of it.'

'Attorney-at-law, with practice in Tremadoc. And old practice, though somewhat restricted. My younger brother has a more lucrative one, for it includes the small port of Portmadoc, as well as Carnavon. His has been our family practice for generations, and in my father's lifetime it increased greatly under his care. His Tremadoc work he did not take so seriously.'

'May I say,' asked Doctor Syn, 'without seeming to pry into family affairs, that it is surely strange to leave the better practice to the younger son. I take it your brother was the favourite.'

'Not a bit of it, for I believe I was,' replied the other. 'My father was a just man, though perhaps he showed to me as his eldest child the more consideration. He offered me the choice of the two practices, the one sound and large, the other small and with no hope of growing. I chose the latter.'

'Was that foolish or noble of you?' asked the vicar.

'I should tell you that coupled to the small practice was a gamble. Yes, sir, a gamble with death, and it is on this death's gamble that—'

'But I am keeping you standing. Forgive me,' Doctor Syn pointed to the comfortable chair in front of the alcove curtain. 'Pray be seated, and then continue with your family history if it please you, though just where it touches me, I am at a loss to understand.' The Welshman bowed and sat down cautiously. The fact was that he was not used to a pistol at full cock in his pocket and felt mightily scared of it.

'You need have no fear of that chair, Mr. Jones,' smiled the vicar. 'Our squire is a heavy man and always hurls himself into it without harm.'

Doctor Syn stood behind the high-backed chair on which the cushion was balanced. The stranger took a quick glance round the room and then whispered, 'We are alone?' Syn smiled. 'As you see. These books are all genuine tomes of learning and conceal no secret doors.'

'Will that sexton of yours return?' Doctor Syn shook his head. 'I think I can safely say that he will not return.

When he has locked up the church, he has a habit of dropping the keys into his pocket, and making his way to the Ship Inn.'

'But I heard you tell him to bring back your keys,' said the Welshman.

'Ah yes, so I did, but a thirsty man has a short memory of things that keep him from his drink. If he should remember that he has my keys, he would only take them to the kitchen door and give them to my housekeeper.'

'Then you are not married?' asked the Welshman.

'No, are you?' asked the vicar.

'No. But first of all can you give me any proof that you are Doctor Syn? I assure you it is necessary.'

'The legal mind, eh?' replied the vicar, and pointed to a large volume that lay open on the writing table beside him. 'I have just been filling up the Register of Burial here. We have a funeral tomorrow.'

'Ah yes,' nodded the Welshman. 'The murdered excise officer. That man of yours told me something of it.' Syn held the book up for the other to see. 'I must not sign it, of course, till after the funeral, but you can see my signature on the previous pages. Any amount of them. You see? Christopher Syn, D.D. and now for your satisfaction, this.' He took up his quill and signed his name on a spare sheet of paper. 'You can see for yourself that it is my signature.'

'Aye, proof enough,' nodded the lawyer.

'I am glad you find it so,' returned the vicar. 'And now perhaps you will tell me the nature of your business, and what this gamble with death has got to do with me, for without wishing to appear rude I must point out that I was working when you came in.''And I trust you will not think me rude-mannered,' answered the lawyer, 'if I take a look outside your door. I wish to prevent our conversation being overheard by a third party at all costs.'

'I will lock the door if you wish it.' Doctor Syn strode past him, opened the door wide, saying, 'You see? An empty hall. We will now lock it.' This he did. He then went behind the Welshman's chair and, feeling behind the curtain, he took his clerical overcoat from a peg, and held it up before the lawyer. As he shook it, he said, 'There is no one inside this you see. No eavesdropper, but a heavy coat. Although it is hot weather, I keep it hanging there in case I am called out at nights to visit the sick. There is a curious malady called marsh-ague. One catches it from the damp of the misty dykes.

Well, since you are satisfied that there is no one inside it, we will hang it up again. Oh yes, and here is a spare cassock too, in the other corner. It is quite harmless, you see. Well, we will put it back behind the curtain and then shut the garden door. You see, sir, that I am more than ready to humour you.' The lawyer, who had turned round in his chair to watch the vicar hang up the garments behind the curtain, did not see Mipps holding a pistol and grinning. Doctor Syn took care of that, pulling the curtain close before crossing to the garden door.

Just as he was about to shut it, the suspicious Welshman asked, 'Any gardener working out there? Or is it too late?'

'Mipps, my good sexton, looks after my vegetable garden, orchard and lawns, but he has finished for today.'

'Has he no assistant? Small lad or anything?'

'No. Just the churchyard donkey to pull the roller. No other helps, though it is my housekeeper who picks the flowers. She lives at the far end of the vicarage, and could not overhear us if she happened to be at home which she is not, for she has gone to the village on some errands.' The vicar shut the door, and once more taking up his stand behind his chair, he peered over the top of it at the lawyer, and said, 'And now, really sir, endeavour to be brief.' The stranger cleared his throat, then, seeming to find it difficult to find the right words for a start, he shut his eyes, opened them again and stared hard at the vicar, who smiled and said, 'Well, sir?'

'It is a very peculiar business and difficult to broach.'

'I await your pleasure, sir,' replied the vicar. 'May I suggest that you plunge into it boldly. You need not mince words.'

'Then let me begin by telling you something, reverend sir, which perhaps you have never noticed.'

'That should be interesting. What?' The lawyer with a great effort spoke emphatically but quickly. 'There are some sorts of men who, once they have made up their minds to accomplish a certain thing, will go to any lengths in order to do so.'

'I think I have noticed that,' replied the vicar. 'You must not think that a country parson is never encountered with desperate men. Since I took Holy Orders many years ago, I have met more than my share, I assure you.'

'And can you tell a desperate man when you meet him?' asked the other.

'Would you for instance take me for one?'

'Why, really, sir, our acquaintance has been of the shortest, but from what I have seen of you, I think that, however desperate you were, you would be too sensible to become a menace to the community.'

The lawyer leaned forward and spoke very gravely. 'I am not so sure about that, Doctor Syn. I sincerely hope that I shall not be forced to do anything criminal, having spent my life on the right side of the law. But of late I have been driven desperate indeed. All the way from Wales, this feeling of desperation has grown, and before it takes disastrous effects, I appeal to you to save me from becoming—well, a "menace", as you say.'

'I wish you would speak plainly,' urged the doctor, growing irritated with all this rigmarole.

Suddenly there was a loud report of a gun. The Welshman sprang up from his chair crying out, 'What's that?' Doctor Syn laughed. 'A gun. A sporting gun. Our squire is giving his seventeen-year-old son a lesson in rook-shooting. I do not permit the churchyard birds to be interfered with in their rookery, partly because they are taking sanctuary in holy ground and partly because I have a likeness to the birds. They are so like black-coated parsons with their wise ways. But I have compromised with the squire by telling him young Denis may fire at the birds outside the churchyard. He has never hit one yet, I am glad to say.'

'I am indebted to him,' replied the Welshman.

Doctor Syn, noticing his right hand as fidgeting in his side-pocket asked him casually, 'In what way? Are you, too, fond of rooks?'

'I am indebted to him, reverend sir, because another shot will not attract attention, and I feared that,' whispered the lawyer tensely. He turned sideways to the doctor. His hand came out of his pocket, and the vicar saw the glint of a barrel. There was a deafening report and the study filled with smoke.

When the smoke cleared, Doctor Syn was still leaning against the tall back of the chair, with a smile upon his face, a smoking pistol in his hand.

Mipps stood beside the lawyer, with his pistol covering him.

The lawyer, with his thumb dripping blood, his pistol with broken butt lying against the foot of the bookcase, watched, with an expression of bewilderment upon his face, the cushion which Doctor Syn had thrown down so dramatically upon the floor, and which he was now with calm leisure picking up again.

Quite frankly Doctor Syn enjoyed the situation, and showed it in his smile; it was so droll.

With equal frankness, Mipps was disgusted by it. That the Welsh lawyer could have had the wicked impertinence to draw a pistol against one whom he thought to have been an unarmed parson made his own trigger finger itch to pull.

It was the lawyer who broke the silence by exclaiming peevishly, 'I knew that I should bungle the whole business! It seems, sir, that you were well prepared for me. I mean the pistol under the cushion, and the cushion jumping on to the floor just at the right time. This man, too, behind the curtain. Now how exactly did I give my secret away? I am curious to know that at least.'

'We were prepared, that is all,' explained the vicar politely. 'We did not know that you intended to gamble with death, as you called it, at my expense.

But we have a way down in this part of the world of not being taken by surprise. You must admit that I was not inhospitable. I hid my pistol beneath this cushion, so that it could give you no offence, and I hid my sexton behind that curtain, to put you at ease, by letting you jump to the conclusion that he had gone out the garden door. And now, sir, when I have attended to your finger, and Mr. Mipps has given you a glass of brandy, which is excellent, I assure you, since it was given me from the squire's cellars, and not from the free-traders, I shall ask you of your charity to satisfy my curiosity, by explaining your motive in thus wishing to murder me in cold blood. I confess that I am glad your gambling with death was not all upon your side.'

'I never wished to murder you, nor could I have done,' grumbled the lawyer.

'Nothing was further from my intentions, I assure you. I merely wish to force you to accompany me to Wales in order that someone up there, more resolute, more unscrupulous than myself, may murder you. For believe me, he wants to and will, unless of course you succeed in murdering him first.'

'May I ask the name of this attentive enemy?' asked Syn.

'Tarroc Dolgenny,' replied the lawyer. 'He has made his name in North Wales, and I may add that he will make it even bigger in hell.'

'Does he pretend to know me?' asked the vicar. 'I never heard his name before, and you must own that Tarroc Dolgenny is a mouthful that one would not readily forget the taste of; but unless he has at some other time gone under another title, I do not know him.'

'He only knows you by name, Doctor Syn, and like myself took you for a medical man. Indeed, divinity in connection with you never entered our heads. I may add that he first heard of your name through me, and I wish I had never told him, since it has put me into this extremely awkward position.'

'But what is your grudge against me, then?' asked the amazed vicar. 'For you I have none. Ah, but here is the brandy. Thank you, Mr. Mipps. And I see you have procured a bandage from the same cupboard. Now sir, if you will allow me, I can ease the pain, for I know something of doctoring, as I have been a mission preacher in the wild parts of America, and to be able to heal the body is a very sure way of healing the soul too, amongst the heathen. Now after we have tied this up, and fortunately I see that it is not at all serious, since the bullet is embedded in the wooden butt of your pistol, we will then have our drink in peace, and talk.' And making a very neat job of the bandage, and signing to Mipps to bring a third glass for himself, which needless to say Mipps had every intention of doing, Doctor Syn raised his glass and said, 'The King and ourselves.' He then smiled again and added, 'And, oh yes, Tarroc Dolgenny, whoever and wherever he may be.'

'No, I'll not drink to him, save to his damnation, which is a sure toast,' replied the Welshman vehemently. Then, changing his expression to one of kindness and goodwill, he also added to the toast, 'In spite of Dolgenny I wish you long life, reverend sir.'

'Aye, aye,' chimed in Mipps, which made the Welshman add with something of an effort to conquer his personal dislike of the sexton, 'And to you also, Mr. Mipps.' He took one sip of the brandy and nodded his appreciation, and as the others drank, Doctor Syn slowly, Mipps at one gulp, he asked suddenly, 'Did you ever hear tell of a bloody field called Culloden?' Doctor Syn looked surprised, but answered gravely, 'I have reason to remember it well, sir, and with much sadness. My father was killed there, fighting upon what must now be considered the wrong side.'

'Aye, and three of his brothers killed with him,' went on the lawyer with some bitterness. 'The Bonny Prince robbed you of a father and of three good uncles too.'

'That is so,' said Doctor Syn.

'May they all rest in peace,' continued the lawyer, 'for I have heard tell that they were worthy men. Your father, Septimus Syn, was especially admired by my good father. They had much in common, those two gentlemen, for they were both clever lawyers, and they both fought for the Prince.'

'Do you mean to tell me that they met at Culloden?' asked the vicar.

The lawyer nodded. 'Aye, reverend sir, and before that too. But at the great disaster to the cause, it was the same cannon ball that killed your father which wounded my father too. Did you ever hear how very gallantly your father died?' Doctor Syn pointed to the panelling behind the lawyer's back. 'That sword which you see hanging there was his. A Dymchurch man who followed my father brought it back with him, and told my mother that he had taken it from his dead hand. So we knew he died fighting to the last.'

'When he was struck,' continued the lawyer, 'that weapon was sent flying several yards away. At that very moment the redcoats launched another attack, and though mortally wounded, Septimus Syn crawled after his sword, waved it in the air, and with his last breath cried out to those around him to advance.

The Scots line rallied under his encouragement, leaped forward and met the bayonets with their claymores, as he died. One of your uncles happened to fall dead upon the body of my wounded father, who till the day of his death, some fifteen years ago, always maintained that it was due to this that he was saved, for a party of the enemy who were killing the wounded passed him by as dead.

Your other two uncles were shot during the retreat.'

'You are better informed of all this than I,' replied the doctor, 'for all I knew was that my father died honourably with that sword in his hand. Though a man of peace myself, I keep that blade not only bright but sharp in my good father's honour. With me it went to the Americas, where in spite of my cloth I was often glad of such a weapon. I thank you, sir, for this information, and we will fill our glasses once more to drink to our fathers, though not perhaps to the cause for which they fought.' Mipps readily refilled the glasses, including his own, and when they had drunk the doctor set down his glass and said, 'But now, sir, taking it for granted that you have not undertaken this long journey of yours to improve my knowledge of our family histories, I am eager to understand why you should come here to force me up north in order that a man you hate should murder me.'

'I am coming to that explanation, sir,' replied the lawyer, once more sitting down in the chair facing the window. 'It is a long and curious story, sir, but I will endeavour to keep it as brief as possible.'

As Doctor Syn was about to sit down too, he noticed that his housekeeper was passing the window on her return from the village, and this put him in mind of supper.

'I fear, sir,' he said, 'that you must be very hungry after your long coach ride, and I know that you have not yet supped.'

'I shall eat later at the inn, sir,' replied the lawyer. 'I was told that I could have something cold with hot punch at any hour I liked. Though I have no desire to detain you from your food, I must own that I should like to explain myself before taking leave of you, so that you may have the night to consider what I propose. I promise you that I will not weary you. On the contrary I think what I have to say will awaken your very liveliest interests.' The vicar nodded. 'Your cold supper at the inn can easily be cancelled by Mr. Mipps. Take another glass of brandy, my good Mipps, and then tell my housekeeper that I shall have a hungry guest to sup with me, and will she lay two covers as soon as possible. Perhaps you will lend her a hand before carrying the message to the "Ship", where no doubt you can eat your supper while we are eating ours.' Mipps looked at the stranger doubtfully, and then picked up the damaged pistol. 'Shall I see first if the gentleman from Wales has any more artillery in his other pockets, sir?'

'Have no fear of me, Mister Sexton,' said the lawyer.

'Caution ain't fear, sir,' replied Mipps.

'And believe me, I never intended to murder your master,' added the lawyer.

'And "Opportunity's a fine thing" is a good proverb,' snapped the sexton.

'There, there,' laughed Doctor Syn, 'if I can take this gentleman's word that his pistol was only to threaten, why, so must you. You can call round later and give me any news of the parish. By the way, have you heard any more from Mother Handaway?'

'Slight improvement, sir,' replied the sexton solemnly. 'Doctor Pepper has seen her and has given her something to make her sleep well tonight, but he asked me to say that he would be pleased if you could visit her tomorrow at the usual hour, as your conversing of the scriptures gives her more relief than his physics.'

'Tomorrow will suit me better, for I can now give longer time to Mr. Jones here. Thank you, Mr. Mipps.' Doctor Syn waved his hand towards the door. Just as Mipps was opening it, he added, 'And I am sure Mr. Jones would urge it just as much as I do, that we do not say a word about this pistol business. Mrs. Fowey is extremely attached to me, and if you mention it and she did not grasp Mr. Jones's motive, she might either spoil his supper with bad cooking or even poison.'

'If you say so, sir, then not a word will be uttered by me.' Saying which, Mipps sidled round the door and was about to close it, when he popped his head round again and said to the Welshman, 'If so be you was to gain confidence, me being away this time really, and starts threatening again, let me tell you, sir, that the ways of the Marsh are tricky, all beset with deep dykes where strangers can be lost and cut off. We Marshmen knows the ways of them, and we also is very fond of our vicar's safety and dignity. Good evening, sir, and I have given you the warning of the Marsh.'

'Be off with you,' laughed the doctor, and then as the door closed he said to the Welshman, 'a droll character, sir!'

'Very droll, certainly,' agreed the lawyer. 'But faithful, I should imagine. A one man's servant, eh?'

'Exactly,' nodded Syn. 'We have both been deeply indebted to one another more times than I can say.' The vicar's mind wandered back to the days they had spent in the Caribbean Seas. Picture after picture; adventurous and terrible situations, in which either he was saving Mipps, or Mipps was rescuing him; Indians, pirates, and huge seas.

The Welshman set his glass down beside him, and the movement brought the vicar back to his present obligations.

'I declare your remark sent me into a daydream, or rather a series of day nightmares, for my servant and I have seen strange things in our time. But it occurs to me that, instead of discussing my sexton, we had better take another drink to whet our appetites, since my housekeeper gets vastly offended if justice is not done to what she prepares. Now I have a very excellent sherry that I should like you to try.'

'Sherry is good, when it is good,' replied the lawyer.

Doctor Syn strode to the door to fetch the drink in question, but as he opened it he perceived Mipps carrying a tray with three glasses and a bottle of sherry, for he had anticipated the vicar's wish. The latter crossed the hall to meet him.

'Supper will be served in five minutes, sir.' Then, sinking his voice to a whisper, he said, 'I brought three glasses, sir, in case you needed an excuse to ask me in as a watch-dog. And shall I stand behind his chair at supper?' The vicar grinned and touched the third glass. 'You may take that away with you and fill it with rum, which I warrant you prefer. There is little danger in this man, and none that I cannot frustrate.'

'Well, if you thinks you can frustrate, whatever that means,' whispered Mipps, 'I'll go and frustrate a noggin or so of rum, which I prefers to wine.' As he took away the third glass Mipps told himself that for once he would have preferred to listen to whatever the Welshman had to say, rather than taste the joy of rum. He thought that the vicar was being over-confident; he himself could not abide the fat little lawyer. It was also annoying that his tongue had been tied about the matter. His cronies at the 'Ship' would expect a good yarn with full details, and he was not in the position to give it to them. However, he was inventive. There was nothing against telling them some tale about the stranger out of his own head. But he would keep it mysterious. And so after telling Mrs. Fowey, the housekeeper, to keep her ears open, and if the stranger did not behave himself to come over to the 'Ship' and he would deal with it, he trotted away to that pleasant house of call.

Meanwhile, Doctor Syn, having re-entered the study armed with the tray, poured out two glasses and toasted the Welshman with, 'Here's to our good fathers, who died for the master they loved. Our Bonny Prince had many good servants, just as I have one.'

'Aye, no doubt they thought so too when they went north,' replied the Welshman. 'I'll drink to your father, but I amend the toast by saying that they died for their own honour at the end and not so much for the Bonny Prince. Did you ever hear, now, what they took north with them besides their loyalty and their swords?'

'If you mean what most of them took—money. Aye, my old uncle, Solomon Syn, the attorney at Romney, told my other that he begrudged the sum that should have come to us, which my father carried with him in the Prince's cause, for since the cause was lost, he considered the money wasted. When my mother asked him how much had been taken, Uncle Solomon told her that she had best be ignorant of that, since it might get our goods distrained by the English Government. So we never knew, but my father being a careful man, we conjectured it would be no great hole in our fortunes that he would make. We knew my father to be well supplied, but he kept money matters to himself and to Uncle Solomon.'

'Aye, he would have the knack. He was a lawyer,' nodded the Welshman.

'He was Clerk to the Court House here, and managed the estate of Sir Charles Cobtree, as well as making collection of Marsh cotts for the maintenance of the wall. He knew money matters well. None better.'

'Aye, that he did,' agreed the lawyer. 'My father too. Now, what sum would you guess that he took north with him? This is no idle curiosity on my part, for I know.'

'Some four or five hundred pounds perhaps,' guessed Syn.

'He took a vast sum, reverend sir. Make your hundreds thousands and you have it. Five thousand pounds! The Prince allowed himself to be influenced, and sometimes very foolishly. Now this was a case in point. He should never have let your father and my father think they had been slighted, for that money and other sums as big might have put him on the English throne.'

'But do you mean the Prince slighted them?' asked the vicar.

'Well I suppose not, not wilfully,' went on the lawyer. 'But they took themselves at their own valuation. Though the Prince never knew about the money they had brought, he lost it, because he did not make enough to-do about our fathers. And what did they do? Why, collected others of the same breed— gentlemen who had brought swords and wealth—and persuaded them that the commands were only given to those who flattered the Prince. This was no doubt true, and our lawyer fathers took a strange attitude. Fight for the Prince they would, since honour demanded that of them as they had passed their word. But there was no obligation, they said, to pay in the money they had never mentioned nor promised. When the Prince was in Edinburgh, our two fathers had discovered a sound banker who could be trusted to keep their counsel, was scrupulously honest with other people's money, respected English Law as well as Scotch, and seldom criticized his client's wishes. Till they saw what the Prince intended to do for them in the way of promotion and honour, they placed their money, five thousand each, in the banker's hands. Your father's three brothers brought five thousand between them. It was easy to get them to follow suit. Two other disgruntled gentlemen were also found who were ready to bide their time and see what the Prince would do. The Prince did nothing. They demanded interviews, but were fobbed off by those around his royal pretended majesty. Once they got word with the Prince, but he was surrounded by his satellites even then, and so the money he would have welcomed and paid for with empty titles was never mentioned. The Prince tried hard to hide his boredom with these amateur soldiers who expected to lead regiments, when they had only a few personal followers. But there was money enough to equip their regiments had the Prince but known. Now, Doctor Syn, what do you suppose they actually did with that money?'

'I have not the faintest conception,' replied the doctor. 'Had they left it where it was in that bank, the banker, if he were as honest as you say, would have traced in each case the man who owned the money, or, if he were dead, his next of kin.' The Welshman shook his head. 'No, for they saved him that immediate trouble. Remember, reverend sir, that all your family under arms were of the legal profession. My father too. They drew up the contract with the banker at a good fair rate. Tell me, did you ever hear of a Neapolitan banker called Nicholas Lorenzo Tonti?' Before Doctor Syn could reply, his sedate old, acid-faced housekeeper, Mrs. Fowey, tapped at the door, then entered and announced that supper was served in the dining-room.

'One more glass of sherry, sir,' cried Syn, 'and then we will drink a bottle with our meal.'

They drank in silence, Doctor Syn thinking deeply, and the lawyer desirous only of continuing his story. When they had set down their glasses, Doctor Syn said, 'This way.' As the Welshman followed his host across the hall towards the candle-lit room, the doctor turned round and, clapping both hands on his guest's shoulders, cried, 'I see where you are driving! They formed a Tontine!' The lawyer nodded. 'They did. And a good one too. But what do you know of Tontines?'

'I'll tell you that, when you tell me what you think of my wine,' laughed the vicar. 'This way.' It was obvious to Doctor Syn that Mipps must have warned the housekeeper to keep an eye upon the guest. Never one to hide resentment, she showed only too plainly her entire disapproval of the Welshman. She carried from the side table the plateful of cold game pie which the vicar carved, and handed it to the lawyer at arm's length. This was not lost upon Doctor Syn, and fearing she might become really unmannerly, he said, 'Thank you, Mrs. Fowey. We need not worry you any further.' With an audible sniff of disapproval, Mrs. Fowey departed for the kitchen, while Doctor Syn poured out the wine. The lawyer was for continuing his narrative, but his host forbade, saying that it would keep very well till the port or brandy, but must not delay the appeasing of this guest's appetite.

When the table was finally cleared and both gentlemen were becoming mellow over their wine, Doctor Syn repeated, 'And so they formed a Tontine? As I said before.'

'And as I said before,' said the lawyer, 'what do you know of Tontines?'

'Oh, I know all about them,' replied the vicar, 'for my father often spoke of that Neapolitan banker who introduced his system into France during the last century. A legacy left amongst several persons in such a way that, as any one dies, his share goes to the survivors till the last alive inherits all.'

'Ably put,' nodded the lawyer. 'You are will-informed. And so was the Edinburgh banker I mentioned, as regards investments. That twenty-five thousand pounds as invested by our warrior fathers, your uncles and two other companions of arms, has already trebled itself. There is, in fact, the sum of approximately seventy-five thousand waiting to be claimed by the surviving son of the founders, and there are only two men left alive with a claim—myself and yourself. All the rest are dead.'

'Good heavens. And was that the reason you thought to kill me? A motive certainly,' Doctor Syn laughed.

The Welshman looked nettled. 'No, no,' he answered testily, 'I have told you I had no intention of doing so, and you must take my word for it. But the man who persuaded me to threaten your life in order that I might get you to accompany me to Wales, ah now, he will murder you if he gets the chance, and then murder me too.'

'And supposing he did,' asked Doctor Syn, 'what possible claim would he have on the money?'

'The right of a husband over the property of his wife,' replied the lawyer.

'And unless I can beat him by law, which I fear I shall not do, he will marry my heiress in order to get that property.'

'You stated that you were unmarried,' remarked Syn. 'Then this heiress.

Who is she?'

'My niece. My only sister's child. She is an orphan and I am her guardian.

The most beautiful girl in Wales. Her name is Ann Sudden. Her father, a Cheshire man, appointed head of the customs for the North Wales ports, was killed by the same man who wants to kill you.'

'Do you know that?' demanded the vicar.

'In my mind, yes; but I have no proofs. Tarroc Dolgenny is not the sort of man to leave a clue against him.'

'And how was your brother-in-law killed?' asked the vicar.

'Disappeared after a visit to Dolgenny's estate. My sister, her husband, and daughter, had supped with him. He took them home to my sister's house in a phaeton which he drove himself. There was no room for my brother-in-law, so he said he would walk the short cut across the sands. There was a moon and the tide was out. He knew the safe path, and none better, but his hat came floating into the harbour the next day.'

'And he was drowned?' asked the vicar.

'It was generally agreed that he had been caught in the quicksands,' replied the lawyer. 'That is probably true, for the quicksands on Tremadoc Bay take a heavy toll of life. At low tide when there is but a river running through the yellow-floored estuary, it is only the few that can pass safely, for the devil in the sand shifts quickly from tide to tide, and what is safe walking one day is deadly the next. It is well named the Devil's Larder, and there is a devil in human shape who supplies much food for it. Yes, reverend sir, Tarroc Dolgenny, who murders his enemies and throws their bodies into the Devil's Larder!'

'Where he wants to throw us in order that he may claim the Tontine of our fathers?' Doctor Syn began to chuckle. 'Shall we play a hand against this devil? You say he sent you down here to threaten me?' The lawyer nodded gravely. 'He told me to seek you out, when I heard from the Edinburgh banker that the son of one of our fathers' companions was dead. This left us two.'

'But why did not the banker try to find me?' asked Syn.

'He wrote a year or so ago to Lydd, where Solomon Syn, your guardian, lived. The banker gave no reason, and was informed that you had gone to America and were believed to be dead. The banker insisted upon some proof of this, so I decided to travel down to see if I could find anything, for you were the only bar to my good fortune. When Dolgenny heard of my purpose, he said, "If he is alive, kill him." When I protested, he said, "Then bring him up here on some pretext and I will." A dangerous man, Doctor Syn. He lives in a castle that is built in the estuary on a rising ridge that is well-wooded. Here he supports a band of men, who are said to make great livings as smugglers. A desperate lot of rascals, who at his command would never shrink from murdering his enemies. Perhaps my brother-in-law stumbled upon some proof of this the night he was murdered. My poor sister did not survive her husband more than a few months. Since her death Dolgenny has pestered my niece to marry him. I could wish he had never heard of the Tontine, since it has made him all the more determined to marry poor Ann. Both she and her mother were impressed by him at first, but now Ann realizes what he is. Well, she is safe enough while I am away, for she is staying at my brother's house, and there is no necessity for her to leave the grounds, which are extensive. Indeed I urged her not to, and she promised. He would not hesitate to force her into marriage if he saw the chance. A dangerous man!'

'My legal friend,' replied the doctor with a smile, 'I might be dangerous too. In fact, I rather think I shall be if I ever meet this man. And a smuggler, you say? Oh, how reprehensible!'

Chapter 4. Doctor Syn arranges to be in two places at once

That night Doctor Syn and his guest talked late, for after they had consumed a quantity of good port and brandy, the vicar mixed a pungent bowl of punch, and as they consumed it, he extracted from the Welshman many stories of Tarroc Dolgenny's smuggling activities. He then entertained his guest by narrating some of the daring adventures of the mysterious Scarecrow.

'And you have no sort of notion who this fellow is?' asked the Welshman.

'I have been over the Marsh many times at night visiting the sick,' replied the doctor, 'but I have never yet seen this Scarecrow. I have, however, had frequent warnings not to venture out on certain nights, but of course I have taken no heed of them when duty has called. It is strange, too, that my poor little pony has never been commandeered by his Night-riders, whereas the horse belonging to our physician has very often been missing from his stable, just as the squire's horses have. Perhaps our mysterious smuggler has a soft spot for the old parson.'

'Well, there's some good in most wicked men,' returned the Welshman, 'though I never found any in the leader of our smugglers. Tarroc Dolgenny has nothing to recommend him but a devilishly handsome face and a quick and daring brain. He is not even a faithful leader when his own interests are like to be thwarted, and he would as soon murder a follower as any enemy. The strange part is that, knowing his character, his men remain faithful to him.'

'Is it known that he is a smuggler,' asked Syn, 'or just suspected?'

'The rascal works openly enough for anybody with eyes and ears,' went on the lawyer. 'At night you can hear his horses galloping through Portmadoc, on a wild rush to Black Rock a mile or so away. No one informs against him. He is too feared, and the new excise officer had better first look to his own safety rather than a warrant. Besides, what can one man do against Dolgenny's crew?'

'Aye, it is the same here,' said Doctor Syn sadly. 'True, we sometimes are billeted with dragoons, but in the usual way what can one lone excise officer do who tries to lay the elusive Scarecrow

by the heels? It means death to him. Not that I think any of our
Marshmen had a hand in it, though they say the Scarecrow is of
Kent, but the scoundrels from Sussex got him. I shall deliver an
address tomorrow over his coffin and pray God that the
Government will see fit to strengthen our coastguards and revenue
men!' It was nearly midnight when Mipps called at the vicarage
once more, bringing back the vicar's keys and a message from Mrs.
Waggetts that she was waiting up to let the lawyer in before
closing. The vicar asked Mipps to escort the gentleman with a
lantern, whereupon Mipps began to rub his sides very vigorously,
and at each rub he let out a groan of pain.

'Have you had a fall or something, my good Mipps?' asked the
vicar.

Mipps grinned and shook his head. 'It's come out again from the
churchyard wall, sir. Honest! It was waiting for me in the dark. And
it got me on the thigh as I passed. Very vicious it got me too, sir.'

'What was it? A dog?' asked the Welshman.

Doctor Syn chuckled. 'You mean the bone?' Mipps nodded again
and answered ruefully, 'Aye sir. As I always has maintained its the
"worrumps" what pushes it. They'll work it right out on to the road
one of these fine nights and then some dog will get it.' Doctor Syn
turned to his guest and explained, 'Mr. Mipps has a great trouble
with this bone in question. It is a thigh-bone, human of course,
and it manages to work its way out through a crack in the
churchyard wall. He is of the opinion that the ghost owner of the
bone is trying to trip him up. My advice to you, Mipps, is to bury it
some fathoms deep, and let it rest in peace.' Mipps wagged his
head. 'Aye, aye, sir. I'll drop it into the excise officer's grave in the
morning. He should keep it in order, should poor George Plattman.
I will do it.'

'Where is it now?' asked Syn.

'By the churchyard wall at the north-east corner,' answered
Mipps.

'Go and put it into the open grave,' ordered the vicar. 'You can
dig it in tomorrow before the funeral. Then go and tell Mrs.
Waggetts that my guest will not keep her for longer than ten more
minutes. We will finish this brew, sir, before you turn in, and upon
your return, Mipps, I will indulge you with a night-cap.'

Now although the lawyer was highly amused at the sexton's
misadventure with the bone, Doctor Syn knew very well that it was
all a fabrication, and for his benefit, being in other words the
private language of the men of Dymchurch to pass a message. It

meant that Jimmie Bone, the highwayman, was waiting to have words with him at the north-east corner of the churchyard wall. Mipps in his turn understood, from Doctor Syn's order about placing the bone in the grave, that he in turn was to tell Mr. Bone to take hiding in the open grave prepared for the excise-man's coffin. Mipps therefore departed towards the 'Ship', telling the waiting highwayman to get into the grave for hiding, until he had escorted the Welshman to the inn; then he and the vicar would join him in the churchyard. Bone found it well to be extremely careful in his goings and comings, for although it was not known by any save the Scarecrow and Hellspite that the highwayman sometimes rode in the Scarecrow's name, he was a proscribed thief of the highway, with a large reward offered for his capture alive or dead.

On this particular night, he had come to the vicarage on foot, so not having his horse to look to, he was glad of the open grave as a hiding-place. Mipps told him he would not have to wait long, and that as soon as the Welshman was safe, he would be released. A few minutes later, having delivered his message to Mrs. Waggetts, and accepted a noggin of rum for his pains, Mipps returned back to the vicarage, where Doctor Syn poured him out a glass of hot grog.

'Did you put the bone into the grave?' asked the vicar.

'I did sir. All safe down deep,' and from the sexton's reply Syn knew that Jimmie Bone was tucked out of the Welshman's sight.

A quarter of an hour later Doctor Syn carefully closed the vicarage door behind the tall, masked highwayman and little grinning Mipps. With his finger on his lips to ensure silence, he led them to his study, and produced another bottle of brandy.

'And how goes your business, Mister Bone?' asked the vicar.

'A coach-load last week, as no doubt you heard, sir,' replied the gentleman of the road. 'Since then nothing at all, sir, what couldn't proceed in peace was not worth the holding, which no doubt has been a good thing, as it has been well for me to lie low.'

'I shall need you to ride tomorrow in my place, Jimmie,' said Syn. 'There is a Welsh lawyer staying at the "Ship", who has been telling me the adventures of a smuggling leader in his mountains, and in my own conceit I have a mind that he should see the Scarecrow's men at work. I warrant he will then not be quite so full of his local hero, who by the way seems to be a scoundrel of the first order. Also I have a mind to test the courage of this Welshman, and for my own protection, since my immediate future may be bound up with his.'

'Will you ride as the Scarecrow at all?' asked Bone.

'No. I shall be on the Marsh as myself, though no doubt I shall find opportunity to give orders should anything go wrong. I shall be visiting Mother Handaway as the vicar, and I think the Welsh lawyer, Mr. Jones, will accompany me. I will arrange with you where to take us by surprise, for I wish you to capture us both, and after threatening to take our lives, you will lash us back to back to the signpost at the corner of Mipps's coffin shop. An uncanny spot will be good for our stranger. I will prepare a notice for you to nail up over my head, which will give the reason for my punishment.'

'And what will the reason be?' asked the highwayman.

'Why, you see, at the funeral tomorrow I shall take the opportunity of condemning lawbreakers,' explained Syn. 'I shall in particular attack the Scarecrow, and so that gentleman, or devil, resenting the meddlesome parson, will show his authority too.'

'Aye, I understand,' replied Bone. 'Much such a game as we played before.' Syn chuckled at the remembrance and nodded. 'It is well for people to know that I am an enemy of the Scarecrow. But we must be careful of our playing this time, for, unless I am mistaken, our Welsh friend is not such a fool as he looks.

But now let us arrange the route to be taken by the pack-ponies. The cargo will be landed beyond Dungeness, while the decoy boats make a false landing at Littlestone. If the revenue cutter appears, which I do not anticipate, the decoys will lead her in a running fight towards Sandgate. The pack-ponies will take the Brooklands way, and we shall use the "hides" at the "Royal Oak". Mipps will see that the sign of the Scarecrow is chalked on all stable doors, so that the ostlers will leave them unbarred.'

'Has the word been passed to all concerned?' asked Mr. Bone.

'All concerned,' nodded Mipps.

'And the Night-riders will assemble on Aldington Knoll,' continued Doctor Syn, 'and when the flare is shown from the boats, they will ride down to the lower level. The pack-ponies will be at the foot of the Knoll and will cross the marsh to the sea-wall under cover of the dyke mists. You will arrest the Welshman and myself at Mother Handaway's. Mipps, as Hellspite, will take the parson up behind his horse, and Curlew shall take the lawyer. On reaching Dungeness you will put it to the vote with pebbles—two pebbles death; one pebble life. You will announce the votes are equal, so that you will have the casting vote yourself. You will read me a homily against meddling in affairs which do not concern me, and you will tell me to be better-mannered in future when preaching.

You know the line to take, Jimmie. And by the way, Mipps, this lawyer. He sleeps light, he tells me. See to it that the stable boys talk beneath his window, which he keeps open. I wish him to stumble on news of the "run" for tomorrow night. And now let us go over the details before parting.' After some two hours' survey over Doctor Syn's great map of the Marsh, Gentleman James, or Jimmie Bone as he was known amongst his intimates, took leave of the vicar with Mipps, and, left to himself, Doctor Syn trimmed his quill pen, and chuckled as he wrote out his address for the funeral.

An hour later, the contents of the brandy bottle consumed, he climbed up the stairs to bed, well satisfied that he would be able to be in two places at once upon the next night, for on Hellspite's horse he would ride with Mipps alongside the false Scarecrow, and be able to give such orders as might be necessary, while in the eyes of the Welsh lawyer he would be nobody except a very ill-used old parson, who in the exercise of his duty had stumbled upon a misadventure.

Chapter 5. Doctor Syn does not appear to be frightened

The next day the weather broke and the Marsh lay wet under a fine drizzle.

Doctor Syn, in spite of late nights at work in his study, was an early riser. He had long since trained himself to need little sleep. Directly he came downstairs he would step out into his porch and survey the weather. Like his master, Mipps, too, needed little sleep, and the vicar was amused to see him crossing the churchyard to the open grave, shouldering spade and pick.

But Mipps was not the first there. The Welsh lawyer, in a heavy coat against the rain, was gazing into the deep cavity.

Doctor Syn, who, much to the anxiety of his housekeeper, was impervious to the dirtiest weather, strolled from beneath the porch without hat or top coat.

Crossing into the churchyard, he overheard the following conversation.

'You are out early, sir,' remarked Mipps to the lawyer. 'Interested in graves? You'd not be if you'd dug as many as I have.'

'Likely not,' replied the lawyer. 'I had a curiosity to see the haunted bone you spoke of last night. But it is not there.'

'Ain't it?' said Mipps, assuming an astonishment he did not feel. 'Well, now, where's it got to? Back in its old haunt no doubt.' He peered into the grave. 'Are you sure it ain't there? No, you're right, sir. And I'm not surprised when I comes to think of it. It's no use trying to regulate that old bone. It's just set on aggravating me.'

'Good morning,' said the vicar cheerfully, 'though I fear it is a wet one. A funeral is a sad and a bad business in the best of weather, but in the rain—most miserable. Have you come to dig in your old enemy, the bone, Mr. Mipps?'

'It's gone, sir,' replied the sexton. 'Spirited itself away. Some might say a dog has took it, but dogs don't care for jumping in and out of graves. No, the old bone has gone of its own accord. I had a notion it wouldn't take kindly to lying under George Plattman's coffin.'

'Are you sure you dropped it in?' asked the vicar.

'Heard it go "plop", sir,' returned Mipps emphatically. 'Very strange.'

'Might be the rooks,' suggested Doctor Syn, looking up at the colony of cawing birds above him.

Mipps shook his head. 'What would they want now with an old dried bone? They'd pick us, but not that. No, sir, I believes in ghosts and such things, and ain't ashamed to say so. The Marsh out there for instance. There's no one can tell me that she ain't haunted by "things" what comes out of every dyke at night. All a-dripping too. Ugh!' Mipps performed a convincing shudder which secretly amused the vicar.

'Ever seen any of these "things"?' asked the lawyer.

'Yes, I has,' retorted Mipps indignantly. 'And them what laughs, wouldn't if they could see what I've seen. Ghosts? Ain't there? There is. It's their happy hunting ground. All this tale of smugglers what some folk believes in is nothing but "them" at their horrid pranks. I've seen the spectral horsemen of Romney Marsh, I has, and on nights too when I have not took so much as half a noggin, and what's more Doctor Pepper can bear me out in it, and who should know better, him crossing the Marsh at all hours of the night a-visiting the sick?'

'But the vicar does that too,' objected the lawyer, 'and he tells me he has seen nothing of them.'

Mipps looked disgusted and answered, 'The vicar's an 'oly man. They couldn't appear to him.'

'Well, we will not make the morning gloomier than it is,' laughed the vicar.

He turned to the lawyer and asked, 'I hope, at any rate, sir, that you slept free from ghosts and such disturbances?'

'The Ship Inn is comfortable enough, sir, and I should have slept uncommon well in compliment to all the excellent drinks you gave me, reverend sir. But to speak truth, I hardly slept at all, but lay awake listening.'

'What to?' demanded Mipps.

The lawyer looked grave. 'Whistles first and then whisperings. Some of them in the passages not far from my door too. And then a long hushed conversation immediately below my window. Whoever they were, they were foolishly prodigal about being overheard.'

'Them ostlers talking horses, that's all, I expects,' suggested the sexton.

'They gossips away all night like a Mothers' Meeting. Mrs. Waggetts has complained about 'em enough.'

'I cannot say who they were,' went on the lawyer. 'But slowly their conversation began to interest me, and I crept from my bed and listened. Men should be careful when they talk against the Government.'

'They were talking about the elections no doubt,' said Mipps.

'It certainly had to do with the Government,' returned the lawyer dryly, 'but all I heard was against it. I'll tell you what it was, and no doubt you, sir' (this to Doctor Syn) 'will take immediate steps against it. There is definitely some sort of smuggling activity going forward, and planned for tonight. I heard words over and over again such as "pack-ponies", "Night-riders", and the "Scarecrow". Then something about all the stable doors being left open.'

'Dear, dear, I trust you were mistaken,' returned Doctor Syn, looking very distressed. 'I can hardly credit it, sir, with poor George Plattman as yet unburied. However I do not feel confident that should such a thing have been planned, the words that I shall speak in my funeral address against lawbreakers will turn all Marsh parishioners from their evil ways. But I see my housekeeper looking out for me, as I have not yet breakfasted, and if you are in the same case, sir, perhaps you will do me the honour of joining me?'

'I have not yet eaten,' returned the lawyer.

'Then Mipps will go to the inn and tell them not to lay cover for you; you shall eat with me. Come along.' Doctor Syn turned to Mipps and added, 'I think it wise not to make any mention of what this gentleman has told us. I will go to the coastguards this morning and warn them privately. I will also inform the squire. And if you will take my advice, Mr. Jones, you will also keep mum about this. Being a stranger, you will readily fall under the suspicion of the villagers, for you must remember that nobody but I knows your business here. I will not pretend to deny but there are desperate men about. For instance there is a highwayman at large with a large reward upon his head. He is popular with those who know him, otherwise he would have been betrayed. It would go hard with any man if the villagers thought he was on the trail of Gentleman James.'

'Is that what the rascal calls himself?' laughed the Welshman.

'Ay, Mr. Jimmie Bone has that high opinion of himself,' explained the vicar, as he led the Welshman out of the churchyard. 'There were some who thought him to be the Scarecrow, but that has been disproved. Like most of his trade, he spends money freely when he has made a hold-up. Do you know, the rascal has the humorous effrontery to pay his tithes.'

'Which you refuse, of course,' retorted the lawyer.

'Which I accept, of course,' corrected Doctor Syn. 'I see no reason for denying his dues to the parish. If he robs a coach, the Sick and Needy fund is benefited. It is better than letting the money be spent in the taverns.'

'No doubt you are wise to take the broad-minded view,' said the lawyer.

'But to change the subject, from our notorious highwayman to yourself,' said Syn, 'I think it would be wise of you to let the folk at the Ship Inn know that you are a lawyer, and are down here on private family business with me.

Otherwise they may put wrong construction on your sudden appearance here, which might well prove dangerous to you.'

'I am not one to be frightened, sir,' replied the lawyer stiffly.

'Well, to be frank, sir,' replied the doctor, as he led his guest into the house, 'I was somewhat wondering about that, because it strikes me that this Dolgenny of yours was able to frighten you down south.'

'Not through fear of my own skin, but for love of my niece,' exclaimed the lawyer. 'There would be none so pleased as I, if Dolgenny could be brought to book, and had he not cast a favourable eye upon my niece, I should have defied him openly, and no doubt paid the penalty ere now.'

'Well, as I hinted to you last night,' said the doctor, 'it is a long time since I had a vacation. I suggest that I may persuade the squire to release me for some weeks, in order that we may establish our joint claims to the Tontine at the Edinburgh bank. We could visit your mountains on the way back and, who knows, break a lance or two against your local villain. Is he a good swordsman, by the way?'

'The finest I ever saw,' exclaimed the lawyer, 'and he'll quarrel with anyone at the slightest provocation, for he prefers to kill openly so that he may be sheltered by the so-called gentlemanly rules of duelling, and the death he gives, though deplored by all honest folk, can in no way touch his liberty.

Besides, there is no gaol in North Wales that would hold him. He's a wizard.

No, sir, if we are to win against him, we must do it with subtlety and not with force. Certainly not with an open quarrel.'

'I may beg to differ there,' said the vicar, smiling. 'I allow that you see in me just an ordinary country parson, helping you to breakfast. But it may surprise you to know that I have killed my man.'

'I have seen some proof of your shooting,' laughed the lawyer, 'but the sword needs youth and strength, and both of these Dolgenny has.' Doctor Syn shrugged his shoulders. 'The sword needs a strong wrist, sir, with a brain directing it. It needs an agile body, not necessarily a youthful one. I once killed a noted duellist when I was at the University of Oxford. He was older than I, but a fine swordsman. I had the youth certainly, but it was not that which beat him. He lost at last because he could not stay the course. It was a long fight, but his body had been pampered. Now, despite my age, I have never given in to it. I think I am as agile as ever I was. I know I have more knowledge, and that only comes from experience. I have always had the knack of knowing what my antagonist will do next, and one that knowledge I act. I have ever had a liking for pretty sword play, and have never considered myself too old to keep in practice.' After breakfast Mipps brought the news that the revenue officers from Sandgate and Dover had arrived at the Coastguard Station. They had bespoken dinner at the 'Ship', and it was their intention to attend the funeral first.

'See that they are received well, my good Mipps,' ordered the vicar. 'Keep an eye on their comfort yourself.' Mipps knew from this that he was to keep an eye upon them and not upon their comfort.

The funeral, despite the rain, was attended not only by all the Dymchurch folk, but by people of all classes from the Marsh villages. The little church was full, and a good crowd gathered in the churchyard around the grave, while others waited to follow the coffin when it was lifted out from the Coastguard Station. In front of the coffin walked the beadle, the squire, the Lords of the Level, and the Clerk of the Court. The mourners followed. Now the coffin, draped in a flag, was to have been placed upon a boat's launching wheels and drawn by six coastguards, but at the last moment this arrangement was altered by one of the revenue officers, who, after a whispered consultation with the beadle, ordered a covered wagon to be substituted for the wheels. The mourners, thinking that something must have gone wrong with the boatlaunching wheels, took little notice of the alteration. Nor did they see that the beadle handed a large key to the officer, who, as it afterwards transpired, had a very good reason for his action.

Although it was still raining, Doctor Syn did not deliver his address inside the church, where the first part of the service was held. He wished everyone to hear what he had to say, and so postponed it till after the committal.

Then he raised his voice and spoke to the assembly. After

praising George Plattman's strict adherence to duty and the Crown, he bade his listeners take to heart the dreadful lesson which some recreants had brought before them that day. 'Although the good things of this world are given to us by a kindly Providence for our comfort and delight, we must always bow to the authorities set over us, who, for the good of our country's revenue, have placed lawful taxation upon certain commodities. It is not the consumption of these commodities or use of them that is sinful, but the evading of their legal dues.

The money which such evasion brings in to private individuals is a sore temptation to those who do not scruple to cheat the Government and such cupidity is apt to turn to violence, hatred, and base deceits. A man who fears the gallows of justice must needs become desperate. The agents of the devil are amongst us, ever seeking to win over men of weak and covetous characters. I thank God that there are none such in my parish. If the crime of smuggling is ever carried on amidst the dykes and beaches of our blessed and prosperous Romney Marsh, I could take my oath that surely the criminals are of foreign soil, and not respected folk who live and toil upon our pasture lands. These wretches may come and go in the night when honest folk are asleep. Some say that they do. I know not. And yet, it has been my privilege to minister here for many years, and no one knows everyone hereabouts as well as I, and certainly there is no one whom I can think of who could be so smooth a hypocrite as this spectral rider who calls himself the Scarecrow. Man or devil, I feel confident that he does not belong to us. That such a creature exists, some doubt. To those I say that I have on this day of sorrow received a letter from him. My good housekeeper discovered it beneath a pile of new-laid eggs in her collecting basket. It is an arrogant threat to me, as your vicar, that if I speak against him at this solemn service, it will be the worse for me. One cannot allow such a one to stop the mouth of God's church. I shall therefore speak. I solemnly denounce him here before you all as a miscreant, and let him do his worst to me, if it is God's will that he should have the power to harm me. I adjure you to avoid him, my brethren. Say unto him and unto all his tribe, "Get thee behind me, Satan". And let the example of brave George Plattman in this grave steel our hearts against all such wickedness; and even at the risk of our lives, let us stamp out this outrage of smuggling from our midst, which can only lead eventually to the scaffold and hell-gates.' Mipps, leaning on his spade, looked at the inspired face of the vicar as his grand voice thundered out to the rain-soaked mourners. He looked round, too, at the faces of the villagers he knew so well. They all appeared to be absorbed by the saint's address, and in full agreement with his brave exhortation. Mipps chuckled in his heart, knowing that those who wore the holiest expression on this sad occasion rode beside him with the Scarecrow's Night-riders, or walked at night with the long cavalcade of pack-ponies. At the conclusion of the service, the first to thank the vicar for his brave and patriotic words were the revenue officers. He showed them the Scarecrow's warning he had received, and they in turn showed it to the Clerk of the Dymchurch Court, hoping he might get a clue from the writing. But it was obviously a hand disguised. The Clerk said so, and Doctor Syn shared his opinion; and who knew better than he who had written it himself the night before and placed it in the basket that very morning behind his housekeeper's back? As the crowds slowly disbursed, Doctor Syn noticed that the Welshman had got into conversation with the two revenue officers, who were strolling with him towards the Ship Inn.

'I want you in the vestry, Mr. Mipps,' said the vicar. 'Were you going to fill in this grave at once?'

'Better do it soon, sir,' replied the sexton. 'With all this rain about, poor George is like to be flooded out.'

'Come to the vestry first, however,' ordered the vicar.

The squire, before returning to the Court House, asked Doctor Syn to join him there as soon as possible for a glass of sherry before dinner. He had heard of the Welshman's arrival, and had noticed him at the funeral, and wished to know what the vicar knew of him.

'I will follow you, Tony,' said the vicar. 'I can tell you strange news about this Welshman, but I must first sign the register of burial for Mr. Mipps.' The vicar closed the vestry door and looked at Mipps, who helped him to divest himself of his Geneva gown in which he had been officiating.

'As I am going to the squire's,' he said, 'perhaps you will take this to the vicarage to be dried?'

'Aye, sir,' replied Mipps. 'It's as wet as we used to get on the poop in a seastorm.'

'That Welshman may talk,' went on Syn. 'Find out whether those revenue fellows ask him to dine at their table. He refused my offer to introduce him to the squire at dinner, saying he was for eating by himself at the "Ship". If he does talk, in spite of my asking him not to, and I think it likely that he will, we shall have

those two officers to deal with on the "run" tonight. We may as well
know beforehand.'

'Aye, aye, vicar,' replied Mipps. 'I'll first take your wet gown to
be dried.

Then I'll take a look at the "Ship" and them gentlemen, and
after that fill in the grave. If them revenue men comes "out"
tonight, and we has no choice but to deal with 'em the same as
poor Plattman, I take it that they'd not be buried here, but one in
Sandgate, and one in Dover.'

'Aye,' nodded Syn. 'And I noted that the officer from Hythe was
there too.

He was standing at the edge of the crowd, and I have no doubt
but that these three birds of ill-omen will now be gathering
together. I expect he went to the "Ship" to wait for them. He would
be buried in Hythe. I fear you will not get any commission for
coffins from them, should the worst happen.' Mipps grinned. 'Well,
we don't want no more funerals in this sort of weather. In fact, I
feel so cold that I think a little something warming will be sensible.'

'They say rum is an excellent medicine against the cold,' replied
Syn, smiling.

Having signed the register and bidden Mipps lock up the book,
the vicar put on his top coat and walked from the church to the
Court House.

This building, which was the official residence of the squire as
chief magistrate, was a fine rambling old mansion, and contained
the Court Room and offices connected with the ruling of Romney
Marsh, besides housing the beadle, in rooms above the cells, and
quarters for the Clerk of the Court.

During his lifelong friendship with Sir Antony Cobtree, Doctor
Syn had free access to the house at all times. His own position as
chaplain to the Court gave him a key to all the official rooms, and
to their own private apartments the Cobtrees never expected him
to be announced, but just to walk in when he was so disposed. He
therefore opened the front door and, crossing the flagstoned hall,
proceeded to the library.

Here he found the squire in a state of great excitement talking
angrily to the revenue officer from Hythe. Doctor Syn was very
surprised to see him in the squire's library, for as he had told
Mipps, he expected that the three officers would be together at the
'Ship'.

The two men, whose heated argument he had interrupted,
presented a marked contrast. The squire, very popular in the

district, was hearty in manner as a rule, but though he still rode to hounds, his face and figure were already showing signs of good living, and the heartiness for which he was famed was banished from his florid face only when he was suffering from irritating twinges of gout. On entering the room, Doctor Syn thought that the exposure from the funeral had brought on one of these attacks. On seeing the vicar, the squire immediately stopped speaking, though he still glared angrily at the officer, a stolid, serious-looking man of forty, with a weather-beaten face, dark hair tied back in a neat queue, dark eyes, hard and penetrating, and a hooked nose. His limbs might have been framed from gnarled oak, and there was a tenacity of purpose about him which had raised him from the ranks of customs' men to the post of an officer of some importance. Doctor Syn wondered what had brought him to the squire. By his friend's rage he gathered it to be something unpleasant.

'I hope there is nothing wrong,' he said with a sympathetic smile.

'Well, yes,' admitted the squire, still glaring at the officer, who sat stiffly on a high-backed chair without arms.

'Oh, for heaven's sake,' exploded the squire, 'get into a more comfortable seat! The sight of you sitting there on that unarmed contraption brings on my gout. There are plenty of good armchairs as you can see, without choosing that thing.'

'It is quite to my liking, sir,' replied the officer. 'But if it pleases you, I will change, since I am your guest.'

'Let the good fellow sit where it pleases him, Tony,' reproved the doctor.

He then added with a smile, 'You need not look at him, if the sight of his chair gives you the gout.'

'I'll have the chair taken out of here for good, when he's gone,' replied the squire testily, as he poured himself out another glass of sherry and tossed it down.

'My dear friend,' laughed Doctor Syn, 'when you have remembered your manners and given your guests a glass of your excellent wine, perhaps you will tell me what is wrong. I think you said there was something wrong?'

'So there is. So there is,' grumbled the squire. 'As ever there was.' He poured out a glass of wine and handed it to the vicar, who was about to pass it to the officer when the squire stopped him with: 'Oh, I offered him one, but he wouldn't have it any more than he will have a comfortable seat.'

'And yet I have seen you drinking at the "Ship", sir,' said Doctor

Syn.

'Aye, sir. Off duty, but not on it as now,' replied the officer curtly.

'So you are here on duty, eh?' inquired the vicar. 'Not come to arrest the squire, I hope. Indeed, you could not have the authority in Dymchurch.'

'It's almost as bad,' exploded the squire again. 'I'll tell you.' There was an interruption, however. A discreet tap on the door, and the squire shouted, 'Come in.' The door opened slowly and Mipps looked round it, touching his forelock to the squire. Mipps shared with Doctor Syn the right of entry to the Court House at all times.

'Begging your pardon, squire,' said the sexton, and then he saw the officer and broke off with, 'Oh, there you are!'

'Are you looking for this man?' asked the squire. Then, realizing that the man in question was a commoner who had risen from the ranks, he now occupied an honoured post, he amended his question with, 'Are you looking for this gentleman? Have you business with him?'

'Not business, sir. Oh dear no!' replied Mipps. 'Just a message which I undertook to deliver to this er—gentleman. He's wanted.'

'By whom?' asked the officer.

'By the customs,' said Mipps significantly. 'Not only are you wanted by the Sandgate officer, but by the Dover one too. At the "Ship". So when the squire's finished with you, go quiet and don't let Mrs. Waggetts have no scene.' No doubt the squire should have reproved this facetiousness, but he was always amused by Mipps and invariably encouraged him to be funny.

'Well, don't stand there, jambed in the door,' ordered the squire. 'Come in and take a glass of wine. I think at least that you are not squeamish like this gentleman, who refuses to drink on duty.'

'I'll drink in most places, sir, duty or no,' replied Mipps, coming into the room and closing the door. Then, turning to the vicar, he added, 'Except on holy ground or in holy buildings.'

'Not even in the crypt, you rogue?' laughed the squire, who was already getting over his temper.

'Sometimes, sir, in the crypt or vaults if they smells dankish,' replied the sexton. 'I then takes something not to drink, but as medicine to keep out the cold vapours.'

'Aye, rum is a good medicine for that,' said the squire with a wink. 'But sherry is none so bad either,' and he handed the sexton a glassful.

'But what is this bad news you were about to tell us, Sir Antony?' asked the vicar. 'I take it you can speak before our sexton?'

'The news is not bad at all, sir,' said the officer emphatically. 'Merely a piece of routine which can be adjusted no doubt to please all parties.'

'It will not please me unless it goes to my way of thinking,' retorted the squire, getting angry once more.

'Aye, that was ever your way,' laughed Doctor Syn.

'If the Squire of Dymchurch tries to impress you that I have brought him ill news,' went on the officer, addressing the vicar, 'I venture to think that you will agree with me that I have brought him very good news. In fact, sir, the best news not only for my humble purse, but for the bettering of this neighbourhood.

In short, reverend sir, I have caught and arrested Gentleman James, the some time prize-fighter, better known as Jimmie Bone the highwayman.' Mipps shot a quick glance at the vicar, and saw that he showed no reaction to this staggering piece of news, except to raise his eyebrows in mild surprise.

The officer went on. 'In twelve hours the reward of five hundred pounds will be in my pocket, and when I use certain methods which seldom fail to make the strongest squeal and speak, I may add another thousand for information which will lead to the arrest of the Scarecrow. That is my good news, sir, and I hope you agree that it is so. The Church supports the law, I know.'

'The Church preserves the law, sir,' corrected the vicar. 'We gave it to you in our translation of the Bible. But now that we have heard your good news, what is the bad? But first where is this highwayman guarded?'

'That is the whole point, reverend sir, of what the squire calls "bad" news,' continued the officer. 'He is in the cells here of the Court House, and no one knows of it save this present company, the coastguards whom I have bound to silence, and the beadle from whom I got the key. I think you will admit that I carried out the arrest in the neatest way. This scoundrel is very popular, like anyone who is free with their money. But in his so-called generosity, he overreached himself. He had heard of an old woman who was dying in poverty in Hythe. Her case was desperate, though she had not applied to the parish for help, through mistaken pride. This Bone heard of her distress, and since she had once done him a service, he sets off like a fool in broad daylight to carry her money and nourishment. I got the information from a neighbour who had visited the invalid. She heard the old woman mumbling her thanks to God and to this scoundrel.'

'And informed you, yes?' put in the vicar.

The officer nodded. 'Now I could have arrested him in that house. I suppose a too cautious officer would have done so. He would then have been locked up in the cells at Hythe. But it occurred to me that if I could find his hiding-place I mighty be able to recover a haul of what he had robbed. I and six of my men waited for him to come out of the house, and sure enough he presently comes out.'

'Was he masked?' interrupted the vicar. 'I ask because I have been told that no one has ever seen his face.'

'No,' went on the officer. 'But he was well muffled up, which was excusable, against the driving rain. He sets off through the town towards the Marsh. I followed him. At the end of the High Street I signalled to my men, who were hidden in a covered wagon. This was at the corner by the "Red Lion". We kept behind. So long as he kept to the road we were sure of him, and I was hoping that his hiding-place would be one of the lonely cottages beneath the sea-wall. Whether he felt suspicious of our wagon crawling in his wake, I don't know, but when we reached the sea-wall and had gone a few hundred yards in its shelter, he turned right and crossed a plank bridge on to the empty Marsh. It was impossible for us to drive after him, so I gave up the idea of tracking him to his lair, and ordered by men out of the cart. His suspicions were aroused then, for he began to hurry, glancing behind him. I sang out to him, asking the way to Dymchurch. I saw him slip his hands into his side pockets, feeling for his pistols. He evidently knew that we had recognized him, for I presume he knows me well enough as his enemy. He pulled up his mask, which was under his cravat, and started to run. For such a big fellow, he was as fleet as a deer. I ordered my men in pursuit, sending two of the best runners out like a fan to hedge him off. I think he would have got away but for a mishap which was his undoing. He ran down a dyke bank to cross the water, caught his foot in some bulrushes, and down he went with a sprained ankle and his head under water. By the time he had extricated himself we were on him. His pistols both missed fire from the damp, and I flung my heavy cudgel, which struck him on the forehead and knocked him out. After that it was easy to pull him unconscious from the water and lash him up. We carried him to the road and lifted him into the wagon. Blood had stained his mask, and I thrust my 'kerchief beneath it, which staunched the wound. But I took one peep beneath the mask to see if I could identify him. I had seen him once before in a Hythe inn and had been told he was a grain merchant from Maidstone. It was good fortune that he could not come riding into Hythe on that famous horse of his.'

'But how did you bring him here without attracting attention?' asked the squire.

'You'll never guess,' laughed the officer.

'Must have been very clever,' put in Mipps, who, taking the lead from Doctor Syn, was striving to hide the dismay upon his face. 'Gentleman James is very popular. You'd never have got him to the cells without some of that mob attending the funeral trying to rescue him. He's been good to the poor, they say.'

'It was clever,' said the officer. 'I warrant, too, it will raise a laugh in court.'

'I think I see how it was done,' remarked the vicar. 'You brought him in the wagon that carried the coffin?' The officer grinned and nodded. 'Told my colleagues that orders had been changed and that the coffin was to be taken to the churchyard in our horse wagon. I'd taken the precaution to gag the highwayman's mouth while he was unconscious, which he was till we got him into the cell.'

'You might have suffocated the man,' said Doctor Syn.

'I think a hempen rope will do that, sir,' replied the officer. 'When the coffin was lifted out I drove the wagon past the Court House and backed it up against the entrance to the cells. The mourners were too interested in the funeral to trouble about us. We lifted the body out screened from view by the wagon, and when Jimmie Bone came round he was lying on the floor of the cell. That is, you will agree, good news.'

'Certainly,' nodded Doctor Syn readily, to the great astonishment of Mipps, who had expected his master to plead for their close colleague. Mipps, in fact, was badly frightened at the turn of events. He knew very well that Jimmie Bone would never willingly betray what he knew, but a man under torture is not always master of his will. Doctor Syn continued, 'But what is the bad news that has so upset the squire?'

'Why, sir,' replied the officer, 'I intend taking the prisoner to a stronger cell. To Hythe, I hope, where I can keep an eye on him. The alternatives are Dover or Sandgate Castle. But since he is my captive, I am for Hythe. I wish to break his spirit in my own way.'

'But no one can move a prisoner once put into my cells,' burst out the squire. 'He is there and it will be my duty to try him at the Dymchurch Court House.'

'That is Romney Marsh law, certainly,' agreed the vicar. 'I must go and see him. At least I may be able to bring him to a better frame of mind by a confession.' The officer nodded. 'Aye, a parson might get something out of him.' Mipps also nodded, but with an effort repressed the grin which he felt was about to spread over his face. If his master had words with Jimmie Bone, it meant that he had already formed some plan of effecting their friend's escape.

'If he talks to me,' went on the vicar, 'I must of course reserve the right of keeping silence according to the dictates of my conscience.'

'You need have no conscience against upholding the full rigour of the law.

The man is a proscribed scoundrel.' Doctor Syn looked at the officer and said, 'Perhaps. We shall see. But the man has not yet spoken. As to the advisability of removing him elsewhere, it might be for the peace of our parish to encourage it, Tony. In any case he would have to be moved secretly, and, I should suggest, at night. I fancy Mipps is right, and that there are many who would attempt a rescue, and I should loath to see any of my flock mixed up in such an adventure against the law. It would make them accomplices. I fear, sir, that your success is robbing not only the poor of a good friend, but of considerable tithes which he sends me after each robbery.'

'You mean you accept it?' gasped the officer.

'Certainly,' replied the vicar innocently. 'I am not to know it is stolen money, though of course one suspects it. But I always ease my conscience by thinking it is better in the funds of the sick and needy than either being spent in the taverns by Mister Bone, or in the pockets of the rich for dicing and cards.

You will please arrange, sir, that I visit the prisoner.'

'Well, sir,' said the officer, 'I suppose I have no authority to stop you if you wish it, since you are chaplain to the Court. But I think you will have to bide a little. He recovered his consciousness all right, but refused food and asked for brandy. I provided this for him at my own expense, seeing that he would earn me a good deal more than the price of a bottle. I sent the beadle for it, and when he returned the prisoner had the effrontery to drink half the contents in one long swallow. He then offered it to me, and when I refused as being on duty, down he tilts the other half. It would have killed some men, but not Bone, who said he was plaguey sleepy and would like to be rid of my company.

Whereupon he curls himself up on the floor, and falls into an immediate and drunken sleep.'

'Then when he wakes from it you will have the goodness to send for me,' said the vicar. 'I shall be dining here with the squire, but afterwards I shall be working at the vicarage.' The officer bowed to the squire, who returned the courtesy distantly; and Doctor Syn, followed by Mipps, accompanied the officer to the front door. 'I am fully in agreement with you, sir,' said the vicar, 'over the question of removing the prisoner from Dymchurch. But, as I said, it must be done very carefully and under the strictest secrecy.'

'The squire was very indignant at the idea,' replied the officer.

'Well, he is naturally jealous of his rule here,' explained Doctor Syn. 'His position is somewhat unique, since he holds it direct from the Crown. But I fancy I can persuade him to our way of thinking. By the way, how is your prisoner guarded? Not by your coastguards, I hope? for then the news will be all over the village.'

'No, sir, for I thought the same,' replied the officer. 'Besides, the squire forbade it, and pointed out that although Bone was a law-breaker, he was a highwayman and not a smuggler. Of that I have my own opinion, and shall, I think, discover more later. No, sir, my prisoner is guarded at the moment by an empty bottle of brandy which will keep him quiet for a long time, a crack on the head, a sprained or strained ankle, an oak door with strong bolts, and your beadle. That is enough for me to be able to snatch a morsel of dinner at the inn.'

'But will you let me know when I can visit him?' asked the vicar.

'Are you really determined to?' asked the officer. 'It is not without danger.

However, I shall be there and armed.'

Doctor Syn shook his head. 'That I will not permit. You may stand outside the door if you will, but inside I insist on privacy. I go there as a parson, and I hope to get a confession from a penitent. It is my duty to visit any prisoner in the Court House cell, and I always see them alone.'

'I warn you against it, reverend sir,' said the officer.

'I am in the Lord's hands, who will deliver His servants from the wicked,' said the vicar solemnly.

The officer shrugged his shoulders and strode away.

Doctor Syn imitated his shrug, and looked at Mipps, who realized that the gesture in the officer's case meant contempt for the parson's faith in God's protection; but he also knew from past experience that when the vicar used the gesture of shrugging his shoulders and looking at him with wide-open eyes as he had then done, they were both called upon to crack a very hard nut.

Mipps sighed. 'Poor James! Now what did he want to go airing his charity for on a day like this, full of Preventive men thinking of poor George's funeral? He's tied a rope round his neck this time.' Doctor Syn closed the front door quietly behind him and strolled with Mipps towards the churchyard wall. 'I rather think our friend is not worrying about that,' he said softly. 'He trusts us to untie it for him, and so, like an experienced soldier, he is snatching a good sleep before his is called by us into action.'

'What's the orders then, sir?' asked Mipps. 'For I see no way out of it.

According to plans we need Jimmie tonight. In fact, without him the "run" will be marred, and we'll have to signal the boats back to France.'

'We'll do nothing of the kind,' replied Syn. 'To get James out of the cells will not be so difficult as my own escape which I managed from Dover Castle, but it will be something after that fashion. I shall need my Geneva gown and a good length of cord to tie beneath it. A gag, too. Well, Jimmie is wearing a 'kerchief. That will serve. It should be simple if our luck holds.' Mipps grinned. 'And I suppose you thought that out directly you heard the news, eh, sir? You never turned a hair, and I owns I was badly frightened.' He then looked solemn and added, 'There's that officer, though. He could hardly miss, if he thought anything was wrong.'

'But if he does think so and attempts to fire,' said Syn, 'you as a good churchman, Mipps, could naturally be horrified at bloodshed, which would be an excuse for spoiling his aim.' Mipps grinned again. 'I'm glad I'm to be there, sir.'

'Of course. With the beadle and officer, while I enter the cell. Jimmie will lash me up, and put on my gown and wig, and the moment he knocks and the beadle unlocks the door, you must attract the attention of the officer. He will cover his face as he comes out as though in prayer. Should the officer recognize him, while your arm turns his aim, he can use his fists, I hope. There's no heed to be taken of the beadle. I never knew him to look for trouble yet. Now, I shall be back in the vicarage within the next two hours, for I have much to talk over with the squire. You must fill in that grave, but give orders that ears are to listen at the "Ship". I wish to know whether my Welshman holds conversation with the excise men.'

'And if he does, you wish to know what it's about, eh?' Doctor Syn nodded. 'I will find out from Jimmie Bone if anyone else saw his face when he was taken. If so that person or persons will, I fear, have to accompany the Hythe officer upon a very long journey.' Anyone noticing Doctor Syn at that moment as he spoke to his sexton with such a gentle, saintly smile upon his face, would have imagined that he was but talking upon parochial matters. No one would have suspected that he had just pronounced a grim sentence of death.

With a respectful, 'Aye, aye, sir,' Mipps strolled away towards the Ship Inn.

Doctor Syn watched him and listened to a nautical air that the little sexton was whistling, and forgetting for the moment the predicament the highwayman was in and forced them all to share, he said to himself, 'There goes a curious piece of humanity if ever there was one. As faithful as a dog; as useful as a horse; as brave as a mongoose; as sly as a monkey; as fierce as a rat; as gentle as a lamb, and as wise and as foolish, according to requirement, as an owl. We've been through more together than the average, that's certain. Battle, murder, and sudden death. We came here at length for a quiet life, and what have we gained? Battle, murder, and sudden death all over again. And so it will go on till the end of one of us.' When Mipps had disappeared into the coaching-yard of the 'Ship', Doctor Syn took a quick look towards the cells; then he opened the Court House door, and rejoined the squire in the library. The latter, unlike the rest of the neighbouring gentry, had a sneaking regard for the audacious highwayman.

True, he had never suffered at his hands, which was, of course, entirely due to the fact that Jimmie Bone, knowing that Sir Antony was Doctor Syn's old college friend, had always let the squire's coach go by in peace. Certainly the squire had often fumed outwardly against the highwayman for daring to break the laws upon his own Romney Marsh, but since his irritation a few minutes before against the Hythe officer, he began to range himself on the prisoner's side, and confessed as much by saying, when Doctor Syn came back, 'I could almost wish that the rascal would escape.'

'What, Jimmie Bone the highwayman?' cried Doctor Syn, astonished.

'He's also known as "Gentleman James",' corrected the squire. 'And, plague take him, he was certainly arrested doing a gentlemanly action. Besides, I admire the way the fellow accepted defeat and asked for a bottle of the best.

The man is a philosopher.'

'I must say that I should not care to be in your seat when you condemn him to death,' answered the vicar sadly. 'He is a man much loved by the poor, and for them he does as much good in his way as you do in yours. But you will be able to do nothing less than condemn him, of course. General Troubridge has never forgiven him for holding him up in the Archbishop's coach.'

'Troubridge will not dictate to me,' exploded the squire. 'No, my friend, not in my own Court Room.'

'But we must not deceive ourselves,' went on the vicar persuasively. 'This man Bone has frequently robbed His Majesty's mails. Even the Chief Magistrate of the Marsh could hardly overlook that. There would certainly not be one of the Lords of the Level who would support you in leniency, which could only appear to them as high treason. No, Tony, you know as well as I do that death or the plantations would be the only sentence you could pass.'

'You are in the right of it there,' exclaimed the squire. 'And I must own that when you put it like that I should be unpopular either way. Not that I give a fig for old Troubridge or what he thinks! He has a grievance against the rascal. But if he can't look after himself, it's his own fault. The highwayman has never attacked me, and I travel about a good deal. I think I would far sooner lose the regard of that blustering old dragon than my popularity with the poor.'

'Aye, you have ever been the father to your parish, Tony. But they will take this arrest badly, and I could wish that you would allow this Hythe officer to take him elsewhere to be tried. It would not then be laid to your door. Besides, we know that Bone is an ingenious rascal. The more he is moved from prison to trial, the better chance he has to escape.' Suddenly the squire began to chuckle. He was about to speak, but seemed to think better of it and poured out more sherry instead.

'Well, highwayman or no,' said Doctor Syn, 'he is a game fighter, and I for one never regret having fought against such a magnificent specimen.'

'And remember it was you who helped him escape that time,' laughed the squire.

'My conscience is easy on that score,' replied the vicar. 'The dragoons pursuing him were no parishioners of mine, whereas Bone has always had the humour to pay his tithes. Besides, as he told me that day, he has never robbed a parson.'

'Nor a good squire,' said Sir Antony. 'And now perhaps you guess the reason for my chuckling just now.' The vicar shook his head. 'Well, no, Tony, I picture a fine figure of a man like this Bone swinging in chains, and I see no cause for levity in it.'

'Christopher, you old fool,' whispered the squire, and his eyes twinkled with mischievous merriment, 'I dislike that Hythe officer, and I will not say that for the highwayman. Suppose someone—a man like Mipps might do it— but suppose someone let it leak out that the popular highwayman was being removed tonight from Dymchurch to another prison. Suppose that someone— and I still suggest Mipps, as he can be as secret as the devil when he likes— anyway this someone hinted that it meant the rope. Are there brave enough spirits, think you, in Dymchurch, who in sufficient body and under cover of disguises and the darkness would effect a rescue? We would know nothing of it, of course, though we should be secretly glad the highwayman was free, and I confess that I should like to see that Hythe officer, who will not drink on duty, looking even sillier than he did on that chair.' The butler came in to announce dinner.

'Take that chair out into the hall,' ordered the squire. 'It is too stiff for a comfortable library.'

The two friends passed into the dining-room, Doctor Syn continuing in a matter-of-fact tone, 'Yes, Tony, I think something of the sort might be arranged, and I dare swear Mipps might know the man to do it.' Throughout the meal the butler noticed that the squire continued to chuckle, and after the most sedate remarks from the good vicar too. Once when Doctor Syn had been telling him of some poor invalid who would appreciate an early visit from Lady Cobtree when she returned from London, the squire so far forgot himself as to let out a loud and hearty chuckle.

'Whatever amuses you in that?' asked the vicar. 'I tell you that the old body is in need of the comfort which Lady Cobtree can give so well.'

'My thoughts were straying back to that excise officer and how damned silly he was to refuse my good sherry,' explained the squire. Syn, however, was glad to know that if Jimmie Bone escaped, the squire would not be displeased.

When the butler had left the gentlemen to their port, the vicar told the squire what he had heard from the Welshman concerning the Tontine.

'Now that is strange,' said Sir Antony. 'It must have happened. I could not have dreamt it, but many years ago when you were lost to us in America, I had a letter from a banker in Edinburgh, asking whether I could tell him anything of your whereabouts, should you be alive. That I was unable to do. I had given you up for dead, though in my reply I said that we had every hope that you would one day return to us. I asked my correspondent if there was anything I could do, and might I know the nature of the business. His reply was that there was no immediate urgency, and that the matter might never benefit you, but being a secret matter he could give me no details. You may depend it was this Tontine.'

'Very likely,' replied the vicar.

'And you say this Welshman is the only other claimant?' asked Sir Antony.

'That appears to be so,' replied the vicar.

'Then let us hang him instead of Mr. Bone,' laughed the squire. 'What are you going to do about it?' Doctor Syn smiled, fingering the stem of his glass, then leaned across the table. 'Were I not a parson and a man of honour, I could easily find a means of removing the Welshman, without being directly stained by his blood, for he tells me quite seriously that there is a wild smuggler in his home mountains, who wishes not only to murder him, but me as well. In fact, this Welsh lawyer was sent by this gentleman to lure me to Wales for that very purpose!'

'If only he murders him and not you,' laughed the squire, 'the long journey might be worth the making, and, by God, Christopher, I have a mind to accompany you. It would make you a very wealthy man, and all we have to do is to let him murder the lawyer and then fasten a quarrel on the smuggler and kill him in revenge.'

The vicar shook his head. 'We could hardly both be spared from Dymchurch, Tony. Not at the same time. But I must own to a curiosity which prompts me to this journey north. In fact, I proposed to the lawyer that, as rivals for this money, we should cry quits, visit Edinburgh and each draw half the Tontine.'

'And his answer to that?' inquired the squire.

'That the banker is obstinate. In fact, he would not advance one guinea on the Tontine's security, because he had not got proof positive of my death, and it was to obtain this proof that the lawyer has journeyed here to find out for himself. As to his tale of the smuggling rascal up there, well, it sounds fantastic to me.'

'I should not be happy to see you go with him,' said the squire. 'It might be easy enough to arrange an accident in the Welsh passes which might be very convenient to him. How do you know whether the fellow can be trusted?'

'I have ever had a way of looking after myself,' replied the vicar. 'But we will both of us size up this man's character before I start.'

'And you could take Mipps with you,' said the squire. 'Just so soon as the affair of Mr. Bone is settled, we will discuss this seriously. In fact, you had better bring this lawyer to me, and I will hear what he has got to say. Only, after your experience of him, see that he does not carry artillery in his pocket. I have no love for people who point pistols at me.'

'I can promise that he will not make such a fool of himself again,' laughed the vicar.

A few minutes later, Doctor Syn left the Court House for the vicarage.

Mipps was already awaiting him.

'Is there any sign of Jimmie Bone awaking from his drunken sleep?' he asked.

'Not yet, sir,' replied Mipps. 'The Hythe officer left the cell some quarter of an hour ago, and instead of coming here, as I expected, he went to the Ship Inn.'

'Now I wonder why he went there?' said the vicar.

Mipps winked. 'Dirty work which I can't fathom. The Welshman has been very mateyfied with them excise officers. He dined with 'em. I took a drink at the next table, but they talked in whispers. I listened hard, according to your orders, sir, but all I could gather was that they was connecting poor Jimmie Bone with the Scarecrow.'

'Our Welsh friend needs watching, then,' said Doctor Syn. 'I am in the mind to put his courage to the test tonight. I shall know then how far we can depend upon him, for certainly the way he bungled the pistol business did not increase my good opinion of him.'

'But you see, sir, you shot first,' said Mipps with a grin. 'He'd have to be quick indeed who could shoot quicker than Clegg.'

'We will leave the name of that old pirate out of it,' said Doctor Syn. 'I think we agreed to forget that such a man ever lived.'

'Well, sir, it's difficult to remember to forget when you keeps that old harpoon of his hanging above your fireplace.' Syn looked up at the weapon in question, and chuckled. 'I had forgotten that,' he said. 'Now listen, Mipps, I am going to visit Jimmie Bone, and I have thought of a way for his escape. He will put on my robes and come out as me. It must be your part to see that he is not detected. Follow him to the church, and I will give him the keys of the crypt. There are hiding places there, as we know.

Then tonight we will smuggle him to Mother Handaway's and

the "run" can go forward as planned.' Mipps rubbed his hands with relief, just as a man passed the study window.

'It is the Hythe officer,' warned Doctor Syn. 'Our friend is evidently awake at last. I shall need the cord around my waist, and it will be hidden under my Geneva gown.'

'Here they are, sir, and there's that rascal knocking on the door.' Doctor Syn took off his clerical coat quickly, and wound the cord which Mipps had produced from a cupboard securely around his waist. Mipps then helped him into his gown, which fell in full folds, concealing all sign of the cord.

'Have you your blunderbuss, Mipps?' whispered the vicar.

'All loaded, sir, and I'll take care to aim at whoever is stopping Jimmie Bone's escape. And whoever that he won't take me out shooting rabbits with him.'

'Now open the door,' ordered Syn. 'Find out first if the prisoner be awake.

Then come and tell me in here.'

Mipps did as he was ordered, admitted the Hythe officer, who told him that the prisoner was awake and very amused to hear that he was to be visited by the parson. 'A scoffing sinner, Mister Mipps, and so you can tell your master. I will await you outside.'

'Just as you please,' replied Mipps. 'I'll tell the vicar.' The officer strolled out into the front garden, and looked across at the low wall of the churchyard. What he saw, or rather what he did not see, seemed to give him satisfaction, for the six good coastguards he had posted there were lying completely hidden in the grass the other side of the wall. Another coastguard he could see, smoking a pipe and sitting upon a mounting block at the corner of the 'Ship' yard, and he knew that despite the man's appearance of unconcern, he was keeping a sharp lookout and was ready to signal to his mates beneath the wall if he saw any danger of the prisoner being rescued.

Doctor Syn handed Mipps a loaded pistol. 'If Jimmie Bone is suspected, present this at his head, and I'll warn him to grab it. You will let him take it.

He may need it to fight his way out.'

'Aye, aye, sir, and after he's fired it, a pistol butt in his hand is a good weapon. He'll use his fists too. He wasn't named "Gentleman James" for nothing.'

'Should he not be detected as he comes out,' went on the vicar, 'never mind.

You will then keep the pistol hidden and accompany Jimmie to the church. I shall not move till the beadle looks in on me, and by that time I hope Jimmie will be safely hidden.' Saying which, Doctor Syn picked up his Bible, and, followed by Mipps, joined the officer in the garden. All three went towards the cells.

Fat and pompous, the beadle was there ready to unlock the cell door.

'Has he given you any trouble?' asked the officer.

'I have not given him the chance, for I have not been inside,' replied the beadle. 'I have my own skin to think on, and since you unlashed his legs because of his sprained ankle, and then his hands so that he could swill himself in good brandy, I have been taking no chances with Gentleman James. He could still hold his own in the ring, and could break me with ease, though he cannot break this door.'

'Well, open it,' demanded the officer, 'and I will inform him that the chaplain is visiting him.' So saying, the officer entered the cell alone and closed the door behind him.

The prisoner was lying on a heap of straw that was piled in the corner behind a rough table. A stool completed the furniture. He lay covered by his overcoat, and as he peeped over the edge of it, he groaned with disgust on recognizing his visitor.'

The officer paid no heed to this, but said civilly enough, 'I am allowing you to see the parson, Doctor Syn. Do you wish to see him?'

'I have no respect for revenue officers,' answered the highwayman, 'but strange as it may seem to you, I have a regard for parsons, for they are on the whole friendly disposed towards the sinner condemned by the law. That is why I have never robbed one in my life. You need have no fear, therefore, that I shall be dangerous. I would like to see this Doctor Syn. I was wrong to scoff at the idea when you first told me he would visit me. I rather fancy I shall confess my sins to him: aye, and in all humbleness; whereas to you and your kind, you hangmen, I'd just glory in 'em.'

'Then the parson will be more welcome than I am,' retorted the officer. 'I wish he would allow me to stay in the cell, but he refuses, and I have no power to go against his authority in that. But if your love of parsons is feigned, and you offer him any violence, be sure that I shall be at hand, and armed, so you had better behave yourself.'

'Oh, I'll behave,' answered Jimmie Bone. 'I'll not risk having you come in more than necessary, believe me! Besides, if you think I'd confess my sins in front of you, you're mistaken. I have my pride.'

'Then I'll send in the parson,' said the officer, opening the door and beckoning to Doctor Syn, who stood in the passage, which was fortunately very dark.

'The prisoner will see you, sir,' he said, and as Doctor Syn entered he added, 'And as I hoped, he will confess.'

'Not to you. Only to the parson,' cried Jimmie Bone. 'I wants therefore to see him alone, and I has the rights of a prisoner so to do. I know I'm for Jack Ketch; you'll see to that, and with the shadow of death upon me, I'll make no peace with you, though with the reverend gentleman I will.'

'You certainly may, my poor fellow,' said Doctor Syn sympathetically, as he laid his Bible on the table. 'How dark this cell is, to be sure. That little grating up yonder only makes it seem the darker.'

'It is for ventilation, not for light, reverend sir,' explained the officer.

'I think every prison cell should allow the inmate to see the blessed sun,' replied Syn reprovingly. 'Besides, a prisoner should be allowed to read the Holy Writ. What is the use of a grating that looks on to a wall like that? I must speak to the squire about it.'

'And he'll say what I says,' returned the officer. 'A cell is a place of punishment, and the darkness is a fitting reminder to the condemned man of the eternal darkness he is about to enter.'

'I cannot hold with that, sir,' retorted the vicar sharply. 'There is no eternal darkness in the Hereafter, but only eternal light, though perhaps to the wicked man of no penitence the first darkness of death may last longer. Besides, this poor fellow has not yet come to trial, so is not condemned now.'

'But he will be,' laughed the officer, 'and I ain't here to discuss the Hereafter. That's your department.'

'Then go and see to yours,' snapped the prisoner. 'Go and find the rope and skip with Ketch. One day he may fix it round your own neck. I hope he does.'

'A revengeful spirit is no fitting preparation to confession,' rebuked the vicar. Then, turning to the officer, he ordered him to leave them and to lock the door on the outside. 'When I wish to withdraw, I will knock three times.' The officer went out, closing the door, which he ordered the beadle to lock.

As the key turned and the lock creaked home, Doctor Syn winked at the highwayman.

'I have tested this cell with Mipps,' he whispered. 'We often thought one of our fellows might be prisoned here, and I consequently made sure that a whispered conversation could not be heard through that door. Now quickly! Listen to what I have to say. First of all is your ankle too painful for walking?'

'I made it out worse than it was, thinking it might put them off their guard,' said Bone. 'But I can walk on it, for better a strain on the foot than a stretch round the neck. What's the plan?' Doctor Syn had taken off his wig and laid it on the table. He then pulled off his Geneva gown and ordered Jimmie Bone to put it on. 'And keep mumbling a pretended conversation while we get ready.'

'I have been a bad and wicked man,' said the highwayman aloud, as Doctor Syn unwound the cord from around his waist.

'Go on,' he urged, 'you're doing splendidly,' and as the prisoner launched into a great recital of his many crimes upon the highway, Doctor Syn between many loud ejaculations of 'poor fellow', 'my poor sinner', gave his whispered orders.

'Lash me up tight. But first let me adjust my wig on your head. It fits well enough. Now my hat pulled down over your brow. So! I took care to wear it that way on purpose, and it hides the gash on your forehead, which we will attend to later with any luck. It is quite dark in the passage. If the officer suspects you, he may fire, but Mipps is there to turn his aim. Mipps will then present a pistol at you, which he will let you grab from him. Then use your discretion. Fire if you must, though a good blow would be better than using a weapon. It is a mistake to fire against an officer of the law, for that the law does not forgive easily.'

'But if I am caught, how do I explain the rope I am supposed to have tied you with?' asked the prisoner. 'I was searched when I was taken, and there was no rope then.'

'A sympathizer or accomplice let it down through the grating,' explained Syn. 'You can say that you pretended to be drunk for the purpose. That will clear me.'

'And what do I do if I get clear of the outer door?'

'Walk with Mipps to the church, and he will hide you in the crypt,' said the vicar. 'We will free you when it is time for taking horse tonight. Can you ride with that ankle?'

'My ankle is nothing. I could run on it to get away if I had to.'

'You will only have to walk, I think,' replied Syn. 'Now go on with your confession, while you tie me up, and be quick. Gag me with your 'kerchief. Put your mask in your pocket. You may need that tonight. As you leave, keep your hands over your face as though in prayer. And take comfort, for should this escape fail, we have another planned for tonight, when you will be moved from here to be taken to the cells at Hythe. You will be rescued, never fear. But such necessity will be a pity, since it will mean changing many of our settled plans.' All through this conversation, Jimmie Bone had been busy tressing up his master with the cord.

'Tie it tighter; tighter,' Syn ordered. 'That's better. Now gag me with your 'kerchief. Then tie my mouth tight with your neck-cloth. Then cover me with your overcoat, and when you are ready to go knock three times upon the door.' Jimmie Bone, acting his part well, talked in a high-pitched whine of penitence, while he obeyed. After looking at the prostrate parson, and testing the cord which looked very convincing, he covered him over with his great riding coat. He then went to the door and beat three times upon it with his fist.

Both men in the cell heard the key creak in the lock, and the beadle opened the door for the officer to enter.

'Are you finished, reverend sir?' he asked.

Jimmie Bone with head bent and one hand covering his face as though overcome with emotion, nodded gravely, and passed the officer out of the door.

'Glad to see you safe and sound, sir,' remarked Mipps, feigning unutterable relief in his voice.

'Aye, it was a risky thing to do,' said the beadle. 'The vicar should have thought of the value his good life is to the parish, and not have risked it with such a villain.' The officer, having glanced across at the prostrate figure in the dark corner, shrugged his shoulders and said, 'You are in your sulks, I see, because I am here, but believe me I have no wish to see you till I accuse you in the Courts.

You'll be moved out of here tonight and taken to a safer place where there will be no chance of a rescue. Till then I shall not trouble you.' He went out, ordering the beadle to lock the door. Mipps was then climbing the stairs behind the black-robed parson. The officer followed.

'Did he make a confession of his various crimes, reverend sir?' he asked.

The figure of the parson did not turn nor answer, but continued to mount the steps. It was Mipps who turned round and said, 'Leave the vicar alone, for goodness' sake! This sort of thing upsets him. He takes others' misfortunes to heart and don't lick his chops over Jack Ketch as you do.'

'Is that any reason why he cannot answer me?' returned the officer.

'Call up him later on,' advised Mipps. 'Whenever he gets a spiritual turn like this 'ere one, he goes into the church and has a bit of communing with himself. What the prisoner confessed—and it may be murder, and oh, don't you hope it is, you old vulture!—is a matter for the vicar to decide upon and deal with. It don't concern you. Nothing spiritual concerns you. Only got to look at your face to know it simply couldn't. So leave the vicar alone and have respect to the church, is my advice to you, my man.'

'The church must have respect for the law then,' replied the officer. 'I say I have the right to know whether or not the prisoner confessed. Not that I don't know his crimes well enough. I do. But his own confession helps the prosecution and helps the prisoner too.'

'You talk of help,' echoed Mipps. 'You wouldn't help your own greatgrandmother out of a horse-pond, you wouldn't. No hypocrisy now!' At the top of the steps the parson was waiting for the beadle to unlock the outer door. The officer hurried after them unsuccessfully to brush past Mipps.

Failing to do so, he called up, 'Just a moment please, reverend sir.'

'Didn't I tell you that the vicar is communing with himself?' snapped Mipps over his shoulder. 'Come to the vicarage in half an hour if you must, and wait for him. Then p'raps he'll tell you what the prisoner said, or p'raps he won't. I don't know. You must let him commune about it first.' Mipps, having reached the top of the steps, thrust his head past the officer towards the beadle who was too fat to pass. 'You'll never squash yourself to the floor. Give me the key.' Jimmie Bone waited patiently, muttering, 'Poor fellow! Poor fellow!'

'Don't take it so to heart, sir,' pleaded Mipps, as he stooped and unlocked the outer door. He then swung it open and the figure of the parson with his back towards the officer was framed in the light of the evening sun.

'Mind the stone jamb of the door, sir,' warned Mipps.

Unused to walking in a long gown, Jimmie Bone lifted it in order not to stumble over the step in question. The action showed the officer a muddy boot, and he remembered distinctly that Doctor Syn had worn buckled shoes.

Pulling his pistol from his belt and cocking it, he cried, 'Stop!' Like lightning Mipps struck the weapon from his hand, saying sharply, 'Don't point that thing at the vicar.'

'It's not the vicar! It's Bone, you fool!' roared the officer, trying to push past Mipps in his anger. Unable to do so, for Mipps stood his ground firmly, and being a step above the officer had every advantage, the officer whipped a whistle attached to his uniform by a lanyard to his lips and blew it shrilly.

'Here, you ain't Bone, are you, vicar?' cried Mipps, pointing his own pistol at the prisoner.

Bone turned and wrenched it from his hand, as agreed, and then, with his left, he struck the officer under the jaw with all his mighty force. Down went the officer backwards with the whistle still between his teeth. The beadle, who had retreated a few steps at this alarm, was unable to stand the weight of the falling officer who crashed on to his back, and with a gasp he fell headlong down the steps with the officer on the top of him.

'Attempt to follow me, you rats, and I'll shoot,' hissed Bone, pointing his pistol down the steps.

'Don't let him fire!' stammered the beadle.

'Keep where you are, for pity's sake,' whined Mipps, 'or he'll kill us all.'

'Keep your mouth shut, you dirty little sexton,' snarled Bone, 'or I'll treat you worse than I've done the vicar.'

'Oh, he's killed the poor vicar,' moaned Mipps. 'Kill me then, for I can't live without my beloved vicar. Oh, my poor master! You villain!'

'Shut your mouth or I'll put a bullet down your throat to stop your tongue.' And with this warning, uttered to clear Mipps in the mind of the officer, the highwayman passed out into the full light, pulling the door behind him.

He hurried across the Court House drive towards the churchyard gate. He did not dare to run, in case anyone should be watching from the road.

Meantime Mipps kept moaning in the darkness, 'Oh, my poor wrist! The villain has near broken it, snatching my pistol away.'

'Don't clutch hold of me,' cried the officer from the darkness below, for the frightened beadle was gripping him tightly as a shield for his own body in case the prisoner fired.

'Hi, you sexton,' went on the struggling officer, 'pick up my pistol, open the door and fire at him. This fool won't let me up. Fire the pistol outside the door.

I have men who will hear the alarm and help you.' Mipps opened the door, and by the light picked up the fallen pistol. 'I'll get him. Have no fear,' he said bravely, and out he went, not forgetting to pull the door to behind him, in order that the others should be hampered by the darkness. Nor did he wish their cries to be overheard, for the officer was cursing the terrified beadle loudly.

It was at this moment that the squire happened to step out of his front door to take the air, for he had drunk much port and wished to clear his head.

Seeing, he thought, Doctor Syn hurrying towards the church, and wishing to know how he had fared with the prisoner, he called out to him to stop.

'Hi, vicar! Doctor! Christopher!' he called, and was puzzled that the parson did not turn. 'Doctor! Doctor Syn!' he shouted.

What followed astonished his fuddled brain the more, for as the black-robed figure passed the churchyard gate, six customs men rose up from behind the wall and surrounded the 'parson'.

'What was that whistle for?' asked their leader. 'Something wrong?' His answer was a smashing blow on the chin which sent him sprawling.

This was followed by the flash of a pistol which brought down another with a bullet in his leg, as the figure of the 'parson' jumped in leaps for the church door. One of the others fired and missed, while the other three rushed after the figure, who, hampered by his bad ankle, was overtaken and tackled in the porch. Bone flung his empty pistol in the face of one, but the other two gripped him, and they fell in a struggling mass on the pavement.

Mipps, who had run past the squire, reached the porch, just as one of the antagonists managed to press his knee upon the prisoner's bad ankle, causing him to let out a howl of pain and rage. Seeing that the odds were now against his friend, Mipps decided that for the moment they must accept defeat, especially as the two men were astride is friend's back and lashing his wrists up tight with a cord. When this was done one of them asked, 'What happened, sexton?'

'Goodness knows,' replied Mipps. 'I thought it was the beloved vicar. Then suddenly he knocks the officer and beadle down the steps. I pulled out my pistol, but he was too quick for me. Seized it, he did, and gets away. I didn't know it was Jimmie Bone till he did that. I just thought it was the saintly vicar who had got sudden bats in his holy belfry.' By this time the squire had joined them and had listened to the sexton's recital. 'Then where's the vicar?' he demanded.

'Dunno, sir,' replied Mipps. 'Horrible nightmare, the whole thing. Oh what a wicked, desperate villain! He must have killed the vicar and left the body in the cell after stealing his holy robes.'

'We must hurry there at once,' exclaimed the squire. Then, turning to the two men, he added, 'Bring back you prisoner, and, Mipps, come with me.' The squire ignored the groaning man who had been shot in the leg, merely saying to Mipps, 'This is a bad business.' Mipps gathered that the squire was disappointed that the prisoner had been re-taken, and had no fear that the vicar had been injured by him. Meanwhile the wounded man lay groaning with his mate sitting beside him nursing his jaw. It was no joke to be struck by Gentleman James, ex-pugilist.

As the squire and sexton reached the Court House they met the officer coming out of the cell door.

'Have they got him, sir?' he demanded.

The squire did not answer, but asked, 'Where is the vicar, you bungler? It will be well for you if he is safe, but otherwise—'

'He's in the cell. Tied up,' interrupted the officer. 'Where is my prisoner?'

'To hell with your prisoner!' exploded the squire. 'I am a magistrate, not a gaoler. Why did you not release the poor vicar?'

'The beadle is attending to him,' retorted the other. 'I was against the reverend gentleman going to the cell alone. It is on his own head, and of the two of us, I need more attention, since that rascal has nigh broken my jaw. He struck me with my whistle between my lips as I was blowing the alarm.'

'You'll find another of your fellows with a broken jaw, and one with a bullet in him,' said the squire. 'You should have attended to the vicar yourself, since it was all your own bungling.'

'I have my duty to do first, sir,' snapped the officer. 'Ah, but I see that they have got my prisoner. I think there is no doubt now that Gentleman James's next fight will be with the hangman, and the rope will hang him up who has held up so many.'

The squire showed honest indignation on his face and turned to Mipps with, 'Come, we will attend upon the vicar.' The outer door of the cells was open and as they groped their way down the steps they heard a prodigious groaning.

'I care little for the groans of the revenue men, but this distresses me,' said the squire.

'Trust Doctor Syn to be more or less all right, sir,' remarked Mipps.

'Jimmie Bone would never want to do damage to him, and even if he did, the good vicar has a way of looking after himself.' As they entered the cell, the door of which was open, their eyes, growing accustomed to the darkness, made out by the filtering light of the grating the bulky figure of the beadle sitting on the stool with his head between his hands.

The groaning was coming from him and not from the trussed figure of the parson, who lay on his back staring over his gagged nose and mouth.

'My poor Christopher!' exclaimed the squire. Then, turning upon the beadle, he vented his rage by saying sharply, 'Why have you not attended to the vicar? Don't sit there blubbering, man!'

'I tried to attend to him, sir, but the knots was too tight,' replied the wretched man. 'I am in much pain too. I was knocked all the way down the steps with that officer on top of me. The vicar had no rougher passage than that, I swears.'

'Every male baby should be sent to sea, I says,' said Mipps scornfully.

'Then they'd learn how to tackle knots. Besides, you wouldn't have been so fat and lazy neither.' Despite the gloom, it took Mipps little time to unfasten the cord, and to help Doctor Syn to his feet.

'That's better!' said the vicar, rubbing his wrists, and stretching himself.

'What an adventure, Tony! But did the prisoner get away?'

'No, he got caught in the church porch, sir,' explained Mipps, not quite able to hide the disappointment in his voice. 'Revenue men was hiding behind the wall. Six of 'em. But Gentleman James gave a very good account of himself.

Them as hasn't been too smashed up will no doubt be bringing him along.

They've tied him up, so he can't escape again.'

'Then let us get into the air,' said Doctor Syn. 'I have had enough of this place.'

'And as for you, sir,' said the squire to the beadle, 'you can stay here and groan, as they will need you to lock up the cell when the prisoner is brought back. But how did this all happen, Christopher?'

'Very quickly,' replied the vicar with a smile. 'In fact, so quickly that I hardly know what did happen. But I hear them coming. We had better wait for them.'

Despite his bad ankle, which was now paining him considerably, the prisoner was forced to walk down the steps with the revenue men behind him.

As he entered the little cell first, he saw the parson and laughed. 'As I told you I had never robbed a parson, sir,' he said, 'I thought I had better make good my words, and have come back on purpose to return you your gown, wig, and hat. I allowed these poor fellows to bring me back, for they ain't much good at fighting, and I was sorry for 'em. No fun knocking down skittles.'

'There is no explanation necessary, James Bone,' returned the parson coldly. 'Neither do I wish to hear your excuses, which only spring from your wounded vanity. True, you were outnumbered, but that is no reason for belittling these men who have done their duty and done it well. As for myself and your rough treatment of me, I will point out that I was only trying to help you, and you took unfair advantage of it. However, I am still willing to help you, only I warn you that when I visit you in a stronger prison than this, I shall be closely guarded, for you are to be taken away secretly tonight to a place where you will be kept in safe custody till you stand your trial. In that place I will do what I can to bring your mind into a fitter state, so that should you be called upon to meet your final Judge suddenly, you may appear before Him in true penitence.'

'And I intend to find out who dropped that cord through the grating,' said the officer. 'I'll have that rascal in the dock beside you. And now take off the vicar's things and let the reverend gentleman make himself respectable.'

'I'll be delighted,' replied Jimmie Bone. 'But you must first undo my hands.

Pity to cut this beautiful gown off with a knife.' The officer gave orders for his hands to be freed, but took the precaution of standing in the doorway to prevent any further escape. Two of his men fumbled with the knots, which again irritated Mipps. He stepped forward with a 'Ain't none of you been to sea? Let me,' quickly untied the cord, and then, having removed the hat and wig from the highwayman's head, pulled the gown off, and helped the vicar to robe.

'Now, Bone,' the officer said, 'who let down that rope?'

'I am unlike you, sir, in this respect,' replied the smiling Bone. 'For I have many a good friend in spite of the fact that I am a rascal. As it happens, I could not tell you who it was, so torture would not be able to get the information out of me.'

'Now, vicar, we'll get out of here,' said the squire.

The beadle locked the door, then escorted the party up the steps, and having locked the outer door, waited till the others were out of sight and then trotted off to the Ship Inn for a little medicine to stay his shaken joints.

Doctor Syn, having refused the squire's invitation to play a game of backgammon on the plea that he had important parochial matters to discuss with his sexton at the vicarage, which the squire knew would have to do with a further attempt at rescuing the prisoner, then persuaded the officer to have a covered wagon at the Court House door by eleven o'clock, when the prisoner could be removed secretly to Hythe. He also advised the escort of two riding officers and two armed men in the wagon with the prisoner.Syn and Mipps went off to the vicarage, entering the study by the garden door.

'Well, you took all that very cool, sir,' remarked Mipps.

'I must own that I thought he had got away,' replied the vicar. 'I heard the crash as the officer and the beadle fell, and I chuckled. Then to my disappointment, the officer looked in on me as I lay groaning, and said, "I have men hidden behind the wall. I have taken precautions." Then I confess I was a little frightened.'

'What!' echoed Mipps. 'Well, you didn't appear to be frightened at all.'

Chapter 6. Doctor Syn appears to be frightened

Later that evening Doctor Syn strolled into the bar of the Ship Inn, and called for drinks all round with a pipe of tobacco for himself.

Mrs. Waggetts filled his churchwarden clay and brought it to him with a glass of brandy. He rested according to his custom in his favourite corner of an ingle seat, and summoned the yokels one at a time to sit with him and chat. It was in this manner that he kept in touch with all the news of his widely scattered parish. While he was thus engaged the Welsh lawyer, Mr. Jones, entered the bar, followed unobtrusively by Mipps.

Mr. Jones bowed to Doctor Syn and invited him to take another drink. The fisherman sitting next to Doctor Syn politely and respectfully got up to make room for the stranger on the settle, and himself joined Mipps at the bar.

When the drinks had been served, Mr. Jones whispered behind his glass, 'I should like a word with you in private, reverend sir, for I have something to say which I fancy will interest you.' The vicar smiled and then asked in an undertone, 'About the Tontine?' Jones shook his head, looked across the bar to see that he was not being watched, and whispered back, 'No! The Scarecrow!'

'Really?' queried the doctor, raising his eyebrows in surprise. 'Well then, suppose we finish our drinks and take a stroll across to the sea-wall.' The Welshman agreeing, they left the inn together, and as soon as they were out of hearing from the villagers grouped about the door the Welshman said, 'Aye, Doctor, the Scarecrow is expected to ride this very night, and the revenue men are to be out in full strength. Now I confess to you that I am in the mind to see the fun.'

'If what you say is true, I should advise no such thing,' returned the vicar.

'Have you considered the danger? There will be fighting if the parties clash, and suppose, now, that a bullet strayed into your own head, you would leave me with the Tontine.'

'Now, that is certainly an idea, and one that you may profit by,' laughed the other. 'Indeed, were you to accompany me, you might press the trigger yourself, and being a holy man, the blame would fall on the rascal smugglers.'

'Yes, that is certainly an idea as you say,' nodded the vicar with a smile. 'Or perhaps you are persuading me to go with you in order that you may squeeze the trigger quicker than you did yesterday. For indeed, unless one of us kills the other, we may have to wait a plaguey long time for the other to die.'

'I think there is no danger of foul play between us now,' replied the Welshman. 'I have taken rather a liking to you.'

'Then you should not put temptation into my brain,' laughed the vicar. 'But to be serious, when did you get this information about the Scarecrow? And where?'

'I was told by the revenue officer from Hythe during dinner,' explained the Welshman. 'He urged me to keep the information to myself, but I take it that this injunction did not apply to you, and I consider that if anyone deserves to see this Scarecrow taken, it is the vicar of his parish.'

'Well, if you are bent on seeing the adventure,' went on the parson, 'you may be the safer for my presence, for certainly I have the excuse of visiting the Marsh at night. The fear of smugglers has never yet interfered with my duty to the sick, and at this time there happens to be an old woman very ailing in the mind and body, who I know would welcome my ministration in the night hours.

Indeed, having learned this very evening that she has taken a turn for the worse, I had intended to journey to her after dark, for the poor old soul fears the darkness and needs more comfort then.'

'Then make it as late as you can,' exclaimed the Welshman, 'and we may not only comfort her, but see something of he adventure too. My informant tells me that they expect something to happen between midnight and one in the morning. Apparently the Hythe officer is so confident about this time that he has arranged to take his highwayman prisoner from the cells here at eleven, and get him into safety at Hythe, before he need think of joining his fellows at Dymchurch again.'

'So he told you about the removing of the prisoner too, eh?' asked Doctor Syn. 'I know all is safe with you, but it seems to me that the fellow talks something freely for an officer of the Crown. However, I wonder now that he does not think it somewhat risky to move this popular rascal while the smugglers are on the move. They might attempt a rescue.'

'I said as much too,' agreed the other. 'But he maintains that these smugglers are a selfish lot of dogs, and would think first of their own gains.

Indeed, he says that they will have their minds so set upon their own business that he considers it the most propitious night in which to move his victim.'

'I hope he finds it so, with all my heart,' said Doctor Syn fervently. As they strolled along the sea-wall, Doctor Syn pointed out a fast-sailing cuter. 'Look,' he said, 'that is the revenue boat. How these fellows give away their own official game to their enemy! I know little of strategy, but surely it would have been better to have lain low, till the hour of action arrived! I begin to think that this Scarecrow manages his side more wisely.'

'I shall be very curious to see whether he is as clever as our great smuggler of the North Wales coast. But I think not,' said the lawyer.

They walked back to the vicarage, where they parted, Doctor Syn saying that he had work to do on a sermon, but it was agreed that the Welshman should call upon him at a quarter past midnight, and that they should then cross the weird Marsh and see for themselves whether there was truth or not in the information gleaned by the Hythe officer.

'We will cross the Marsh to old Mother Handaway's then,' said the vicar as he waved farewell. 'Whether we see anything or no, we shall at least be doing a small deed of mercy to a sick old woman who loves to hear the words of Blessed Scripture in the night hours.'

'I shall be with you, sir,' cried the other. 'At a quarter past midnight?'

'A quarter past midnight,' repeated Doctor Syn.

Doctor Syn, however, set out for Mother Handaway's directly it was dark.

He left the study door locked behind him, and he rode upon his fat little white pony with the two panniers full of good provisions to comfort an old woman.

He turned from the road, avoiding it, and rode across the fields, crossing the dykes by the many bridges, some of them old brick, but many of them a few planks. He knew them all in the dark. He found three of the larger bridges guarded by revenue men, who, on recognizing the good parson, warned him that the Scarecrow's wild riders were expected to be out later that night. One of these pickets, indeed, advised him to get home at once and out of danger.

'Whether there is such a person as this Scarecrow or not,' replied the parson, 'he shall never interfere with my bounden duty,' and with a cheerful good night, he jogged away into the deep darkness of the Marsh.

'There goes a brave parson and a good,' remarked on of the men.

Doctor Syn at last reached the hovel where the old woman lived, and after handing over the provisions he had brought for her, and giving her instructions as to how she was to behave under certain circumstances, he led his pony to the hidden stable, where the old witch lighted a lantern. He closed the secret door in the screen of bulrushes.

A quarter of an hour later this door opened again, and a tall, fantastically clad figure, wearing a hideous mask that shone with phosphorous, led out the wild black horse known as Gehenna. The weird rider, hearing the old woman close the door behind him, leapt on to Gehenna's back, dashed out of the dry dyke in which the stable was situated and then galloped away across the fields, leaping the dykes in the darkness. Neither horse nor rider needed sight upon the Marsh. They knew it only too well. Doctor Syn knew it by day. This tall devil knew it by night. Aye, my masters! The revenue man was right in this, for the Scarecrow was indeed once more 'out' upon the Marsh.

At a quarter past eleven, a covered cart was pulled up outside the Court House cells. It was drawn by two horses, and two men sat on the box seat. One of these was the Hythe officer, the other the driver. Two riding officers, well mounted, and with pistols in their holsters, completed the party.

The beadle was awaiting them with his keys, and standing by him was the Welsh lawyer, his hat pulled down to his eyes and his figure muffled in a great driving coat.

The Hythe officer jumped down and addressed him with, 'So you are as good as your word, sir, and have come out to see the whole of the fun? The drive to Hythe will be dark, for the moon does not rise till later. But you'll see our prisoner safely gaoled, and then you may drive back with us in ample time to call for Doctor Syn. Has the reverend gentleman consented to accompany you?'

'He has,' replied the lawyer. 'But since I promised to wait upon him in one hour from now, I shall most likely be late.'

'We shall not waste time, you'll see,' laughed the officer. 'We shall go at the gallop. I have no wish to be late, either, as I intend to have the Scarecrow under lock and key with Jimmie Bone before the morning. That is, of course, if the Scarecrow rides tonight.'

'I hope so,' said the Welshman, 'for I shall then have two worthy adventures to recount when I get home again.'

'Don't raise your voice,' warned the officer. 'I have no wish to attract any attention.'

'All's quiet enough,' whispered one of the mounted men.

As though giving him the lie, there suddenly arose a peal of distant laughter.

'In the name of God what's that?' asked the lawyer.

'Drunken rascals in the "Ship's" bar,' explained the officer. 'I am glad to hear them. The village itself is a deal too still. Not a light; not a sound. But that roystering persuades me that they have had no hint of what we are about to do.

Rescue or no, the removal of the highwayman would at least have attracted a crowd. So let us hurry, and get him away while we may.' The beadle wanted no second bidding, for he was as anxious as any to be rid of a prisoner who had caused him so much pain and anxiety. Of Jimmie Bone he was definitely afraid. So he unlocked the outer door and led the way to the cell. No sooner had he swung the door open, than the officer with two of his men ordered the prisoner to mount the steps. His arms were tied behind his back, but his legs were loosened so that he could walk and mount the cart the quicker. The Hythe officer wanted no delay, and he saw to this himself in a brutal manner, for as the prisoner was heaved up by the front step of the cart, and ordered to climb over the box seat and lie down beneath the cover, the officer gave him a sudden push which brought the wretched man down on his face. One of the men climbed after him and sat on the box seat with his back to the horses, so that he could keep an eye on the prisoner. The Welshman was told to seat himself beside the driver and cling on tightly, as the pace would be fast. The officer himself, when all was ready, clambered on to the tail board and stood guard from the back.

Then with the riding officers on either side of the cart and keeping close to the great wheels, the party drew out on the high road and broke into a trot. Past the Ship Inn they went, and hearing loud laughter issuing from the bar, the officer was satisfied that all was well, for had a rescue been planned, he told himself that the rascals would keep quiet.

'As far as you like,' he called to the driver, and the horses were put to a gallop.

He felt further satisfied when they had passed the last of the Dymchurch farmhouses, for it was only in Dymchurch that he had held any fear of an attack.

For a mile or so on their way the road runs directly under the shadow of the great sea-wall—a straight road with which the driver and horsemen were familiar even on dark nights. Indeed so dark was it on this particular night that the whiteness of the road was invisible, but the blackness of the wall was guide enough, and the horses were driven and ridden at a full-stretched gallop.

When nearing the end of this long stretch, the officer cried out the warning, 'Be careful of the bend. We are nearing it.' The driver laughed back. 'Never fear, sir, I can take it full-pace, and we owe our prisoner a shaking.' The bend referred to was a sharp right-angled sweep, which the ancient road-makers had turned in order to avoid a dangerous swamp on the left hand, and a rising slope towards the sea-wall on the other. It is the spot where a few years later the sunken fortress known as the Great Redoubt was built to withstand the threatened landing of Bonaparte.

'Cling on tight, sir!' cried the driver to the officer, and then added to the Welshman at his side, 'Take care not to be unseated. You can see the sharpness of the turn, by the whiteness of the road there beyond. But trust me, I know the corner well.' The Welshman, though not able to distinguish the road along which they were now dashing, could not make out the white ribbon where it turned inland out of the shadow of the wall, while beyond which flickered the distant lights of Hythe.

Far from slackening his pace, the driver, wishing to show his skill, lashed his animals to an even greater speed.

Round the spun, the great right-hand wheel leaving the road. But before they were clear of the black shadow, the horses came down with a crash, the cart, jerking into the air, toppled out on to the road. The riding officer on the right side suffered the same fate, and was flung over his horse's head, whilst his companion on the left was pinned with his horse beneath the cart. The Hythe officer on the back lost his balance and fell into the edge of the marshy pool by the roadside, and was seized by six men who had ambushed themselves below the road, and ere any of the unfortunates realized that the accident had been caused by a taut wire drawn across the corner, they were charged down upon by some fifty hideously masked riders who had been hidden by the lofty slope that led up to the sea-wall.

Before they could recover themselves the whole party were made prisoners by the dismounted men, who like their fellows wore fantastic masks which made them unrecognizable. Then the wire which had thrown the horses was quickly unfastened from the posts on either side of the road, rolled into loops and placed on the saddle of one of the riders.

The Hythe officer, his wrists tied behind his back, was permitted to stand upon his feet, while his men were trussed with cords and laid down by the side of the road. The Welshman was seized by two men, but not tied.

It was then that a tall rider on a fierce black horse rode out from the others and roared in a deep croaking voice, 'The Scarecrow's apologies to Law and Order! We are here to save a valiant rascal from the gallows. Set Mister Jimmie Bone upon his horse!' The highwayman had been lifted from the inside of the overturned cart, and when his hands were freed, he was lifted on to his saddle.

'Where is the Welsh stranger?' asked the mounted Scarecrow.

'I am here,' retorted the little lawyer. 'Shaken up, it is true, but in spite of your violent attentions, unhurt.'

'We will carry you with us some half-way to Dymchurch,' went on the Scarecrow. 'You will then make your own way to the village on foot. We understand that you were to wait upon Doctor Syn. So you shall, and you will tell him that the Scarecrow and his merry Night-riders have rescued the highwayman, and that, should he wish to help these officers of the law whom we are leaving here tied up, he had best send someone to free them at his discretion. If not, here they can lie for all we care till the morning, for there is little likelihood of travellers being abroad on a night when the Scarecrow's men run contraband. If he hastens, these poor fellows will not miss the fun, and we can have another brush with them. Are you able to ride, Mister Bone?'

'Aye, aye, Scarecrow,' laughed the highwayman.

'Then let us get you into safety as quickly as we may. We have to make the beach at Littlestone before the tide is up. Hellspite, you may fix our notice to the cart.'

A little man, who in spite of a witch's disguise put the Welshman strongly in mind, for some reason or other which he could not understand, of Mister Mipps, the Dymchurch sexton, rode forward on a mule and affixed to the wheel of the cart a piece of parchment on which was scrawled the words, 'The Scarecrow has rescued the highwayman.' This message the little figure nailed to the overturned wheel. Meantime others had unharnessed the cart-horses and got them to their feet, as well as the mounts that had carried the riding officers. Since the animals did not appear to be much hurt by the fall, they were mounted by four of the smugglers who had been on foot, the others leaping on to spare horses led by their colleagues. One of these addressed as Curlew

was ordered by the Scarecrow to take the Welshman up behind
him, and another named Raven was told to set the Hythe officer on
a spare led horse.

'Half-way to Dymchurch you will set the Welshman down,'
croaked the leader. 'Should we leave him here, he would untie
these fools before we are ready for them. As to the Hythe officer, he
must ride with us further afield. And now, my merry lads, we will
dash on with our business, and may the night prove profitable!'
Saying which, the Scarecrow, with Jimmie Bone riding behind him,
led the company in a mad gallop along the high road.

Half-way to Dymchurch, when the moon first lighted the sky
above the seawall, a halt was called while Curlew set down the
Welshman, who was ordered to climb the steep bank of the sea-
wall and to walk along the top of it to Dymchurch. He was further
warned that, should he be seen to retrace his steps towards the
scene of the accident, he would be fired at.

The weird cavalcade once more galloped on, and the little
lawyer, clambering up the grassy bank of the wall, trotted along
afoot in their wake.

The Night-riders turning in their saddles laughed as they saw
his little figure silhouetted against the skyline.

It was not long, however, before they reached the outskirts of
the village, where they were lost to sight from the hurrying lawyer,
who did not see that the main body, instead of entering the village,
skirted round behind the rookery on one side of the churchyard,
and took to the Marsh, while the Scarecrow, the highwayman, and
six others rode with their prisoner, the Hythe officer, into the
square facing the Court House. What they did there took little time,
though it occasioned a halt, after which they too followed their
companions out on to the Marsh.

The Welsh lawyer followed stubbornly, and had no thoughts of
turning back to help the trussed men, which was not altogether
due to their threats of shooting, but largely because he was more
than ever determined now to reach the vicarage and accompany
Doctor Syn on to the Marsh. He told himself that his best plan was
to report about the ambush and the highwayman's rescue, and let
Doctor Syn deal with the situation. Despite the shaking he had
endured when thrown so violently from the cart and the rough
riding he had suffered, his chief emotion was that of excitement,
which not only banished his fear, but made him feel proud of his
personal share in such an adventure.

By the time he reached the outskirts of the village, the moon was already showing above the sea-wall, and lighting up the white gravestones in the little churchyard.

He was the more proud of himself when he considered how frequently the strongest man will become unnerved at having to pass by a churchyard at night, and yet here was he, looking at the tombs indifferently. For had he not ridden with the terrible Night-riders? How eager he was to tell this to Doctor Syn. The parson had scored off him at their first encounter, but now it was his turn, for Doctor Syn had assured him that he had never set eyes on the Scarecrow. As he hurried along by the low wall which divided the churchyard from the road, he wondered why the rooks were chattering in the great trees that topped the church. Every nest seemed to be alive, and several large birds were whirling up and down in the vicinity of the Court House. But even these black birds of ill omen failed to shake his nerve until he passed the corner of the wall and saw the reason of this unusual activity from the rookery. Then he was badly frightened.

The birds were swooping down to perch for a few moments upon the gaunt gallows that stood in the Court House Square. He remembered that when he had driven past it in the cart, this grim tree had been barren of its grisly fruit.

But now a man was hanging there, and as he approached, the moonlight showed him who the victim was. It was the Hythe officer.

The little lawyer was by now very badly frightened, but he rushed forwards clapping his hands to scare the gorging birds. As they circled up angrily into the night sky, he stretched up and felt the limbs. Still limp, but of death there was no doubt, for the rooks had been too busy. The hanging had been skilfully carried out. It had also been mercifully swift.

Shaking now in every limb, the lawyer tottered towards the vicarage. Doctor Syn had told him to tap for admission upon the garden door. As it was dark in the garden, since the moon shone upon the other side of the house, Doctor Syn had not shuttered his study window, but had let the candlelight shine out to guide his visitor. The casement also was wide open, and the Welshman, peering in, saw a bat flitting about the room, and darting at the lighted candelabrum. Although Doctor Syn had told him that he would be working till he called for him, the lawyer thought at first he could not be in the room, for surely no one could work with a bat flying about. As he peered further through the casement, however, he heard a gentle snoring. Then, as his eyes accustomed themselves to the dazzling candlelight, which shone upon the open pages of a large Bible, he saw the vicar sitting in his high-backed chair at the far side of the table. A quill pen was in his hand, which rested on the comfortable arm of the chair, and a serene smile lit up his face.

Doctor Syn was sleeping tranquilly, although the bat kept up its fevered flight so close to his face.

'Doctor Syn! Doctor Syn!' The lawyer's voice broke the silence in a hoarse whisper.

The sleeping vicar stirred. Then he gave a little start, and opened his eyes.

'Who's there?' he asked.

'It is I—Jones,' replied the lawyer.

Doctor Syn sat up, and rubbing his eyes, looked towards the open casement.

'Oh, it's you, is it?' he said pleasantly. The bat flew past his face and he jerked back. 'And a bat as well. Did you bring him with you to wake me?'

'Have you slept for long?' asked the lawyer. 'Because if not, I wonder if you have heard any unusual noises within the last half-hour?'

'What is the time?' yawned Doctor Syn. The bat flew close to him again and he rose quickly. 'I never could abide a bat,' he said, with a shudder that convinced the lawyer, who did not know that Doctor Syn had been at great pains to encourage the little creature into the room just before his arrival. 'We must get him out of this.' He picked up the candelabrum and placed it near the casement. 'If you share my dislike, stand aside. Good gracious yes, I have slept for at least an hour and a half.' He looked at the tall clock in the corner as he said this. 'Yes, I was penning a sermon for Sunday, and I glanced at the clock last exactly one hour and a half ago. I will leave the bat to fly out while I come round and open the door for you. Fancy falling asleep over my discourse! I hope it will not have the like effect upon my congregation.'

The Welshman leaned heavily on the casement sill. 'Never mind the bat,' he said, 'but as you are a man of charity, open a bottle of brandy, for the sights I have seen have weakened my knees.'

'I have brandy ready,' replied the vicar, 'for I thought we should need a drop before setting out, and I have also filled a flask to take with us. Ah, and there goes the bat out of the window, so I'll close the casement and let you in.' As soon as the Welshman entered the room he sank down heavily into a comfortable chair, while Doctor Syn poured out the brandy, which the lawyer drank greedily. 'That puts the heart into one again,' he said as his host refilled his glass.

'I cannot think how I could have slept so peacefully and for so long, with that nasty little creature flitting so close to me,' said the vicar.

'I venture to think, sir,' replied the other, 'that I have had the worse experience,' whereupon he plunged into the full details of his adventure, interrupted by Doctor Syn muttering such phrases as, 'Dear, dear! Is it possible? You amaze me! Astounding! Impertinent rascals!' At the end of the narrator's description of how he was set down to walk along the sea-wall, Doctor Syn said, 'No wonder you were frightened, sir, and needed brandy.'

'But I was not frightened then, sir,' exclaimed the lawyer, 'though I confess the sight of those hideously masked riders was fearsome enough. Indeed I was congratulating myself that I had taken part in such a unique adventure, which will afford me a good story for the rest of my life. No, sir, I was not afraid until I turned the corner of the churchyard and came straight up against the gallows with a corpse hanging from it.'

'What?' ejaculated Doctor Syn.

'Yes, sir,' cried the lawyer, 'and the damned rooks were already busy on the body. And it was the body of one of the men who had driven with me on the cart, and who had been carried off with me and the highwayman. To see a man you have spoken with only half an hour before in full vigour of manhood suddenly changed into food for churchyard rooks, is frightening in the extreme.'

'You don't tell me that the smugglers have hanged a revenue man?'

'Yes, sir. The Hythe officer is swinging from your gallows tree.' Doctor Syn's face pictured horror, righteous indignation, and then sorrow.

'Truly the ways of Providence are wrapt in mystery,' he said. 'This poor fellow may have been a hard man, but at least he followed his duty and died in the execution of it, just as the unfortunate and popular George Plattman did. And I have doubts that the criminals will ever be laid by the heels. That Providence should fight on the side of the law-breakers almost persuades one that the law must be wrong. But we must go immediately and lay this ghastly information at the Court House. The squire must be told of it, and the beadle sent to look after the body. Let us go.'

On the way to the Court House, Doctor Syn stepped across and gazed at the gallows. Then rejoining his companion, he shuddered as he said, 'You are right, sir. The poor fellow is beyond our help.

We can only protect his body from the birds. That is the beadle's duty.' He rang the bell and learnt from the footman who admitted them that the squire had already been carried up to bed.

An acute attack of gout had followed a plentiful enjoyment of port, and Sir Antony Cobtree had thus been prevented from mounting the stairs without help.

Doctor Syn, in sending up a suitable message of sympathy, added that he had brought along with him Mr. Jones, the Welsh lawyer residing at the Ship Inn, who had imparted to him the gravest news which in his opinion the squire should be apprised of immediately.

The returning footman brought back word that the squire would receive them in his bedroom; whereupon Doctor Syn took upon himself to dismiss the footman in order that he might instantly rouse the beadle from his lodgings above the cells. He then told the Welshman to follow him upstairs.

They found the squire propped up with pillows and wearing a quilted dressing-gown over his nightshirt. His wig was on a stand hard by the bed and his head was crowned in a tall night-cap.

'Forgive me receiving you in bed, gentlemen,' he said, 'but this accursed gout is my excuse. Now what is this bad news you speak of, Doctor? Your servant, Mr. Jones.'

'Briefly this, sir. The highwayman, Bone, has been rescued and carried off by no less a person than the Scarecrow.' The squire chuckled. 'You call this grave news, old friend, but for myself, and laying aside my legal calling for the moment, I am not sorry that that fool of a Hythe officer has got it in the neck.' Doctor Syn sighed and shook his head gravely.

'Well, are you?' exploded the squire. 'Naturally, as a magistrate, I must not approve the escape of a prisoner of the Crown. But that wretched officer from Hythe was a deal too officious for my liking. I knew there was something very weak and pig-headed about him, when he refused a comfortable chair and my good sherry. It seems he has now made a real fool of himself, and I expect he will get it right in the neck from his superiors. He'll get one in the eye too from me at the inquiry.' Doctor Syn once more gravely shook his head. 'The Hythe officer has got a rope round his neck and rooks' beaks in his eye sockets. At the moment his corpse is swinging on the gallows of Dymchurch outside your window there.' The doctor's terrible announcement caused the squire to forget the attack of gout, as he cried out, 'What?' and leapt from his bed, tottering to the window which he opened wide, leaning out so that he could get a view in the moonlight of the gallows.

"Pon my soul you're in the right of it,' he said. 'There's a body hanging there. But who did it?'

'When you have heard Mr. Jones's narrative,' explained the vicar, 'you will agree with me that there is only one person who could have carried this out.

The dreaded and mysterious Scarecrow.'

'Well, if there really is such a person, and I have yet to know it,' snapped the squire, 'he goes too far when he uses the official gallows from whence to hang his enemies. I suppose I should do something at once, eh, vicar? But what the devil can I do?'

'The obvious thing is to summon the beadle,' replied the vicar, 'and in your name I have sent to rouse him. It is his function to deal with the body.'

'Of course it is,' agreed the squire. 'Tell him to deal with it at once. He must lodge it in the cells for the night. He must get men to help him.'

'I will go and instruct him,' said the vicar. 'He should be here by now. In the meantime I will leave you with this gentleman, Mr. Jones. As I told you, he has come to Dymchurch to inform me about the Tontine of which my father was a member. Mr. Jones was an eye-witness this night of Jimmie Bone's rescue, and can furnish you with all the details. He has actually spoken to the Scarecrow.'

'Yes sir,' nodded the lawyer. 'And I woke up Doctor Syn to tell him what I shall now have the honour of telling you.' The squire limped back to his bed, and seeing that the vicar was about to leave the room in order to instruct the beadle, he called out, 'Just a minute, Christopher! Before you leave me, I should like to be sure that Mr. Jones has not got any artillery in his pockets?' Doctor Syn smiled and shook his head, while the squire, turning on the Welshman, added, 'I have a decided objection to being made a target of, Mr. Jones. I will take my chance of being winged at any time in fair fight, but I like shooting to be organized in a gentlemanly fashion.'

'I am not armed,' replied the Welshman. 'I see that you have heard how foolishly I behaved to the good doctor here, but believe me I shall not make such a fool of myself again.'

'No, you might be more successful and hit me,' retorted the squire.

The Welshman flushed with anger as he took off his heavy coat and threw it behind him on the floor. He then proceeded to take off his under-coat.

'All right! All right!' cried the squire testily. 'Just pat your breeches pockets, and I am satisfied. I can see that there is nothing dangerous in your waistcoat.' For the little Welshman was unbuttoning his waistcoat to show that he had no pistols concealed.

'All right, doctor,' said the squire. 'Get the beadle and give him his orders, and this gentleman can then tell me his story.'

It was a very frightened beadle that accompanied Doctor Syn and two of the squire's manservants to cut down the body from the gallows.

'I tell you, sir,' he whispered to Doctor Syn, 'that while this Scarecrow lives, not a man of us is safe. We shall all be murdered in our beds. He's a scoundrel, sir! A scoundrel!'

'I should not talk too loud against him if I were you,' warned the vicar, 'for this Scarecrow has given us full proof of his uncanny powers. If these rooks cawing above us hear what you say, they will tell the Scarecrow you are his enemy, and then they will be pecking at you next.' The grisly work was carried out under the supervision of Doctor Syn, who kept muttering, 'Poor fellow! Poor fellow!' while the beadle, sweating with fear lest the Scarecrow should suddenly appear and see what they were doing, urged them to hurry.

At last the body was placed in one of the cells and locked up, the beadle so scared that he refused Doctor Syn's invitation to take a drink in the Court House with the manservants, for the dread of having to walk the few yards back to his lodgings by himself. Instead he ran up to his bedroom and bolted himself in.

When Doctor Syn re-entered the squire's bedroom, the Welshman had just finished his detailed description of the night's adventure, and the squire was criticizing his behaviour with, 'But why didn't you approach the Scarecrow and pull his mask off so that we should know who the scoundrel is? Since your curiosity prompted you to go so far in what hardly concerns you, I think you might have let it carry you to a more useful termination.'

'I venture to suggest, sir,' returned the Welshman, 'that were you or any other to encounter that dreadful apparition on that black horse, you would not run the risk of supposing that the hideous face, lighted up as it appears by hell's fires, could be anything but the devil's own face. To find that it was no mask would be a shock to one's soul.'

'Nonsense and fiddlesticks!' exploded the squire. 'Of course it's a mask smeared over with sand phosphorus to scare feeble-minded

and curious people from his unlawful business. The phosphorus
from Dymchurch sands at low tide is famous the world over.
Simplest thing in the world to daub a mask with it and make it
glow! That sort of thing would never frighten me, though I confess
I fear lunatic gentlemen who let off fire-arms for no excuse. But I
have never been afeared of a Guy Fawkes on November the fifth.'

'Tut, tut, Tony!' admonished the vicar, who had entered
unnoticed and had overheard the squire's peevishness. 'You must
not suppose that this good gentleman from Wales is frighted by
such things either. At least he is anxious to accompany me across
the Marsh, for I have to visit old Mother Handaway, who lies so
grievous sick. Mr. Jones is concerned with a notorious smuggler in
his own country, and wishes to see what he can of our Marsh law-
breakers. He has been informed by the unfortunate Hythe officer
that a "run" is contemplated this very night at the time of high tide,
and if we are to witness it, we should be setting forth immediately.'

'Oh, and pray what good will it do to the community at large if
you do clap eyes on this Scarecrow?' asked the squire.

'Well, perhaps the two of us may find the courage to unmask
him,' smiled the vicar. 'But I doubt very much whether he will have
the impertinence to appear on the Marsh tonight, after what has
happened. However, apart from the Scarecrow and whether we see
him or no, I have my duty to perform to a sick old woman, and that
I have every intention of carrying out.'

'Well, if you want me wake me,' yawned the squire. 'I shall have
trouble enough in the morning when I shall have to deal with
tonight's tragic happenings. It will mean an extensive inquiry and
the calling together of the Lords of the Level. I assure you I have no
intention of accompanying you, and I think you are mad to cross
the Marsh at this hour. But you were ever an obstinate devil,
doctor, and may no harm befall you.'

'Amen,' laughed Doctor Syn, leading the Welshman from the
squire's bedchamber. As they left the Court House he informed his
companion that he must first call in at the vicarage.

'You wish to arm yourself I presume,' said the Welshman. 'If you
loan me a pistol, too, we shall be the more secure.' The doctor kept
his reply till they were once more in his cozy study.

'Whenever I go out on duty, I arm myself with these—a Bible in
one pocket and a flask of brandy in the other. My good sexton has
already taken a basket of nourishment to the sick woman we are
to visit, and it only needs a comforting exposition of the scriptures
to complete her comfort. The brandy flask is for our own comfort,

and to combat the Marsh ague which is so dangerous in these parts. Two of God's greatest gifts, Mr. Jones.'

'The Bible and brandy, eh?' queried the lawyer. 'Aye, Amen, for I think you are not far wrong.' Doctor Syn thought it best to leave by the garden door, which he locked from the outside, and dropping the key into his heavy coat pocket, he led the way through the garden and across the Glebe Field, which was flanked by a deep dyke and bridged by the masonry of the Romans.

At this ancient bridge were two coastguards who challenged their approach, but on recognizing the parson, warned him that it was perilous to cross the Marsh on a night when the Scarecrow's men were expected to be 'out'.

Doctor Syn silently congratulated himself that neither of the men belonged to the parties who had seen and spoken to him earlier on the Marsh that night.

'Aye, I know that they are "out",' returned Doctor Syn, 'for my companion here was an eye-witness when the highwayman was rescued and carried off.'

'What, sir? Has Jimmie Bone escaped us then?' asked one of them.

'There's no doubt about that,' replied the vicar gravely.

'Then the gallows tree will have one piece of fruit the less,' answered the coastguard, 'and for that I am not sorry.'

'You are wrong there,' said Doctor Syn. 'The gallows fruit has been cut down not an hour since, and in my sight, too, for the Scarecrow has hanged the officer from Hythe.'

'Good God, sir!' muttered the other man. 'If that is so then none of us are safe from the scoundrel.'

'Are you alone here?' asked Doctor Syn, 'or are any of your fellows within call?'

'They have been recalling the pickets to the sea-wall, sir,' replied the coastguard. 'We are awaiting our signal now from a "flasher".'

'And what might a "flasher" be?' asked the Welshman.

'A flint-lock without a barrel,' explained the doctor. 'So you are mustering on the sea-wall, eh?'

'Aye, sir, we'll need every man there, if the Scarecrow attempts a landing.'

'Well, let us hope the night passes safely for all concerned,' said the parson.

'There has been enough violence, God knows. Poor George Plattman and now the Hythe officer. Your fellows who escorted the highwayman towards Hythe were left by the smugglers trussed up upon the roadside, according to my friend here, so unless they have escaped, your force will be the weaker.'

'We are under-forced as it is, sir,' said the man. 'No doubt this night's work will cause the Dymchurch squire to apply for a troop of dragoons from Dover Castle.'

'The Scarecrow has outwitted the dragoons before,' replied Doctor Syn sadly. 'I fear that the only chance of catching the scoundrel comes from himself.

His impertinent daring may one of these nights over-reach itself, and then we shall have a hanging in Dymchurch at which all good citizens will rejoice.

Well, good night, my friends, and may God keep you from its perils!' The two companions then proceeded on their way towards Botolph's Bridge, which crossed dyke water to enable wayfarers to reach a lonely Marsh inn called 'The Shepherd and Crook'.

As they approached the bridge they saw a party of men in the moonlight.

'More coastguards,' said Doctor Syn. 'I suppose they are also awaiting their recall. They are wearing masks. I never knew them do that before. The other fellows were not wearing them. These are evidently more cautious, and don't wish to be recognized by the smugglers if they encounter them, for the Scarecrow has a way of taking revenge upon his enemies, and once seen taking an active part against him, they are marked men. I think under the circumstances, I should feel inclined to wear a mask myself.'

'And so should I,' agreed the Welshman. 'This Scarecrow seems the very devil to deal with.' It was a party of six guarding the bridge and one of them cried out, 'Who goes there?' Doctor Syn called back, 'I am the vicar of Dymchurch, and this is a friend of mine. We are on our way to visit a sick old woman who lives on the Marsh between Burmarsh and St. Mary's.'

'Then our information is correct,' remarked the man who had challenged them. 'I take it, reverend sir, that your friend's name is Jones, a stranger to these parts.'

Doctor Syn looked at the Welshman with a mystified expression. 'That is quite right, my man,' he said to the coastguard. 'Mr. Jones hails from the mountains of North Wales. A far cry from our beloved Marsh.'

'Then you will both put your hands above your heads,' ordered the coastguard.

'What on earth for?' asked the doctor, nevertheless obeying since he perceived that two of the party were covering them with pistols.

'Scarecrow's orders, and he'll tell you what for himself,' was the astounding answer. 'We are about to take you to him. Search them for weapons!'

'We are not armed, I assure you,' promised the doctor. 'And why should we be searched when you know who we are? Are coastguards also in this devil's pay?'

'Aye, we know you well enough, but you do not know us,' replied the other.

'We are no coastguards, though we look like them, no doubt. We are loyal members of the Scarecrow's band, and you can consider yourselves his prisoners.'

'But neither coastguard nor smuggler has ever hindered me in the execution of my sacred calling,' objected the vicar. 'I tell you I am not out upon the Marsh to spy, but to bring comfort to an ailing member of my flock.' The masked man laughed. 'Aye, we know all about old Mother Handaway.

As to her comfort, it has already been provided for. Mr. Mipps, your sexton, took her some provisions earlier in the night.'

'You are well informed,' replied Doctor Syn.

'The Scarecrow knows everything,' said the other. 'And that you will know full well when you meet him, as you are about to do. But in order to meet him you must consent to have your eyes bandaged, so that you do not know the whereabouts of his secret meeting-place.'

Doctor Syn turned to his companion with a smile and a shrug of his shoulders. 'I suppose we must submit with a good grace,' he said.

Their next half-hour was uncomfortable. With two of the smugglers on either side of him and their eyes securely blindfolded, the prisoners were hurried along across the fields. They were pushed down steep banks and plunged into dyke-water, then dragged across and hoisted up the opposite banks, while tall bulrushes tripped their feet and lashed their faces. At last, however, a halt was called. They heard a key turn in a squeaky lock and a further squeaking of an old door being swung open on rusty hinges. They were then warned that they had to mount steps and were supported up a short flight, when they were again halted while the door was locked behind them.

Doctor Syn sniffed and muttered to the Welshman, 'Hops! It would seem that we are in an oast-house.'

It was then that a deep voice boomed out, 'Uncover their eyes, and since they have spied upon the Scarecrow, they shall have the privilege of seeing him before going to their death.' The bandages were immediately torn from their faces, and it was a fearsome spectacle that confronted them. By the light of torches which four fantastically dressed figures held above their heads, the prisoners saw a semi-circle of some dozen men, masked, cloaked and booted, who were grouped behind a hideouslooking devil who sat upon a barrel.

A painted mask that gleamed with phosphorus hid his real features, and gave him a terrifying appearance. From his shoulders a ragged but voluminous cloak served as a hellish background to his agile figure, clad in a weatherbeaten black riding suit which was completed with tight-fitting black boots drawn up to the thighs. Upon his head was a high-brimmed black three-corner hat from which flowed long whisps of horse-hair and was trimmed with a tail of ravens'feathers. From the side pockets of the jacket there showed the heavy butts of horse pistols, and from a heavy belt, which supported a brace of small pistols, hung a long sword.

'Doctor Syn,' croaked this terrible figure, 'if I had not heard the best opinions of you from the poor of Romney Marsh, who are the richer for serving me, you would long since have been sleeping in your own churchyard, with an epitaph of violent death upon the headstone. I have been lenient with you. But when you use the excuse of your sacred calling to spy out the mysteries of the Marsh, you have presumed too far, and no more tolerance can be shown to you.

Since it is your wish to witness the Scarecrow's men landing a cargo, you shall be put in a position to do so. And a safe position as far as we are concerned, for the very sand and sea which you shall watch will carry your soul away on the full tide. For your companion, this stranger, who accompanies you on your long journey, I have no regrets. He has chosen to thrust his nose into matters that in no way concern him, and must therefore take the consequence. Your fate will teach others to fear the Scarecrow and to leave his business alone, and so, since you are doing me a service just as that Hythe officer I hanged tonight has done, I do you both the compliment to wish you a pleasant journey on the running tide. Good night.' He then turned to his followers and added, 'Their graves are ready dug by the last posts of the breakwater by Henley's Herring Hang. I think that at the next low tide the green crabs will have rendered them unrecognizable. Those who are named for the funeral party will complete their work and then rejoin us on the beachy stretch of Littlestone. Cover their eyes.'

'I warn you,' cried the vicar, 'that if any harm befalls us there will be such an outcry on the Marsh as even your ingenuity will not silence. Every house will be searched and every hiding-place laid bare by the military. You will be betrayed by your own arrogance, and just as surely as George Plattman and the Hythe officer have been murdered by you, so will you hang upon the Dymchurch gallows.'

'Stow your croaking, you old rook,' ordered the Scarecrow, 'or I shall have your beak covered as well as your eyes!'

'But you cannot possibly mean to kill us,' faltered the Welshman. 'I am willing to pay a good sum for ransom.'

'If you think to bribe me you are mistaken. The Scarecrow is above that.'

'But not above murder, it would seem,' replied the lawyer. 'I have powerful friends in Wales who will soon set the machinery of the law against you, even though they fail to do so here.'

'It is a far cry from Wales, sir,' laughed the Scarecrow, 'and I have never yet feared a piece of toasted cheese. And let me warn you that if you talk any more your death shall be even more ghastly than the one I have planned for you.

Cover their eyes, my merry devils, and let us be done with this delay.'

The next journey was even more trying to the prisoners than the previous one, for on being led out of the oast-house with their eyes once more blindfolded, they were hoisted on to two spare horses and told to take a firm grip on the manes, as the reins were held by the riders detailed to lead them.

They travelled at a good pace, and in silence, for when Doctor Syn sniffed and remarked that his nose told him they were heading across the Marsh in the direction of the sea, he was rudely ordered to keep his mouth shut.

For the most part the party moved quickly at a sharp canter. Every now and again the prisoners were warned to hold tighter and the pace was increased to a gallop to enable the horses to leap the dykes; but a good deal of the way was made along the Marsh roads, which were smoother going than the dyked fields.

At last the prisoners were told to lean forward, and the horses climbed a steep slipway that brought them on to the top of the sea-wall. Along the way they trotted for a hundred yards or so, and then down another slipway which brought them to the beach. On the hard sand the going was straightforward. After a short gallop the party drew rein, and the prisoners were dragged from their horses. Opposite the tall wooden building known as Henley's Herring Hang, where the fish have been dried and smoked from time immemorial, there is a breakwater which runs out from the sea-wall. It is fashioned from the oak of wrecks, and consists of two rows of heavy planks reinforced with planks, holding together great boulders and masses of pebbles whose weight breaks the force of the fiercest waves.

Around the end piles nearest the sea two pits had been dug, uncovering some four foot or so of the stakes below sand level. Into these pits the prisoners were dropped, and their feet were lashed securely to the posts. Still blindfolded, their arms were dragged behind them and tightly lashed with cords around their wrists. Many coils of rope were then wound round their bodies and the posts, and with two spade that had been hidden under the heaped-up sand the pits were quickly filled up again. Piled up to their chins, the sand was then beaten down hard.

It was then that Doctor Syn broke the silence. 'We can at least claim the promise of your dastardly Scarecrow that our eyes should be uncovered, for he said that we should have the privilege of witnessing his landing of the cargoes.

For my own part, I would rather watch death coming with open eyes.' Promptly the bandages were wrenched from their eyes, and it was then that the Welshman fully realized the horror of their situation, for as he saw the long lines of wave after wave floating towards them on the level sand, he let out one piercing scream in desperation. One of the smugglers dug a spadeful of sand and flung it in his face. 'Stop that, or I'll pile sand over your head, and the crabs will get you before the salt-water. Why don't you take it calm, like the reverend gentleman?'

The threat silenced the Welshman's voice, though his terror was still made manifest by his chattering teeth.

'We must hurry,' whispered the spokesman of the smugglers. 'Look!' Round the promontory of Dungeness a string of five sailing boats appeared.

As they swept round into the bay the moonlight caught their canvas. They were the Scarecrow's luggers bringing the brandy kegs from France. Then they disappeared into the black background of the land.

'Time we joined the Scarecrow,' went on the leader of the party. 'Get to your horses, all but Curlew. Have you looked to the priming of your pistols, Curlew?'

'Aye, aye, Raven, and I've borrowed a third from Seagull, in case of a misfire.'

'You know what you have to do?' asked Raven.

'Aye, aye,' replied Curlew. 'If the prisoners cry out for help, I puts bullets in the backs of their heads.'

'Your horse is tethered under the sea-wall,' went on Raven, 'and cannot be seen. You sit behind 'em in the shadow of the breakwater and then you'll be out of sight too.'

'We've forgot one of the Scarecrow's orders, Raven,' said one of the smugglers who had picked up the spades.

'What's that, Seagull?' asked the Raven.

'The board. It's hid where Curlew sits, and I have the hammer and nails.'

'Bring it here, Curlew, and show it to the prisoners.' Curlew handed Raven a board on which was crudely pained the following inscription:

'So rot the bones of all the Scarecrow's enemies.'

This the Raven held before the prisoners' eyes, ordering the parson to read it aloud, which Doctor Syn did in a firm voice, which caused a burst of laughter from the now mounted smugglers.

'Silence, you fools!' ordered the Raven. 'Nail it up, Curlew, and not too much noise with it either.' Seagull produced a hammer and two nails from his pocket, and helped Curlew to fix it across the tops of the posts, high above the prisoners' heads.

On the last stroke of the hammer, Raven said with a chuckle, 'There's the last nail in your coffins, gentlemen. As for you, Mister Parson, you'll shortly know whether there's any truth or not in the Heaven you're so fond of preaching about. It will be a cold clammy journey there, I'm thinking.'

'Look, Raven,' cried Seagull, who had now mounted. 'There's the flasher from Limestone Beach. It's going in "twos". That means the Revenue men are somewheres on the sea-wall between us. We'd best take to the Marsh and come out behind 'em.'

'No, we'll gallop the beach, and chance a stray shot or so,' ordered Raven.

'We'll waste good time on the Marsh. Follow me and keep your horses to the sea edge as far from the wall as possible. A splashing or so won't hurt us. It ain't as if we have to drink sea-water like these gentlemen. Now I wonders which of them four eyes the crabs will feast on first. There's the flasher again.

Three times! That means ride like hell.' Saying which the Raven kicked up his horse, headed for the wave, and followed by his fast-flying companions, swerved round in the water's edge and galloped away.

The wretched prisoners watched them cover some half of the journey and then saw a line of flashing from the sea-wall, followed by a crackling report.

'It's the revenue men firing at them,' whispered Doctor Syn. 'If only they'd come our way!'

'It would only mean a bullet in your heads,' whispered the voice of Curlew.

'I knows my orders.' A scattered volley was returned by the galloping smugglers in the direction of the wall, which the revenue men promptly answered. This resulted in a scream, as a horse plunged forwards and fell kicking in the waves. The others rode on.

'They got one of the spare horses, that's all,' chuckled the voice of Curlew.

'Well, horse-flesh is cheaper than man's.' The spare horse was left to its fate, and the smugglers, after letting off a few more shots, were out of range, heading for Littlestone.

'Scarecrow's luck as usual,' laughed Curlew. 'They'd best not follow or they'll find themselves outnumbered. There's two hundred marshmen "out" tonight.'

'I only pray that they do not number any of my parishioners,' said Doctor Syn.

'There's more from Dymchurch than from anywheres,' replied Curlew. 'I'm one myself, though you'd never guess who. Perhaps you never guessed that the most pious-looking of your congregation was the Scarecrow's men.'

'I should have been a sad man had I suspected it,' returned the vicar. 'And I could almost wish that you had kept me ignorant. I should have liked to go to my death believing in my people.'

'Well, you can't, and that's a sure thing. Mind you, we ain't supposed to know who's who ourselves, and we don't know, though we has our notions.

Raven, for instance. Now I bet a guinea I do know who he is. I may tell you when the waves are in your nostrils, just by way of cheering you up and giving you a surprise. Regular attendance he gives at church, and no one sings the hymns louder. Did it never strike you as remarkable that so many poor fishermen and farm hands was able to put so much money in your collecting bags? You've the Scarecrow to thank for that! Be generous of a "Sunday in the bag" was one of his favourite orders, and the Scarecrow's orders must always be carried out.'

'Dear, dear,' sighed Doctor Syn, 'and I have even thanked God for the noble efforts my poor have made to help the poorer. No doubt, then, I have often spoken to this man you call the Raven. No doubt also that you guess at the identity of the Scarecrow.'

'No, I have no idea. No more has no one else,' returned Curlew. 'Our own identities are secret and known only to him and his go-between-us, who shall be nameless. I think this go-between knows who he is, but he's the only one, and that's how he works it all so safe.'

'But not safe for very long,' replied the doctor. 'They say that dying men are often privileged to prophesy about the future, and I who see the tide of death approaching am about to prophesy to you of your leader. This night's black work will finish him and bring him to trial. Your own arrests will follow his.

He will turn King's Evidence against you.'

'Not the Scarecrow!' interrupted Curlew. 'He has never forsaken his men who have been faithful.'

'That is no matter,' retorted Doctor Syn. 'Without his leadership you will betray yourselves, and all of you will hang. Now, Mister Curlew, and I call you that name for want of your better one, has it occurred to you that you can save your neck by freeing us, here and now? I give you my sacred word that only good will come to you by the action.'

'You heard what the Scarecrow said about bribery,' replied the guard. 'I think there is none of us who would betray him, even with the rope about our necks.'

'Then you throw away your own life as well as ours,' warned Doctor Syn.

'That's as may be. But I would rather suffer the punishment of the law than the penalty for disobeying the Scarecrow.' Meanwhile with every wave the water drew nearer to the prisoners, and as the relentless line approached the Welshman kept up a low whimpering groan.

'Won't be long before that moaning of yours will turn to gurgling,' said Curlew. 'Why don't you take it brave like the parson? He ain't frightened same as you.'

'Oh, but indeed I am,' replied the doctor, who was glad of the hint. 'I defy anyone not to be frightened when facing certain death. I could face it bravely enough were I lying sick in bed, but this is too horrible, and I'll not accept credit where none is due. Believe me, I am frightened in the extreme.' This confession made the

Welshman whimper the more violently, which was exactly what Doctor Syn meant it to do, and he registered the opinion that his companion in misfortune was not to be depended upon in peril.

Just then there came another crackle of shots, followed by a tremendous volley. Then across the water they heard a mighty cheer.

'That sounds as though the revenue men are driven off,' chuckled Curlew.

'And it also looks as though further revenue men are going to their help,' said Doctor Syn. 'Unless I am mistaken that long boat tacking from Hythe is the Dover patrol boat, the revenue cutter.'

'Arriving too late as usual,' sneered Curlew. 'She'll never make Littlestone before the cargo is landed and then the Scarecrow's luggers will have gone, and the goods on the backs of the pack-ponies.'

'There's another boat in her wake,' said Doctor Syn. 'But she appears to be taking a shorter tack towards shore.'

'A fishing boat,' explained Curlew. 'Nothing to do with the cutter. Now get this clear into your heads. If you shouts for help I'll empty these into your heads,' and the prisoners felt the barrel of pistols pressing into the backs of their skulls.

'We are not stupid, unless perhaps we decide to make our deaths the more sudden,' replied Doctor Syn. 'Besides, the revenue men are heading the cutter further to sea, and I suppose are trying to head the luggers off on their way to Dungeness and deep water. The little boat is making good way, though.'

'The waves are making good way too,' sneered Curlew.

The water was now only a foot or so from their faces, and the Welshman was chattering with fright. Doctor Syn began the recital of a prayer, but was ordered by Curlew to keep silent.

A few more waves and the water touched their chins, and it was only the pressure of the pistol from behind that prevented the Welshman from screaming.

A few minutes more and the water was round their necks and covering their strained-up chins. In the meantime they saw the fishing boat down sail directly opposite them about fifty yards off shore. They could see the fisherman busying himself with his tackle.

'If you attract his attention,' warned Curlew, 'I'll pistol you and run. But no doubt he's one of the Scarecrow's men, who has been keeping a weather eye on the cutter. In any case you'll get no help from him.'

'I'm frightened,' moaned the Welshman. 'I don't want to die! It's awful!'

'It is awful indeed,' whispered Doctor Syn. 'I am frightened too, but I am trying to pray and should advice you to do the same. May God give you the courage to play the man.'

The Welshman, who, being shorter than the vicar, was lower to the water, spat violently as the first wave reached his mouth.

'God have mercy on you!' whispered Doctor Syn. 'May He give you strength to face the end bravely.' The Welshman spat again.

Chapter 7. Doctor Syn undertakes an amazing quest

It was obvious that the fisherman, preoccupied with his own business, had not noticed the horrible situation upon the beach. He appeared to be searching for something in the bottom of his boat. He picked up an old tin and looked inside it, then dropped it with a clatter and an oath. He then grasped a heavy sweep oar, and thrusting it out over the stern, he propelled the boat towards the beach. As the keel ground into the sand, he swung himself over the side. He was a little man wearing enormous sea-boots. He leaned over the side and picked up the tin he had dropped and a spade. Then he came wading ashore.

'Stay were you are a minute,' ordered Curlew, and the prisoners felt the barrels of the pistols leave their necks. The fisherman was being covered. 'Who are you, and what do you want?' asked Curlew.

'Well now, you look like the devil himself,' replied the fisherman. 'I take it, though, that you're one of the Scarecrow's men. I'm ashore to dig lug, I am, and I'se none other than Mister Mipps, sexton of Dymchurch, and gracious goodness what in the world are you doing of to my vicar and the little gentleman from Wales?'

'Scarecrow's justice,' replied Curlew, 'and let me warn you not to meddle in his business.'

'I don't want to muck about with his business,' replied Mipps, 'but before we knows where we are, the good vicar will be drowned.'

'That is the Scarecrow's idea, sexton,' replied Curlew.

'Well, it ain't a very nice idea, now, is it?'

'You hurry along with your lug-digging and get back to your boat,' ordered Curlew.

'I'd a deal sooner dig for the vicar than lug,' replied Mipps. 'But I expects the moment I started doing any such thing, you'll be letting off them barkers at me. Is that it?'

'That's about the size of it, Mister Sexton,' returned Curlew.

'And being so close,' mused Mipps, 'it strikes me as you could hardly miss.

But what has the poor vicar done to the Scarecrow?'

'Preached against him, and spied on him,' was the curt answer.

'What a pity,' sighed Mipps. 'Well, there's nothing for it, then, but for me to get my lug and back to the old boat. The water's already in the Welsh gentleman's mouth, and though an undertaker and sexton myself, this here funeral ain't to my liking for once. I'll wash out my tin and then go up the beach for the lug.'

'Don't you want low tide for lug?' asked Curlew. 'Sure you ain't using lug as an excuse to poke your long nose into the Scarecrow's business? If so watch out for trouble.'

'I knows lug I does,' replied Mipps, 'and I'll have no Scarecrow's man teaching me about the ways of the little fellows. Also I ain't poking my nose into no danger. With all respects to the vicar, I enjoys life too well.' As he spoke he leaned down and rinsed out his tin with his left hand, holding the spade over his shoulder with his right.

'Then I advise you to go on enjoying it,' warned Curlew.

'Leave us, my good Mipps,' ordered Doctor Syn. 'You can do no good, though I know you would wish it otherwise. But I would spare you the pain of seeing me die. Go!'

What the prisoners saw then was unexpected. Mipps was crouching down and washing the tin, when he suddenly let it go and grasped his spade handle with both hands. Round came the blade in a circular up-bound sweep. There was a crash of metal meeting metal, and a loud explosion, but by then Mipps had leapt over the prisoners' heads with a mighty splash and had closed with Curlew. They heard the sound of heavy breathing as the two men fought behind their heads for the possession of the second pistol. A second explosion told them this was discharged and with no harm to their rescuer, for they heard him cry out, 'Wasting good bullets in the air what should have been in your devil's innards.'

'Look out, Mipps,' warned Doctor Syn. 'He has a third pistol somewhere upon him.'

'I've got it, sir, and him too,' came the reassuring answer. 'Now then, get on that horse quick! I'll not risk your help, for I'd rather see the back of you, and I've a pistol here only waiting your return, for I see you've no holsters at your saddle.' Mipps raised his voice and shouted after the fleeing Curlew, 'Told you I enjoyed life! I does!' Back came Mipps into the prisoners' sight, with a 'He's gone, and now to get you out!'

'Our ankles are tied to the posts, as well as our bodies and wrists,' said Doctor Syn. 'You'll have to cut the cords with your sheath knife which I thank God you are wearing. You'll find trouble digging down so far in the wet sand.

Hurry!'

'Sand's soft enough round these posts,' said Mipps, drawing his

knife and plunging it down behind the post that held the vicar. 'No
trouble, sir, to one who's caught lug all his life. I'd chase an
escaping lug from Dymchurch sands to molten seas of hell, but I'd
get him.'

'Don't talk! Don't talk!' cried the Welshman. 'Get me out, man,
I'm drowning!'

'Now, you keep your mouth shut, sir,' replied Mipps, 'and you
won't do no such thing. Breathe through your nose, and keep calm.
The vicar and me will get you out all in good time.'

'No, Mipps,' corrected Doctor Syn. 'Rescue Mr. Jones first, for,
being shorter than I am, he is lower in the water.'

'Begging your pardon, sir,' went on Mipps, who was now laying
full length in the water with his face half covered, in his frantic
cutting of the lower cords.

'He's in no fit state to help me out with you, whereas you and
me will soon hoist him, and bring him back to life. There's your
ankle rope. Regular tethered! Thank God for a sharp knife and rope
what's rotting in the wet! Stretch your feet, sir. That's it, sir. You're
free. Now, sir, wriggle yourself round and climb up the pole as it
were whiles I give you a hoist.' With the help of Mipps and his
spade, and the firm leverage of the stout post, it did not take
Doctor Syn long to drag himself from the wet sand and the water,
during which operation the Welshman was spouting salt water
from his mouth like a whale, much to the amusement of Mipps,
who had never taken kindly to the stranger since the shooting
episode in the vicarage study.

However, under the encouragement of the vicar, the little man
worked with a will, and although wringing wet, bravely submerged
himself, severing the cords with his knife. It was a good thing for
the Welshman that there were two of them carrying out his rescue,
for by this time he was too exhausted to be able to help himself.

Whether from too much salt water in his stomach, or too much
fright in his heart, the poor little Welshman was unconscious when
the vicar and sexton pulled him clear, but he soon recovered when
Doctor Syn produced his brandy flask from his sand-filled pocket.
Doctor Syn urged that they must hurry in case Curlew returned
with others to carry out the Scarecrow's sentence, from which,
thanks to Providence and Mister Mipps, they had so mercifully
escaped.

Dragging the Welshman between them, they made as much
haste as they could towards the village, keeping under cover of the
sea-wall most of the way.

By the time they had reached the inn, they were a bedraggled-looking trio.

Mipps kept up a continuous sniffling, as a hint to the Welshman that some good liquor at his expense would not be amiss; the Welshman kept up a groaning and a whimpering, while Doctor Syn most piously continued to praise God for their deliverance. 'My good Mipps, it was Providence indeed that called you to go fishing this night. This gentleman and myself are indeed your debtors.' Mipps sniffed again, and remarked, 'A cold in the head ain't so bad when you knows you are going to a spot where they keeps a good drop of liquor. It will take more than was in your flask, vicar, to drive the salt out of us, I'm thinking.' At the Ship Inn Mrs. Waggetts, who was in the habit of sitting up very late when the revenue men were out, in case of business coming her way, made the unfortunate three very welcome, and while preparing hot punch for their comfort, she listened with great indignation to their terrible adventure.

The Welshman lost no time in getting drunk, and was helped up to his room by the vicar and Mipps.

It was not until they had searched under his bed at his request, in case one of the Scarecrow's men might be hiding there, and finally closed the door upon him and heard the key turn in the lock, that the two rascals, vicar and sexton, allowed themselves the pleasure of a grin.

'I think, my good Mipps,' whispered the vicar, 'that we has better repair to the vicarage. Mrs. Waggetts will certainly expect me to be weary, and believe me I have no great wish to recount our trying adventures to the revenue men, should any of them drop in for a night-cap before the dawn. I rather think that the poor fellows will be in need of what the "Ship" can give them. I think also that it is likely we shall receive a different visitor at the vicarage, and when we have driven the salt water from our stomachs with good brandy as you say, I rather anticipate that the three of us will indulge in a good laugh at the expense of our Welsh lawyer and some others who shall be nameless.' So bidding Mrs. Waggetts good night, they left the Ship Inn and walked to the vicarage. In the study they fastened shutters and doors.

'I think, sir,' remarked Mipps, as the vicar handed him a glass of brandy, 'that the planning of this adventure was a extreme. You put yourself in too uncomfortable positions, I think.'

'My good Mipps,' replied the vicar. 'Thanks to you, the adventure could not have been better. The Welshman is entirely deceived. Not only that, but his evidence at the inquiry will convince others that I was his companion in misfortune. He saw the Scarecrow rescue Jimmie Bone. He comes back to this room and finds me very convincingly asleep. In my company he is again faced with the Scarecrow—a different one it is true, but he has no notion of that.

Neither will it enter any of their heads that Jimmie Bone and Doctor Syn can put up such similar performances as the Scarecrow. No one will suspect that I was the first Scarecrow, or that Jimmie Bone was the second. But all will know tomorrow that the poor vicar was exceedingly badly treated by the Scarecrow, and there will be a great hue and cry after the scoundrel this time, I'm thinking.'

'Aye, sir,' nodded Mipps. 'He will not be riding the Marsh for some little time if he is wise.'

'He will not, my good Mipps.' Doctor Syn put up a warning finger, and whispered, 'A scratch on the outer shutter. Open the garden door. It will be Jimmie Bone.' Mipps admitted the highwayman, who reported that the cargoes had all been safely landed and carried on the pack-ponies to the hides. He further reported that the smugglers had suffered only one casualty apart from the horse that had been hit. A tub-carrier had got a stray bullet from a revenue man in his leg, but the bullet had been removed and there would have to be no questions from the inquisitive Doctor Pepper.

'And the casualties to the revenue men?' asked the vicar.

'One got a bullet in the arm,' replied the highwayman. 'One with a broken head who tried to stop the pack-ponies at Botolph's Bridge, and what is more serious, the Hythe revenue officer, who was in charge of my escort, was mysteriously hanged upon Dymchurch gallows. That will cause an outcry, but I think the greatest one will be over the treatment our dear vicar suffered at the hands of these miscreants.' and Jimmie Bone grinned as he drained a glassful of Doctor Syn's brandy.

'It is also pretty certain,' remarked Doctor Syn, 'that a hue and cry will go out for you. They will probably get the dragoons on that search, and I shall feel happier about you when I know you are out of the country for a time. Before the dawn breaks, you must be in the Scarecrow's hiding-place. Mother Handaway will see to your needs, and tomorrow night we will have you smuggled across the Channel. You can shelter on one of our French luggers, and I shall know where and how to communicate with you. Indeed, I rather think, my good friend, that before many moons I shall be sending for you to play a hand against a new adversary. When I have worked out my plans I will let you know. I can only tell you this, that I imagine it will be running the richest cargoes we have yet tackled.'

'But I thought it was agreed, sir,' put in Mipps, 'that the Scarecrow and his men must disappear for a time, and not ride the Marsh till all this has blown over?'

'That is so, Mipps,' returned the vicar. 'The Scarecrow and his Night-riders will disappear from the Marsh, and reappear a far cry from here, where they will ride to very good profit.'

'Wherever you send me,' said Jimmie Bone, 'I shall be waiting for your orders. And in order to do that I had best get into hiding now.'

'Mipps will go with you,' suggested Doctor Syn. 'Or, perhaps better, he will go out first and see if any of the revenue men are still out. I rather think you will find them at the "Ship".'

'If Mipps will come as far as my horse,' said the highwayman, 'I shall be glad of a hoist in mounting, for my ankle is still bad. Once in the saddle it does not matter to me if the revenue men are on the prowl or no. They'll not catch me, and they'll not see how I enter the secret stable.'

'Well, have a care,' warned Doctor Syn, 'for to rescue you again would prove plaguey difficult, though we should have to manage it somehow.'

'Have no worry on that score, sir,' assured Bone. 'I will not be taken again, I promise you.'

'Then good night, my friends,' said Doctor Syn. 'You will receive the Scarecrow's orders tomorrow night, and Mister Mipps will report for parochial orders in the morning at nine. Good night. It has been a strenuous one so far for us all, and a little rest will do us good.' Doctor Syn fastened the door quietly behind them, lit his bedroom candle by the candelabrum, and having extinguished the other lights, he mounted the stairs to his room, where he took off his damp clothes and arrayed himself in a long nightshirt and a tall nightcap. The nightcap reminded him of a more comforting one, and his hand went out to a certain book on the shelf beside his four-post bed. Behind the book was a bottle of brandy.

He took a generous pull and replaced the bottle before climbing into bed.

Having snuffed out the candle, he sat huddled up gazing through the casement at the moon-bathed Marsh. Each field was framed in silvery dyke-water. Even the sheep huddled together as though afraid of the stillness. Presently, in the far distance, a little yellow light appeared, and then moved slowly. Doctor Syn knew what it was, and was glad. Mother Handaway had closed the door of the hidden stable, and was now lighting her way back to her hovel. He knew then that Jimmie Bone was safe. The light disappeared. Doctor Syn's hand once more groped for the bottle, and he silently toasted the Marsh that feared him by night and loved him by day. Back went the bottle behind the book; then, pulling the curtains of his bed, the vicar of Dymchurch and the Scarecrow of Romney Marsh was lying back on the pillows with a sigh of relief. In two or three seconds Doctor Syn was asleep.

Now being renowned as a good parson who cared for his flock, and was ever in the habit of crossing the Marsh at night in cases of illness that needed his spiritual visitations, it was the rule of the vicarage, that unless Mrs. Fowey, the housekeeper, heard his bell ring, which very often happened as early as seven, she should not take up his customary cup of chocolate until nine; and she had the strictest orders that it should never be later. No sooner had Mrs. Fowey called him at this hour, which was the hour for the sexton's visit, than she would say, 'That sexton Mipps is here, and wants his orders, vicar.' However, the morning after these adventures, it was long after nine that Mrs. Fowey brought the chocolate, for Mister Mipps, always very punctual in his dealings with his master, had been telling her some of the horrors which the poor reverend gentleman had gone through on the night previous. Mrs. Fowey had already heard some of this gossip from the inn servants and the butler at the Court House. The beadle also delayed the delivery of the doctor's chocolate, by following on the heels of the sexton and telling his version of the tragedy to Mrs. Fowey through the open casement of the kitchen. He was, he said, mortally afraid of the Scarecrow, and asked Mipps whether he thought it likely that the Night-riders would find out that it was he who took the body of the murdered revenue officer from the gallows.

'Since the Scarecrow seems to know everything what goes on,' replied Mipps, 'and is wonderful clever whatever we thinks about him, I should say he knows already that it was you what done it. And supposing he don't, which I doubt, won't it all come out at the inquest? The squire and the other Lords of the Level will sift every detail, and you'll be a nice fat bit of detail, and a marked man from now on. If we don't get the Scarecrow, the Scarecrow will get us, one by one, and you being the beadle will no doubt be the first to go.'

'But I had to do it,' whispered the beadle, looking fearfully over his shoulder, as though he expected to see the phantom rider appear from the Marsh mist. 'It was my duty.'

'The Scarecrow don't fancy duty what interferes with his plans,' went on Mipps, enjoying the terror of his colleague. 'It was my duty to rescue the good vicar, and I done it, but I'm a marked man for all that. I tell you, Mister Beadle, that we'll be got one by one, and perhaps two or three together, just to save time and make it seem more horrible. But I thinks as how I shall be the last to go. Do you know why?'

'Why?' repeated the wretched beadle.

"Cos he knows I'm the coffin-maker,' said Mipps solemnly. 'He don't want a lot of corpses hanging about all over the place. He wants to see nice little headstones above well-knocked-up coffins deep down and a pretty inscription, like yours will be, "Here lies the Beadle of Dymchurch. Murdered by the Scarecrow, along of his doing his duty which annoyed same considerable. Rest in Peace, Beadle."'

'I don't mind telling you,' said the beadle in a querulous manner, 'that I don't feel ready for my last rest. We all has to go sometime, I admits, but I don't see why one should be pushed into it.'

'Cheer up,' replied Mipps by way of encouragement. 'I won't push you into it. I'll measure you generous-like, and drop you in the coffin I knocks up for you, as gently as I'd drop an infant into a crib. And I tell you what. Have you got any money laid by that you can spare?'

'You think I could bribe the Scarecrow somehow to spare me?' asked the beadle hopefully.

'No, I don't,' snapped Mipps. 'The little Welshman tried to bribe him in the vicar's hearing, and what happened to him? Buried to his neck in the sand and the rising tide! No, he's got too much money, has the Scarecrow, to want yours.

I meant have you got enough to give me, so as I'll be able to give you a nice bit of real oak with a pretty grain, and I'll throw in brass knobs for the same price.'

'I tell you I don't want to go at all,' cried the irritated beadle.

'You'll have to,' snapped Mipps again. 'And I'm sorry to have to say it. I thinks you'll be followed very quick by Doctor Syn, who won't be afraid to say what he thinks about the Scarecrow's behaviour at the inquest, and then by dear Mrs. Fowey whom I shall miss very much. She's always so good to us, and gives us a drop of rum when we calls to see her.'

'The Scarecrow had better not try any of his dirty tricks on me,' exclaimed the housekeeper. 'Oi'd quickly show him Oi had work to do for the dear vicar.

And he'd best not harm the good doctor or Oi'll be after the rogue. He's done enough already. What with last night, and now with your gossip of him, me being late with the chocolate! You know where the rum is, Mister Mipps, so draw a tot for yourself and the beadle while Oi takes up the chocolate.' As she stalked off with the tray and steaming dish, Mipps took her at her word and skipped off into the still-room in order to draw from the rum barrel.

Thither the beadle followed him, for he had no intention of being left to himself any more, until the Scarecrow and his followers were hanged by the neck, and even then, he though he would not be alone too much, for he had a firm belief in wicked spirits, and he shuddered when he thought of the Scarecrow as a ghost seeking him out for revenge.

Doctor Syn was still asleep when the housekeeper knocked on his door. As he did not reply with the customary 'Come in', she was nervous, and, opening the door, crossed to the bed table and set down the tray. She then saw his clothes covered with muddy sand and gave a cry of horror, which awoke the vicar, who pulled aside his bed curtains.

'Is Mipps here yet?' he asked.

'He has been telling me of the dreadful happenings,' she said. 'What a state your reverend clothes are in, to be sure!'

'Yes, Mrs. Fowey,' replied Syn. 'I wish you a good morning. It was not a good night, I assure you.'

'The beadle is below too,' went on the housekeeper. 'He is a very scared man, and that Mipps has been adding to his fears, saying that the Scarecrow will get us all one by one, and the beadle first of any. It is certain no one is safe till the Scarecrow is caught. Do you think, Doctor Syn, that he is a man who pretends to be the devil, or is he the devil himself riding the Marsh in shape of a man?'

'Whichever he may be,' returned the vicar piously, 'we know that his works are of the devil, and therefore we must not fear him, but rather keep our faith in God.'

'You are good and brave, Doctor Syn,' sighed the housekeeper. 'We should all do well to follow your example, but with devils riding in the Marsh and hanging honest men, it makes one doubt in a protecting Providence. What you say in your sermons about guardian angels doesn't seem quite right to me.'

'You must not speak like that, my good woman,' reproved Doctor Syn. 'The ways of Providence are beyond our understanding perhaps, but ever just and right. For some reason that poor Hythe officer was summoned into the Hereafter. His work on earth was finished. He was needed elsewhere. For the same reason, it was not time for me to go, and my guardian angel entered the little body of Mr. Mipps, and directed him to go fishing, in order to save my life. Therefore I must bravely continue here doing my duty. Send the sexton up to me.' Mrs. Fowey found the two men in the still-room, where Mipps crouched over the tap.

'When you've finished the barrel,' she said sharply, 'perhaps you'll attend on the poor vicar while in mends and dries his clothes.'

'We'll have our drink first,' said Mipps with a sly wink to the beadle.

'Something went wrong with the tap. But the beadle will be glad to know that it is now working after a fashion. Will you partake, Mrs. Fowey?'

'Oi will not,' she replied acidly. 'And it seems to me that the tap has worked only too easily, by the looks of you both. Only a minute ago the good vicar was calling you his guardian angel along of saving his life last night, but Oi thinks you a mischievous and lying little devil, and I know the beadle agrees with me.'

'Mr. Mipps likes his little joke, ma'am,' replied the beadle cautiously.

'But it weren't no joke about the Scarecrow getting you,' said Mipps, filling his pannikin quickly once more.

'Well, he did have to twist and turn at the tap, I'll say that for him,' answered the beadle, rather pleased with himself that he could make a sly joke himself, despite the fear in his stomach.

'Aye, and Oi'll be bound it turned and twisted to very good effect,' snapped the housekeeper.

'It finally has, ma'am,' grinned Mipps. 'Wasn't it you what once told me as how rum was the best cure for a stomach full of salt water? No one knows so many cures for ailments as you in this village. Not even old Doctor Pepper. So I'll take your advice, and have just this one more.' Which he proceeded to do.

This was a little too much for the old woman, who picked up a spare spigot and flung it at his head.

Mipps dodged aside to safety without spilling a drop of the

precious liquor, and tossing it down his throat, he handed her the empty pannikin with a polite, 'Thankee ma'am.'

'Put it down yourself,' she ordered, 'and be off with you upstairs.'

'Anything to oblige a pretty girl,' smiled Mipps, and as he sauntered out of the door, he looked back and said, 'Remember, beadle, that my promise holds good. Nice bit of grained oak! With knobs!' Mrs. Fowey vented her rage now upon the beadle, ordering him to be off and not follow her about in her kitchen.

'I though, ma'am, that you might like a man about as a protection. The Scarecrow may take a quicker revenge on the vicarage than you imagine.

There's no one more against the Scarecrow than the vicar.'

'If you thinks that the Scarecrow will come in here when Mrs. Fowey is preparing breakfast, you're wrong. Oi fears no devils in the mornings when Oi has work to do. Be off and do some work too!' Meantime Mipps had closed the vicar's bedroom door behind him, and was inquiring after that reverend gentleman's health.

Doctor Syn handed the sexton his empty dish of chocolate, saying, 'I know you never indulge in this beverage, Mipps, but if you did, I think you would agree with me that it needs something a little stronger to settle it. Pass the brandy. Has Mrs. Fowey been hospitable to you?' Mipps produced the bottle from behind the book. 'Yes and no, sir. Offered me and the beadle a tot of rum which was welcome enough, but you know what here tots is like. There's nothing like a drop of brandy after a good wetting as we had last night. Good for agues, vapours, and spleens!'

'I am sorry to find you suffering from so many disorders,' smiled the vicar.

'Well, you shall have the bottle after me, that is if there is any left. Now I feel very well indeed, and am looking forward to a most amusing day. Though it will not do for me to show I am amused, and it will certainly not do to let anyone but yourself realize that I am in the best of health. I must be today a man who has suffered much both in body and spirit. I shall have to shake with the ague to the extent of deceiving Doctor Pepper, and I shall be broken up with grief that, through the little Welsh lawyer, I have realized that there is such a thing as smuggling going on upon our beloved Marsh. But my spirit will not be broken.' Here the doctor took a long pull at the brandy, before continuing with a radiant smile, 'I shall condemn the sin of smuggling, not only because it defrauds the revenue, but because I find that it leads to one of the deadliest of sins—MURDER. I shall exhort all to unite against these miscreants. I shall urge not only the discovery of the Scarecrow, but the whereabouts of the highwayman.'

'Oh, come now, vicar,' expostulated Doctor Syn's factotum, 'you know you've always admired Mister Bone because he pays his dueful tithes and is kind to the poor poor.'

'My good Mipps, is not the man a criminal?' The vicar was kindly in tone as he asked it. 'There are many admirable qualities in this highwayman, which not only myself but the squire admires. But by breaking the law he causes a greater offence against the law of God. Through his rescue, a murder has been committed. Murder is very dreadful, Mipps. I hope you agree?'

'I think it's horrible,' agreed Mipps. 'But I also thinks that the Hythe officer had to be got rid of for the safety of the Night-riders.'

Syn nodded and smiled, then took another pull at the brandy before handing the bottle to Mipps, who drank greedily.

At this moment they heard a clattering of hoofs outside the adjacent Court House.

'See what that is,' ordered Syn. 'The hunt has started, it seems.' Mipps went to the casement and peered out.

'Four of the squire's grooms mounted, sir,' he reported, 'and the Clerk of the Level is handing 'em sealed documents.'

'The squire is sending them out to summon an extraordinary meeting of the Lords of the Level,' said Doctor Syn. 'It can hardly be today, but certainly tomorrow. That will give us time to do what we have to do. It is essential that I visit old Mother Handaway. She will have to be ill. I cannot risk having her questioned by the lawyers, at least not in the Court House. They might make her tell too many things. Not that any would believe her, but it might put ideas into someone's head, who might one day discover that the old hag is not quite as mad as she is reported.'

'Aye, aye,' replied Mipps. 'She'd be a danger in the Court House. But if they should visit her cottage and question her, I think her love of the guineas she earns will make her faithful to the devil she serves. No offence, sir,' added Mipps in apology, 'but she's mortally afraid of you.' They were interrupted by Mrs. Fowey knocking at the door with hot water, and the news that the vicar must wear his best clothes as it would take her a long time to make his others looks respectable. She also informed Mipps that it was close on ten o'clock, and that the villagers appeared to have no work to do, like she had, for they were crowding into the square, staring at the Court House, the vicarage and the gallows, and that the beadle was making no attempt to send them off upon their business.

'He don't want to be left alone,' said Mipps with a grin, closing the door.

He then proceeded to shave his master, a duty dating from the old days when they had sailed together on the pirate ship, Imogene, as captain and ship's carpenter respectively. As the little sexton helped the doctor to array himself in his est clothes, a note was delivered from the squire, begging his old friend to send word how he found himself, or better, to wait upon him if sufficiently recovered from the misadventure, and to rid him of the Welshman from the Ship Inn, who, although suffering from shock and a sneezing attack, had called early at the Court House to lodge a protest against the treatment he had received 'in my village!' Syn and Mipps chuckled as they read:

'He is putting too sharp an edge upon my nerves. He followed me into the library, where I am now penning this letter to you, and keeps interrupting my train of thought, which is never at its best after an attack of gout, by enlarging upon his grievances, in that irritating accent which he has adopted. My breakfast he ruined, for he would eat nothing. He glared at my grilled kidneys till they turned into saddle leather, and he then took the frizzle out of the bacon by telling me that I ate too much for a man of my girth, whereupon I countered this impertinence by ordering a round of beef and a slice of cold pie which I washed down with a tankard of strong ale. I was in the mind to open a bottle of port, just to show him that we have gentlemen left in England. What with his speeches last night about Jimmie Bone and the Tontine, I do not see why I should endure more. Come to my rescue. I can sympathize with you but not with him. Why on earth, man, did you and Mipps dig him out? It would have been a quick road for winning the Tontine, and no one to blame but the Scarecrow. I have ever hated my legal colleagues who adopt the dry-as-dust attitude. It is worse than a parsony parson. I have already sent out special Request of Attendances to the Lords of the Level, convening them in two days' time. On hearing this he was further peeved that it was not to be today.

Whereupon I informed him that according to my code of manners, an English County Gentleman should never be hurried. You will judge of my feelings by the length of this epistle, which has been penned to relieve them, Your old friend, Tony.'

'And the longest letter the squire ever wrote in his life and with such speed, I'll swear,' laughed Doctor Syn. 'Well, since he never has failed me yet, I will not fail him. But I must not go in haste, for I must remember not to appear as well as I feel. The villagers must see me somewhat bent and tired, so that my resentment against the Scarecrow may be the more convincing. Take word to the squire that I will wait upon him just as soon as I can deceive Mrs. Fowey that I have tried to eat a little breakfast.'

As Mipps walked towards the Court House, he was beset with questions from the villagers, all wanting to know how the good vicar did, to which Mipps replied with a sad shake of his head, 'Very shook! And who wouldn't be? Shockin'!' Presently Doctor Syn himself appeared, and a murmur of sympathy went round as the women curtsied and the men took off their hats. No longer the alert and upright figure which they all admired, but a man broken not only by physical shock, but through bitter spiritual disappointment. Doctor Syn passed through their ranks in a dazed fashion, till he reached the step of the Court House door. It was only here that he seemed to become aware of the crowd, for he turned slowly and surveyed them first in surprise and then in sorrow. Each man who met those penetrating eyes felt that the good vicar was searching his very soul for some hypocrisy. In his best pulpit manner he addressed them.

'My friends, but for the protection of the God I try to serve, you might today have been thus standing round my corpse, hats off and eyes downcast. Had Mister Mipps not been inspired to go a-fishing, and had he not risked his life to save me, it is certain that the bitter waters of death would have passed over my head. But even when I was facing certain death, it was neither physical pain nor fear of drowning that struck a chill to my heart. It was the boastful assurance of my captor that amongst my flock could be numbered many of the Scarecrow's men. I look around now at your honest faces that I know so well, and I find that I cannot suspect one of you to be so dishonest. I can only think that my informant was lying in order to make my end the more bitter. On the other hand should any of you know anything of these Night-riders, do not, I urge you, through fear of their revenge, refrain from coming forward and telling what you know. The good squire and myself will keep your counsel and protect you. For myself, despite the tortures I have suffered at their hands, I range myself publicly as the enemy of these miscreants, and either with your help, or wanting it, I shall not rest content till I have rid the Marsh of this cunning monster called the Scarecrow. And now disperse, my friends, for my friends I hope you'll always be. Go about your daily tasks, and do not give this arrogant Phantom Rider the satisfaction of knowing that he can disorganize the daily life of our peaceful little Dymchurch.' He then raised his hand in blessing and added, 'May the Lord keep us safe under the shadow of His wing. Aye, my friends, we shall be safe under His feathers, so be not afraid for this Terror by night, nor for this Pestilence that walketh in our darkness.' He was about to turn to go into the open door of the Court House, when his eye fell upon the village schoolmaster.

'Mr. Rash,' he said reprovingly, 'I am surprised to see you playing truant with your pupils. Round up your little flock immediately, and continue to train them to be as good Marsh folk as I trust their parents are. So, to your honest trades all of you, and leave these tragic happenings to be dealt with by the proper authorities. Our good squire, at the head of his Lords of the Level, will take such steps as will be found necessary to drive the devil from our midst.' The crowd, many of them shamefaced, broke up into little groups and strolled away, while the schoolmaster, angry at having been called to task before the parish, took revenge upon his charges, by making free use of his cane to drive them out of the squire into the school house.

The gravity which Doctor Syn had assumed to such good effect was broken by a smile as he watched them go, for young Jerry Jerk, the notorious bad lad of the village, dodged away from his schoolmates, and with his master in pursuit, he swarmed up one of the supports of the gallows, and swung by his hands from the cross beam, rolling his eyes up to the sky and pointing his toes down to the ground, while he cried out, 'The Scarecrow has hanged the schoolmaster. I'm old Rash.'

Unfortunately for the enraged pedagogue, who had rushed up and aimed a swinging blow at Jerry's legs, the cane struck the side post and broke in two, whereupon the mischievous scamp dropped to the ground, picked up the two pieces, and handed them politely to their owner with a 'Yours I believe, sir?' He then took to his heels and ran for the school house. Doctor Syn recovered his grave attitude by the time he reached the squire's library door. As he entered quietly, the squire was sitting in his big chair and smoking his long churchwarden pipe, while the Welshman was standing over him and talking wildly. The squire smoked rapidly, as though to hide his guest behind a cloud of tobacco, but on seeing Doctor Syn, he thundered out, regardless of interrupting the angry little lawyer, 'Thank God, my dear Christopher! I am delighted to see you alive.' The emphasis he laid upon the 'you' made it quite clear that he wished the Welshman were not so alive.

The first delight and relief which shone on the squire's jolly face was changed, however, to an expression of grave concern when he stood up and eyed the doctor closely.

'My poor friend!' he said, 'but you look ill. The shock has been too much.'

'We were certainly not treated gently, my good Tony,' replied the vicar, 'as no doubt my companion in misfortune here has told you. Mr. Jones, I trust you are somewhat recovered? I fear that you swallowed more salt water than myself.'

'I was lower in the water than yourself, Doctor Syn,' said the Welshman acidly. 'And may I remind you that I was the last to be dug out of the sand?'

'Mr. Jones,' said the vicar in reply, 'I think there are very few men in the world who can boast of the devotion of such a servant as our friend Mipps. At least do me the justice to own before the squire that I ordered him to deal with you the first as being the lower in the water. He pointed out that he would sooner have my help to rescue you than yours to rescue me. At least he succeeded in saving both our lives, so I think we need not criticize him.'

'Aye, we both owe our lives to the little fellow, I'll not deny,' allowed the Welshman. 'As to your own conduct, I'll own it was good and honest, for you had the best chance in the world to see me dead through no fault of your own, when you could have journeyed to Edinburgh and claimed the Tontine of our fathers. If I do not die of the cold I have contracted, we shall still be rivals in that.'

'When the inquiry is over,' replied Doctor Syn, 'as I have already told the squire, I may journey with you to Edinburgh to identify myself and see how the matter stands, for I am so grieved at what that rascal Curlew told me about Dymchurch men riding with the Scarecrow, that I find I can hardly look my parishioners in the face. It is a dreadful burden on one's soul to doubt those one loves.'

'I'll admit,' put in the squire, 'that a change of scene from the parish would do you good. You have stuck to your pulpit these many years as faithfully as a good captain stands by his ship. But a captain get his shore leave, and you have had none. We shall be lost without you, and you'll have a welcome back. I should be tempted to accompany you were it not for this cursed gout, which would, I fear, make me a burden to you. But Mipps could accompany you, and then I shall know you will be well cared for. Indeed I doubt if the little rascal would be left behind.'

'We will leave it in abeyance till after the trial,' said the vicar, who nevertheless had made up his mind to go.

During that day and the next, he discussed the matter with Mipps, who, although ready enough to obey his master and having no intention of letting him out of his sight, especially in company of the Welshman, expressed his doubts as to the advisability of leaving the parish, or rather their secret organization in it, for so long.

'My good Mipps,' Doctor Syn whispered in spite of the closed shutters of the study where they talked late at night, 'the whole safety of our scheme has been that I have always schemed to eliminate stupid risks. True, we have sometimes had to take them when thrust upon us, but the Scarecrow's rule has been never to seek them wantonly. The hue and cry that is bound to arise after this coming inquiry will force us to suspend further operations for a week or so.

As Chaplain to the Lords of the Level, I shall use all the vehement oratory in accordance with my position, in order to rouse up a mighty search of the neighbourhood. That will put fear into the Night-riders, and they will be only too thankful that their leaders are lying low and not calling them out on a further run. We know also that they would not dare any operation of their own.'

'With you away,' nodded Mipps, 'and Jimmie Bone safe in France, they would have no Scarecrow. No, they would not act without orders.'

'Has the lugger returned?' asked Syn.

'Aye, sir,' replied Mipps. 'I sighted her off Littlestone beach. She come in with an innocent-looking cargo of fish. I spoke to the skipper later, and he told me that the gentleman what took secret passage by night on her, meaning Jimmie Bone, was safe landed t'other side of the Channel, and is safe with the gang there.'

'You should have told me that immediately, Mipps,' said Syn reprovingly. 'I have been anxious about our friend's safety, and with one anxiety the less, one has a free compartment in one's brain for something else.'

'Quite right, and sorry, sir!' replied Mipps. 'You'll have enough to worry you at the Court House tomorrow morning.'

'All I would have you remember, Mipps, is that should you be confronted in the witness box with any evidence that you find awkward to answer, appeal to me on some pretext and follow my lead. One is never quite sure in cases like this what little detail may not be brought up, which might put a different complexion upon the whole case, and become damning. We must keep our weather eye open, Master Carpenter.'

'Aye, aye, Captain,' grinned Mipps, and the two rascals, after a generous night-cap had been brewed by the vicar, parted for an early night's rest, a thing they were certainly not in the habit of doing.

On the following morning, which broke fine and clear, the Court Room was filled to capacity long before the various coaches of the Lords of the Level were due to arrive.

This historic hall of justice, which is a symbol of the independence of the Marsh, is situated on the first floor. It is small; it is dingy, with that musty smell usually hanging about ancient buildings. But for all these disadvantages, it has a dignity which is crowned by the Royal Arms emblazoned over the Throne of the Chief Leveller, or Magistrate. Representing the Crown and the Marsh law, Sir Antony always occupied this seat of high honour, just as his father and a long line of Cobtrees had done before him. Since the beadle had to escort the Lords into the Court House to wait upon Sir Antony, order was maintained in the room, before the judges sat, by the revenue men, who guarded the door and kept the stairway clear.

Excitement and curiosity prevailed amongst the crowd who were lucky enough to gain admission, but it was very noticeable, especially to Mipps who hovered in and out with a wink and a word to everyone, that whereas the women squashed themselves into front seats, their men folk were well content to be separated from them and to crowd the back benches.

Mipps approached Mrs. Waggetts, and whispered, 'Some of them men back there looks a bit sheepish, as though they was afraid to be seen by the lawyers. I only hopes for their sakes that none of them has got mixed up with this trouble, for since they can't catch the Scarecrow, the authorities may be wishful to hang a few others in his place. And this 'ere's a God-fearing village, Mrs. W. Oh, what a wicked world we lives in to be sure!'

'But we knows all the lads back there,' argued Mrs. Waggetts. 'No harm in any of 'em, Mr. Mipps.'

'Let's hope not,' retorted the sexton. 'But nobody really knows what anybody is these days. Who's the Scarecrow, for instance? You don't know, I don't know, nor does nobody know. Might be old Farmer Murrain. Might be the Archbishop of Canterbury.'

'Murrain ain't clever enough,' whispered the landlady of the Ship Inn wisely.

'And the Archbishop would look sillier on horse-back than I does on the churchyard donkey.' Mipps shook his head. 'No, you can rule all three of us out. But whoever the Scarecrow be, I hopes they gets him, for the shameful way he treated our good vicar.'

'Amen!' said the women sitting around, who had overheard.

Mipps, as a very privileged person and an official of the parish, passed beyond the oak barrier that railed off the public from the seats reserved for the principals. He examined the quill pens, the sheets of parchment, and the sandboxes. Satisfied that all was in order, he then left the Court Room in order to put on his verger's gown and fetch the vicar from the vicarage to the squire's apartments.

He passed through the crowds who had not been fortunate enough to gain access to the court but noted that they had plenty of excitement too, for the Lords of the Level drove up in great state in their emblazoned coaches with postilions and outriders. Especially magnificent was the equipage of Sir Henry Pembury, the Lord of Lympne, but perhaps it was General Troubridge from Dover Castle who attracted most attention, for his carriage was surrounded by an escort of dragoons. Both these gentlemen had suffered badly at the hands of the Scarecrow, and were hopeful that this inquiry would be the means of solving the Phantom Rider's identity.

Then there was Admiral Troubridge, commanding the Harbour Guardship.

He accompanied his brother, his naval uniform contrasting with that of the brass-helmeted dragoons.

There were other magnificent figures amongst the Justices. Lord Noel of Aldington, wearing his scarlet gown above the rich brocades, the Mayors of Hythe and Romney, and the Constable of Sandgate Castle. As each of these stately individuals alighted and was ushered through the great door in order to enter the squire's residence, they were loudly and loyally cheered by the crowd, but no one excited more interest than the striking figure of Doctor Syn, dressed in his neat black clerical suit, with the scarlet gown of one of Oxford's Doctors of Divinity.

All these gentlemen, with other privileged Marsh squires, were received by Sir Antony in his library, and regaled with great refreshment in the adjacent dining-room, where a cold buffet was spread, and the best of liquor served.

This, however, was only a prelude to whet their appetites for the banquet to which they knew they would sit down, when the Court rose for the day.

While they ate and drank and gossiped, the crowd outside gaped at the mounted escort of dragoons, and no doubt many shivered in their shoes at the thought that perhaps one day not only the Scarecrow, but all his men might appear at the bar upstairs to be judged by all this finery of the law.

At last two trumpeters appeared upon the Court House steps, dressed in the Romney Marsh Tabard. They sounded a stately fanfare, which was the signal for Doctor Syn, as Dean of the Peculiars and Chaplain to the Lords of the Level, to lead the Justices across the Square into the church, where he delivered the exhortation that God might direct their findings in His wisdom, so that justice might be meted out, and that all might serve God, honour the King, and pay honestly such Scotts as the Maintaining of the Wall should necessitate, for the peace and safety of all good people who dwelt on Romney Marsh.

Then back in procession they walked between the ranks of dragoons, and ushered the squire of Dymchurch up the stairs into the Court Room, to the seat he held as representing the Sovereign upon the Lower Levels of the County of Kent.

Just as the inquiry was about to be opened by Sir Antony, and the humble folk in the body of the hall were discussing in whispers which of the gentry cut the bravest figure, there suddenly appeared a stranger who in sheer magnificence seemed to outshine them all.

Like Lord Noel of Aldington, he was dressed in the latest mode, but, unlike his lordship, he did not wear a wig, but his own hair, a luxuriant auburn, beautifully curled and be-ribboned. His dazzling and effeminate dress could not disguise a colossal strength of body. He was well over six foot, with broad shoulders, well-shaped legs, and a graceful carriage for all his weight. He had a handsome face, though arrogant and with a tendency to sneer; but this fault he could rectify at will by the most engaging smile, which showed perfect teeth.

He entered from the back of the hall and surveyed the assembly critically through a gold-mounted quizzing-glass. He suggested his dislike of the common people around him, by taking a pinch of snuff as an antidote to their perfume.

His long cane cleared him a passage past those who had entered and blocked the aisle after the procession had entered. In silence he approached the barrier, took off his hat to the squire, made him an elegant bow, and said, 'I hope that your Honour will give me permission to sit next to my old friend, Lawyer Jones, who

I hear is in some way connected with this Session. Delighted to see you, Jones. As you perceive I have followed you.' Then, turning to the squire once more, he added, 'I am a student of law and order, sir, and have heard much of your Honour's wisdom in the cause of justice. I therefore crave your permission to be seated, so that I may sit under your Honour at this trial, and learn. I feel sure that my friend Jones will welcome my presence, since he is a stranger here, and I happen to come from his part of the country. Sir Antony Cobtree, I am called Tarroc Dolgenny, and I am very much at your service.' The squire, though somewhat disliking the man's condescending tone, was pleased to have his wisdom praised in such an August assembly, so he turned to the sexton who stood behind Doctor Syn, and said politely, 'Mr. Mipps, place the gentleman a chair.' Mipps obeyed quickly, opening the barrier to admit the stranger in the exalted portion of the hall.

Doctor Syn, screening his face behind a parchment, whispered to Jones who sat next to him, 'Plague take it! It's the fellow who wants to murder us! We must watch him!' This little pleasantry was lost, however, on the Welsh lawyer, who had turned deathly pale, and had much ado to keep his hand from shaking.

Mipps, having closed the barrier once more, managed to pass the squire's throne on his way back to his place, and he whispered audibly, 'Squire, it may be the Scarecrow.' Those who heard looked uncomfortably at the stranger, and Doctor Syn thought that, had he indeed been the Scarecrow, he could hardly have made a more sensational entrance.

Aloud he said, 'Sit down, Mr. Dolgenny! You are welcome! And my friend here will, I know, be glad of your counsel.'

With a bow to the vicar, the stranger took his seat, saying, 'Thank you, Doctor Syn!'

'This is an exceptional fellow,' thought Doctor Syn. 'He has either taken good care to be well-informed, or he jumps very quickly to conclusions.' Throughout the squire's opening speech, Dolgenny contented himself with eyeing the common people beyond the barrier one by one, through his quizzingglass. To Doctor Syn, who was in reality watching him closely though pretending to be absorbed in the speech, it seemed that the stranger was seeking for someone that he could not find, and yet felt confident that the somebody was here. He began his search amongst the men on the back benches.

This took some little time. He then continued his search amongst the women.

This was an altogether quicker operation. It was to Doctor Syn as though the stranger was saying, 'Might be, possibly, but not probably. I don't think so. No, certainly not there.' Having seemingly made up his mind on that score, he deliberately turned his back upon the body of the hall and his attention towards the justices, witnesses, and jurymen, and others like Mipps, the beadle, and clerk of the court, who by reason of their offices were within the barrier.

Underlying the man's manner of casual arrogance and lazy contempt, Doctor Syn detected the sharpest scrutiny, and although the opening speech of the squire was purposely concise, owing to the many witnesses who were to be heard and questioned, Dolgenny, at the end of it, seemed to have weighed up everyone's character in the Court House. Many he seemed to dismiss at once, while others he appeared to reserve for further examination.

When the witnesses took their stand in turn, Dolgenny changed his tactics, for he appropriated the quill pen and blank paper set in front of the Welsh lawyer, and, hardly looking up at all, listened, and made copious notes.

Since there was no criminal present to question, the inquiry, though long, was neither heated, nor complicated.

The Welshman told his story, which fitted in with the stories of Doctor Syn and Mipps. On the private advice of the squire, Mr. Jones did not give the real reason of his visit to Dymchurch, except to say that he came on a legal matter to see the vicar. Doctor Syn had agreed that it would be unwise to mention a Tontine formed by a number of Jacobites in front of so many loyal justices of the peace.

The greatest sympathy was extended to the good vicar, who on the evidence brought forward had suffered such rough treatment from the highwayman as well as from the Scarecrow's men. On speaking of the trials endured by Mr. Jones, the squire, though deploring them, maintained that the gentleman had brought them on his own head, by wilfully seeking trouble in matters that in no way concerned him.

As for Mipps, he came in for the most unstinted praise, especially for his attack upon the highwayman and, later, his rescue of the buried victims.

'It was the act of a valiant man,' said the squire, 'to attack that giant whom you have all heard described as a giant and armed with three pistols. I say it was brave indeed to attack him with nothing but a spade. How you were successful, Mr. Mipps, I do not know except that right was upon your side.' Here Mipps put on the holiest of expressions, as he answered, 'Well, squire, it were like this. Seeing as how he was so big and strong and armed and horrible to look at, and the vicar will bear me out he made you shudder to look at him, I got thinking suddenly of Goliath, and then me being small-like, I thought I'd have a go at being David, and so I just give him one unexpected and quick. That's all, squire.' The whole proceedings were conducted in the kindest spirit, and although the Squire had to own on the various pieces of evidence that smuggling was going on, he beamed upon the crowded court and said that he thanked God for his belief that none of the miscreants were Dymchurch men. Indeed he was only ruffled once, and that with one of the revenue men.

This was the unfortunate who had sustained a heavy blow with a wooden bat or club at Botolph's Bridge. His head was still swathed in bandages, and, fortunately for Doctor Syn, he gave his evidence in a dazed manner, for in the course of being questioned he stated a fact which the vicar was determined to deny, namely that the first person he had challenged that night was the vicar riding alone on his white pony and going to visit someone sick upon the Marsh.

'But did you go into the Marsh alone, sir?' asked the Welsh lawyer. 'I thought, when you left me on the sea-wall, that you went back to pen your sermon, and then I found you asleep in the vicarage.'

'The reverend gentleman,' went on the witness, 'had his baskets on his saddle front, filled with good things for his patient. I warned him not to go further on to the Marsh, since there was a "run" planned and likely to be danger. The reverend gentleman will remember that he answered as to how no danger would keep him from his duty, and I says to my mate, who is now down below on guard at the court door, that there went a good man, or something to that effect.'

'But, my good man,' put in the Welsh lawyer, 'you heard in my evidence that the scoundrels who arrested us said that it was Mipps who had crossed the Marsh with the old lady's comforts.'

'I tell you it weren't Mipps, it were the vicar,' snapped the man.

Doctor Syn smiled. 'It might have been me, but I cannot take credit that belongs to Mipps. I told my sexton that I had altered my plan at the request of Mr. Jones, and that I should be visiting the poor old soul about midnight, for I knew how bad her nights were. Mipps, always thinking of others, said that he would go out and tell her so, and as she might be in need of the nourishments, would take them with him. Mipps will remember his answer when I gave permission. He said, "You look after her old soul, and I'll see to her old body".

Knowing that even the smugglers hold respect for my cloth, I bade Mipps ride my pony which is well known all over the Marsh, and in addition, to wear my second-best clerical wig and coat.'

'That's true, sir,' cried Mipps. 'Bit long in the sleeve, so I had to tuck 'em up to guide the steering reins. Wore the vicar's old hat too, I did. If the bridge hadn't been misty from the dyke water, you'd have seen it were none but old Mipps.'

'I tell you the vicar spoke to me in his very own voice,' argued the man.

'And who is it, mate,' demanded Mipps, 'who hears the vicar's very own voice, as you calls it, more than anyone else? Me! Don't we go through the Psalms and Responses every Matins and Evensong daily? Never notices you there. You'd be a better and a more truthful man if I did. Well then, after hearing him do them long prayers for years, if I can't imitate his voice I ain't as clever as the coastguards' parrot. I was having a game with you, and you was took in.'

'Don't believe it!' retorted the witness. 'Let's hear you do his voice, then.'

'What? In front of the reverend gentleman?' asked Mipps in horror. 'I'm respectful, even if you ain't respectable.' The revenue man got angry. 'Let the squire send for my mate from below.

He'll bear me out that I ain't lying.'

'Stand down,' thundered the squire. 'Both vicar and sexton have contradicted you, and how dare you call their word in question?'

'There, there, squire,' urged the vicar soothingly. 'The poor fellow has had concussion, and as Doctor Pepper there will bear me out, that very often develops the strangest hallucinations in the brain.'

'Is your head bad?' asked the squire.

'Aye, sir,' confessed the revenue man.

'Then don't talk or contradict or—well, in fact, don't make a fool of yourself till it's better.' Saying which, the squire asked if there were any more witnesses, as it was already past dinner-time, and, taking the hint, the clerk of the court said that there were none who could throw any further light upon the affair. Whereupon the squire summed up that the Hythe officer had been brutally murdered by the Scarecrow, who had also attempted to murder by slow torture Doctor Syn and Mr. Jones of North Wales. He ordered, therefore, that the countryside must be searched, the miscreant arrested, and then hanged by the neck till he was dead.

This was so decisive that the gentlemen looked at one another as much as to say, 'Easier said than done.' Asked if there was any further business before adjourning, Sir Henry Pembury said, 'I think we should raise the reward already existing for the arrest not only of this Scarecrow, but also for this dastardly highwayman, who appears to have been the cause of all this trouble.' Lord Noel of Aldington yawned and said, 'Certainly! We can be as generous as we like, for it's my belief that we shall never catch either of them.'

'I rather agree with you, my lord,' laughed Sir Antony. 'Still, we can but go on trying.'

'May I ask how much the reward stands at present, sir?' The speaker was Dolgenny.

'For the smuggler or the highwayman?' asked the squire.

'Well, I was thinking of the smuggler, sir,' he answered. 'But since they are confederates, one might lead to the other. But I was thinking of this so-called Phantom Rider. Have you made the reward sufficiently high to tempt a man to run the risk of unmasking him?'

The squire looked round for information and happening to catch Doctor Syn's eye, asked, 'What does it stand at now? With the reward offered by General Troubridge here, added to the official price on the rascal's head, it stands at a thousand guineas, I think.' Doctor Syn shrugged his shoulders. 'I think that is the figure, but what does it matter? We shall never catch that rascal, the more's the pity. Neither shall we ever pay the price for the highwayman. Five hundred he stands at, but again what is the use of catching him, when the Scarecrow is on his side?'

'Don't lose heart, Parson,' emphasized Dolgenny. 'I rather think we shall get the Scarecrow. Or perhaps I should say, I am pretty confident that I can, should the reward be raised to make it worth the pains. My Lord of Aldington there will agree that a thousand does not carry one far in play at the Coffee Houses.'

'Ah yes, now,' replied Lord Noel, 'I thought I had seen you somewhere, sir.

Now was it White's or Crockford's?' I have seen the luck with you and against you in both houses, my lord,' said Dolgenny.

'And more against me, I'll be sworn,' laughed His Lordship. 'Yes now, and if I recollect rightly, the cards had a way of falling pat for you.' Doctor Syn, detecting a trace of sarcasm in Lord Noel's voice, glanced quickly at Dolgenny. But if insult was meant, the stranger showed no sign of noticing it, but answered amiably, 'I am lucky as a rule. That is why I feel I could match myself against this Scarecrow.'

'Well, gentlemen,' cried the squire testily, 'never mind him now! He has occupied our thoughts enough for this day, and made us hungry for better fare.' He looked Dolgenny over carefully, and finding him at least presentable in clothes and bearing, added, 'If you care to join us, sir, you are welcome. We dine within this building at my residence. Mr. Jones, too, will be welcome if he is in the mind.' Although the procession of entry to the Court House was always stately in the extreme, the departure of the officials, when the work was done and the court dismissed, was entirely informal. The squire certainly led the way, and on this occasion with the two brothers, Admiral and General Troubridge, on each side of him, but not as the chief magistrate, but their host.

Following him was Doctor Syn who had been swooped down upon by Sir Henry Pembury of Lympne. This fat old knight at once complained that these inquiries wasted time.

'There have been so many of them, Doctor,' he said. 'We sit around and listen to the recital of the Scarecrow's latest escapade, but even though murder is added to his crime against the revenue, we get no nearer to catching the wretch.'

On the other side was Lord Noel of Aldington, most eager to know when the good doctor was coming up again to the parish church in order to occupy the pulpit.

'I gave my living to a young cousin of min as you know, doctor,' explained his lordship. 'The choice was a good one. He is quite popular. Exceedingly so with the ladies, by reason of his looks and nice manners. Reasonably liked by the men too, though somewhat young to teach the old ones wisdom. In the pulpit, however, he is more confectioner than preacher. His heaven is an angelcake, with layers of cream covered with texts of sugar. Both hell and sin he ignores, and only mentions Heaven and virtues. I would hear rather the clanging gates of hell and sniff the sulphur, if only by way of a change. Oh, pray come up to us soon, doctor, and damn our congregation for a lot of rogues.

'Tis what we need. In a parish like mine, it is surely somewhat ridiculous to harp on harps, and to lean over the pulpit side assuring rough farm labourers that one day they will be plucking strings in the heavenly choir! Only last Sunday an aged tenant of mine confessed that although he could still wind the straight horn at eighty years of age, he felt he would never get on very well with parson's harps when his time came. I comforted him by saying that the more exalted angels did not play harps but trumpets, which exactly resembled the coach-horn that he used to wind on the Dover mail.'

'And a very good answer too, my lord!' said the vicar.

'I thought so,' went on his lordship. 'You once said that heaven was a place in which only the best of our talents would be developed. That is all right for my old horn-winder, but I should like to be assured that there will be card tables too, for I vow that is my most skilful accomplishment.'

'Why should we try to deprive Heaven of any good thing?' returned the vicar. 'For myself I should feel most uncomfortable if I am to spend eternity in marble halls with floors of gold and pearly gates. Give me a good old coaching inn with oak rafters, a spacious fireplace, and the best of good cheer. Neither do I want to float around in a glorified nightshirt, but to wear the clothes I have been accustomed to.'

'Doctor Syn,' said his lordship, 'upon my soul you should occupy a pulpit in Town. With that sort of theology, you would draw full houses. Paint a heaven like a Vauxhall Gardens, and every Macaroni would sit under you!'

'Aye, in a fashionable church no doubt,' smiled the doctor, 'where they could show off their finery and ogle the women.' Whereupon his lordship began to explain that the vogue for sermons was reviving amongst the best people in town; that many of the dandies listened to the best preachers, partly to study high-sounding phrases, but chiefly to appear surprising in their taste.

'They will boast about their acquaintance with a fashionable preacher and a champion bruiser in the same breath.'

Now, Doctor Syn had long since trained his senses to do two things at the same time, and, as none but Mipps knew, he often worked out difficult dispositions of men, boats, and pack-ponies to be employed in the next run, while actually delivering a sermon. On this occasion he was listening to two conversations. Not only was he perfectly aware of everything his lordship was saying, but he was listening to everything Dolgenny was saying to Jones, who walked just behind him.

'You would ask me what ill-wind has blown me after you so soon?' Dolgenny spoke clearly. Jones replied in whispers. But Doctor Syn detected hatred born of fear in his low tones.

'You came to spy on me, I suppose? To see if I had carried out your wishes? I told you that the first wish was impossible, and as you see I have not carried it out.' As he said this he pointed to Doctor Syn in front of them. 'As to the other wish, or rather order, I think I have succeeded better.'

'You mean he will come north?' It was Dolgenny's turn to whisper.

Doctor Syn did not catch anything then but a mumble. He guessed, however, what Dolgenny conveyed, and knew by instinct that the lawyer nodded.

'You know, little Jones,' went on Dolgenny in a tone which reminded Doctor Syn of a sixth-form schoolboy talking to his fag, 'I have been somewhat mistaken in you, and that annoys me, for I have a most unfailing knack of judging men for what they are and not for what they pretend. Quite honestly I believed you to be the dullest man I had ever met. Well, there is a lot of dullness yet, in spite of a curious undercurrent of romance which I never would have credited. And yet on the evidence I have heard today in this quaint corner of the kingdom, I find that from sheer adventurous curiosity you have been thrusting yourself into dangerous mysteries that have nothing to do with you.

Again, I always took you for a cautious business man. You have executed your will in favour of your most adorable niece, Ann Sudden, who by the way sends you good wishes, and yet with the Tontine so near to your hand, you must needs go and tempt a scoundrel to murder you, in which case, had you not had the greatest luck in being rescued, that vast sum of money would never have benefited Ann or her children when she marries. A more heartless piece of idiocy I never met, burn me if I did. You have told Doctor Syn about the Tontine? I presume so, else he would not trouble to come forth.'

'Yes, he knows all about it,' whispered Jones.

'Then he's as big a fool as you,' whispered Dolgenny in return. 'He knew that you and you only stood between him and a vast sum of money, and through your own obstinate curiosity he sees you all but murdered by other hands than his. Had I been in his shoes, I should have found it impossible to cut those ropes.'

'I do not doubt that for a moment, Tarroc Dolgenny,' said the lawyer sternly.

'Doctor Syn happens to be a man of honour.'

'I rather think I shall soon be able to give the lie to that,' whispered Dolgenny. Then in a louder note he went on, 'And now to your own affairs.

Two winds blew me here in your wake. One good, yes, very good. The other not so good. In fact, bad. Distinctly bad. At least so I think you will take it. Which will you hear first?'

'Both, man, both and quickly,' urged the lawyer.

'Your adorable Ann—'

'No harm has come to her?' asked the lawyer sharply.

'Don't interrupt,' drawled Dolgenny. 'Your adorable Ann is now my adorable Ann. She has consented to marry me.' Jones stopped dead in his walk and faced Dolgenny. 'That would be the worst news I could imagine,' he said. 'Thank God I know it for a lie.' Dolgenny had put his arm through the lawyer's and with sheer strength compelled him to walk on. 'So I am happy, my friend, and as to Ann, why, she is more radiant in her happiness than I have ever known her. How true that old saying is—by the way is it out of the Bible?—Out of evil, good cometh. I forget. Anyway, it's true. For it was the tragedy that brought us to an understanding. She turned to me in her distress, and I was able to turn her grief into joy.'

'What tragedy? What distress? What grief?' asked the bewildered Jones.

'Ah yes! Of course, you don't know. Then let me tell you. The name of your brother's house at Portmadoc should be changed.'

'What? Why? You mean Bron y Garth?'

'Welsh for Breast of the Precipice. No need for me to tell you why.'

'Of course not,' snapped the lawyer. 'Because the house is built behind the Breast Rock, which juts out over the estuary.'

'It juts out no more,' sighed Dolgenny. 'The Breast Rock crashed on to the estuary beach. What is it? A thousand feet?'

'But my brother? Quick, man! Tell me the worst.' Dolgenny continued sadly and slowly. 'Do you know that I often used to watch your brother sitting on the edge of that rock. From the top of my tower I command a great view of the estuary. I am a good mountaineer, but I confess that sight ever gave me the vertigo. I was in the drawing-room with Ann when it happened. For the hundredth time I was proposing, and I confess she was, by sheer force of habit, refusing me again. Suddenly I heard a noise like shale falling down the cliff. Ann asked if it was hailing; it did sound like hailstones.

Then there came a rending, cracking noise, followed by a roar, several crashing bumps, and then as it were a peal of thunder. I looked at Ann, and she at me, and I could see that all her quarrel against me had gone to the face of such a disaster, for we both knew then what had happened. "The Rock has gone over," I remember saying, and she nodded, then with a scream cried out, "Uncle Hugh! Uncle Hugh!" I tried to calm her by saying that although it was a favourite seat of his, I could take my oath that he was not sitting there when I entered by the terrace door. She then said that I had been talking for a good quarter of an hour, and that she knew he much have gone out upon the Rock during that time. "For look," she said, "the waters are beginning to rush back over the estuary, and he always watches to see in what direction that Devil's Larder will shift. Quickly, Tarroc, we must get down there and see." She seized my hand and we raced from the house together like frightened children, and yet I confess that my heart was selfishly singing despite the horror, for she had called me by my Christian name for the first time in our acquaintance, and she was holding my hand as we ran. There was a chance that we could get to Portmadoc Quay in time to summon help before the tide swept up, but this she would not have, urging that we must do it ourselves, and it would be quicker to descend by Borth y Gest. She was right. It was quicker. But the hamlet was deserted. Not a soul in sight! The men were at work n the slate quarries, and the women—well, what could they do? No, the task was mine, and I begged Ann to wait on the rocks till I had finished. She must have known the horror that would confront us, but she was determined to share it with me. "He is past help, but at least I can help you." At that I lost all fear of the nauseating sight awaiting us, for she meant clearly that as she could count on me, so must I depend on her. So on we raced, over the beach, and jumping from rock to rock around the promontory. I will spare your feelings, my dear fellow. Suffice it to say that the sight was more dreadful than we had imagined. It was too much for my brave Ann. She gripped my hand the tighter and then collapsed. I laid her on some soft sand against a rock, and bathed her forehead from a pool. She opened her eyes and whispered, "Oh, I can't help!" I told her to hide there while I went to do what I could. As much of the mangled body as I could wrench from the broken rocks upon it, I laid on a ledge to which I climbed, above high-watermark. It was enough for identification. By the time I returned to my beloved, my fine suit in which I had gone a-wooing was in a deplorable state, and I conjectured that she would shrink from me. Just the contrary, my good fellow! Women are strange creature. Her uncle's blood was on me, and I know she

loved me more for doing him that last service. She knew that I had
always borne a great respect for him, though he had shared your
aversion against me. Well, he was a greater man than either of us,
you'll own. I do most willingly. I then had to make up my mind
quickly what to do. Ann was in my arms, clinging to me like a
frightened child. She was half-swooning and had not the power to
speak, but the manner of her embrace cried out to me for
protection. I looked up at the slate-grey precipice of Bron y Garth,
gloomy and forbidding in the shadow. Across the bay my own
promontory caught the setting sunlight in its gorgeous foliage. That
way spelt peace, the other stark tragedy.

The problem was, could I cross in time before the sea rushed
in? It looked near enough, but as you know the evening light is
deceptive there, and has been the death of many a stranger. I
wondered whether I could gain time on the tide by mounting the
precipice the way we had come down and annexing your brother's
horse from the stable. I dismissed this idea immediately. I knew
that I was unpopular with the servants, who would show me no
favour, and would certainly prevent me carrying their master's
niece across Tremadoc Bay, and I was determined not to be robbed
of my prize now I had won her. But before making the attempt, I
must locate the Devil's Larder. For the past two months the live top
of that death-chamber had been more than ever volatile, shifting
like a great octopus with every tide some hundreds of yards. It had
travelled Harlech way, and back again, and had to my knowledge
twice crossed the river bed to lie beneath your brother's cliff. I
could always find the old devil from my side, just as your brother
could from his. He had told me his method many a time in fierce
argument when I had disagreed to anger him. But I knew that he
was qualified to judge from Bron y Garth. If only I could have
plucked the knowledge from that dead brain behind me. I could
only apply his system, which I did.'

'Be brief, man,' urged Jones. 'What happened?' The little man
was in a fever of anxiety, since the informal procession to dinner
had already entered the private residence of the squire, who was
leading the way towards the library, so that his guests might have
drinks while waiting the announcement of the meal.

They had been, and were, moving very slowly, for both the
squire and Doctor Syn kept stopping to point out some old map or
print upon the walls.

Doctor Syn purposely lingered in front of Dolgenny and Jones,
for he was very much in mind to hear the completion of the story,

and he was thankful that the Court House was such a rambling old building.

Dolgenny was laughing at the reproof from Jones. 'Why, man, you were long-winded enough in your evidence. Let me tell my tale in my own fashion.'

'I want to know what has happened to my niece,' replied the agitated little man.

'She is recovered, and well, and vastly in love with your humble servant.' Dolgenny looked at Jones and made a wry face. "Fore Gad, but there is one point in our marriage that I never considered. You will be my uncle-in-law. I trust you will not be too dictatorial. There is no hurry I perceive, my uncle. This is not the dining-hall, but the library. We are to be served with sherry or negus.

So keep your attention on me, and then well-mannered gentlemen will not interrupt our talk. As I was saying, I watched the flow of the waters as I had seen your brother do. I concentrated on their movements from the deeper pools and from the river banks. I searched the ridges for sand that had no white drift passing the yellowness in the evening breeze. At last I found it. The usual shape like a giant octopus with waving arms of writhing treacherous sand. I knew where the Devil's Larder lay and could avoid it, for I knew it would no shift to any great extent till the tide was full and on the turn. Carrying Ann like a baby in arms, I plunged through the beach lagoon, raced across the sand to the river and forded it. The water reached to my armpits, but I only thought of keeping Ann as dry as possible. Across I ran like the cockle-fishers, zig-zagging along the higher ridges, and all the while the estuary was turning from yellow sand into swirling waters, and the breakers kept rolling towards us on our left, as though to drive us into the Larder on our right. The only sound was the rush of waters, the screams of sea fowl, and cries of people far behind me which I took to be the servants of Bron y Garth, either lamenting the disaster or cursing me for carrying off my prize.'

'Well, you got through, since you are here,' interrupted Jones. 'One can always trust Dolgenny to save his skin, but what of my niece whose life you so selfishly risked? Your own part does not interest me overmuch.'

'Your niece nearly drowned. We both did. For suddenly I realized with horror that the Devil's Larder was shifting and coming towards us as rapidly as the waves were rolling in. Your brother had said it could not happen. He was wrong. I turned my back upon the quicksands and stumbled on towards the waves. Between us was

Hermit's Island, always the last spot to disappear at high tide. When it was abandoned years ago because of the encroaching tides, they left enough stone upon it to make it firm. I had cursed it, as you know, as a danger to shipping, but now I blessed it. Once the sand got me over the knees, but there was some wreckage round the base of the fast-disappearing island and by this I was able to drag our way. The bit of land was firm enough, and I laid Ann down and sat beside her to gain strength for swimming. How I welcomed the respite for I was determined not to leave our refuge till we were swept off it. By then the water would be deep enough to pass over the Devil's Larder if need be. As I watched the waters, I divested myself of coat, waistcoat, and cravat. I kicked off my buckled shoes too. Hearing a sigh behind me, I turned and saw that Ann had not only recovered consciousness, but had so far understood the perilous situation that she was unfastening her heavy velvet riding habit. "It will drag you down," she said. I thanked her and told her that in the face of peril one need not be over nice. I told her that I was waiting for deep water before swimming to Port Merion and my castle and hers. She kept her habit round her till the last minute, then, as the waves lapped about us, a bigger one than we had seen swept my clothes from the rock. She then dropped her frock behind her and quickly entered the water. She swam well, and for the first quarter of a mile employed a strong breast stroke, but the moment she turned to rest by swimming on her back, I followed suit and took her head in my hands. We had only to keep afloat and the rushing tide bore us to land.'

'And you took her to your castle?' asked Jones.

'You don't think I would have left her on the beach for the night, do you? Now, we rested for a few minutes and then I picked her up and carried her through the woods. She was a brave girl, for it was embarrassing for her entering my home, for the first time since her mother died, in sea-soaked undergarments. As I rang the bell, I told her not to worry, because I had always loved her, and it was then that she looked at me unafraid and said, "I love you as well". I handed her over to the care of my house-keeper, and in half an hour's time or so we met in my dining-hall, and she in the daintiest evening frock you could imagine. I did not know such finery was in my place. She then wrote a note while waiting for dinner, in order to put the servants at Bron y Garth at ease about her safety, and I promised her that when I had given evidence at the inquest, I would ride south and inform you of all that had happened.'

'You had not the right to take her to Port Merion,' protested Jones.

'Come now, consider, sir,' urged Dolgenny. 'The child had no parents. The master of Bron y Garth was lying dead. The servants would no doubt be all hysterical. And her rightful guardian was getting into scrapes on Romney Marsh. At least I did my best to comfort and protect her. She has thanked me, and so should you. And since you cannot marry your own niece, why all this jealousy when you hear that she is going to marry me?'

'Because I do not credit your story, Tarroc Dolgenny,' answered Jones decisively.

With the exception of Doctor Syn, who had listened unobtrusively to all this conversation, no one else had taken any heed of the two strangers to Dymchurch, for the library was a scene of much activity. Everyone seemed to be talking at the top of his voice in order to be heard above the buzz and chatter, and while the squire's footmen moved from group to group proffering drinks, the gentlemen's personal servants, who had accompanied their masters to the session, assisted their lordships to disrobe, for their greater comfort at dinner, and with the removal of official gowns and swords, which were carried to an ante-room, general talk became less restrained, as jests were bandied from wit to wit, until the assembly was as hilarious as any host could wish. The squire, leaning heavily upon his stick, stood by the great fireplace and joked about his gout, affirming with many a wink that, had he consumed more good liquor instead of Doctor Pepper's poisonous physics, he would not be so afflicted as he was at present. Around him the groups gravitated, and Lord Noel, who had said all he had to say about sermons, accompanied Sir Henry Pembury to pay respects to their host, thereby leaving Doctor Syn alone, and with no excuse for further eavesdropping. He therefore pretended to notice the Welshmen for the first time since entering the library, and at once proposed that they should recharge their glasses and accompany him to drink a personal toast to the squire, and he signed to a footman to fill up.

'And as a student of law and order, sir,' he asked Dolgenny, 'what do you think of our form of procedure on Romney Marsh? A little quaint to you, no doubt, but you must appreciate that ours is a very ancient as well as independent Court of Justice.'

'I was more than interested, Doctor Syn. I was vastly intrigued. Quaint? Yes, but very picturesque. I fear, however, that this present scene would greatly shock the susceptibilities of our native mountain hymn-singers. I grant you that, following an inquest or a funeral, the hypocrites will drink as much as you do here, but you would hear no laughter or jesting.'

'I think the reason is, sir,' replied the doctor, 'that the death of a revenue man is by no means a novelty in these parts. The more is the pity!'

'And it is by no means a novelty with us either, sir,' laughed Dolgenny. 'My sympathies are against the revenue. What are their men but "hanging judges"? The common hangman is more honest. Should a revenue man come nosing round my private beaches, I should take it as a declaration of war. I should know that his dearest wish would be to send me to the gallows, whether I am guilty or no. Therefore I should have no compunction in killing him out of hand.' By this time they had refilled their glasses, and Doctor Syn proposed that they should move towards the squire.

'Perhaps, Doctor Syn, you would have the goodness to make my excuses to Sir Antony Cobtree, but I drink his health for all that, and wish him and his village well.' The Welsh lawyer swallowed his sherry and set the glass upon a table.

Dolgenny gave his compatriot a black look and asked, 'Would you bring discredit upon North Wales?'

'I regret that I cannot sit at table with you,' replied Jones.

Doctor Syn, although understanding the situation perfectly, pretended great surprise. 'Are you serious? You will not dine? At least give me some reason and I hope that I may set it right, before giving our good squire offence.' It was Dolgenny who replied quickly, 'The fault is mine, sir, for I sometimes have the most unlucky knack of misreading human nature. I came to Dymchurch with news both good and bad, which I felt it was my duty to deliver. Why the plague I did not keep it till after dinner I do not know. I have blundered. I thought the good news would more than compensate for the bad.

Jones's brother has met with a fatal accident. He is dead. One misses a brother naturally. I lost my two, and know. One went just before my father died, and the other within a week. Both my elders. One fell on Snowden, and the other went drunk to the Devil's Larder. The name of a quicksand, Doctor Syn. I missed them of course, but their absence brought me into a fine inheritance.

And Jones here has the like consolation, for his brother was rich and had a fine practice, all of which comes to our disgruntled friend here, and since I am relieving him of the responsibility of his niece, it will all be extra grist to his own mill. Come, Jones, you will have to go to Wales, and to give you strength you must eat.'

'I will eat, but at the inn,' replied the lawyer coldly. 'I had the greatest regard for my brother, and have the greatest love for my niece.'

'And I reciprocate,' cried Dolgenny heartily. 'A steady hack the one, and a spirited filly, t'other! Shall I help you to the inn?'

'I wish to be alone, and can look after myself,' said the lawyer. 'Perhaps later in the day you might find time to wait upon me, Doctor Syn? I should take it kindly, for I wish to talk to you about the Tontine.'

'Ah yes,' said Dolgenny pleasantly. 'You two gentlemen have a great bond between you. I wager that in future you'll be for ever writing to inquire after one another's health. But I see that they are throwing open the doors of the dining-hall yonder, and I must first salute my host and, I suppose, make excuses for my neighbour's flight.'

'Won't you think better of it, sir, and stay?' asked Doctor Syn. But Jones pursed up his lips, and shaking his head vigorously, relied, 'Never!'

'You will not persuade him, doctor,' laughed Dolgenny. 'When once he makes up his mind, he is as obstinate as any mule or lawyer.' Jones watched him sauntering towards the squire with the sherry-glass held high. 'A mule or a lawyer, eh? Had he said a man of honour he would have been in the right of it. I can hardly breathe the same air as the monster, much less sit at the same table. I dare not tell you the reason yet.' Though Doctor Syn took pains to lower his voice, he said quite casually, 'You mean, of course, that a man of honour does not sit with a kidnapping murderer?'

The lawyer was so taken aback that for the moment he could not reply, and Doctor Syn went on in the same ordinary tone which he knew would not attract so much attention in a chattering room as a whisper would. 'I am sure you are right. Dolgenny murdered your brother, in order to carry away your niece by force.'

'You were listening?' asked Jones.

'I make it a habit,' replied the doctor with a smile. 'I have found it a useful one on Romney Marsh. But this Dolgenny has a certain glamour, and as he said, "Woman are strange creatures". Is it likely that your niece has become infatuated?'

'It is utterly impossible!' declared Jones with conviction. 'She has always been a girl of set purpose and once she has made up her mind to a thing, nothing will shake her from it. She is as obstinate as I. Out of many followers she loves but one, and my poor brother and I were in full agreement that he was unsuitable. Mind you, I like Harry Thane. He is steady, strong, brave and welllooking, and of good enough family. But he has nothing but the miserable earnings derived from the most unsatisfactory position in North Wales. He is customs officer for the Tremadoc district, and since the local authorities lend him no support, I would not insure his life at any premium. With Dolgenny's gang of rascals watching for him, the poor lad will soon be finding lodging in the Devil's Larder.'

'We must not let that happen, Mr. Jones,' said Doctor Syn. 'Are Dolgenny's rascals faithful to him?'

'They fear him like the devil.'

'That means then that no further harm can come to your niece while he is from home. They would not dare to harm her, any more than he dare harm you till I am dead. But make no mistake, Mr. Jones. The moment you are in receipt of the Tontine, your life is not worth a penny piece. You will be in graver danger than ever this young customs officer. I will see to it that you get to Wales before him. In fact, we will set out together tomorrow by the mail.'

'I had thought of catching the evening mail today,' said Mr. Jones.

'If we go today we shall be overtaken by Dolgenny before we pass through Hythe,' replied Doctor Syn. 'He has his own carriage, for I sent Mipps from the Court Room to find out. When he took my doctor's robe from me just now, he informed me that he had seen the conveyance. It is built for speed as well as comfort, and his cattle are well matched and magnificent. Well, I must see that his conveyance is delayed, for if we get to London ahead of him, we can also purchase a vehicle made fore speed. Get back to the Ship Inn, and order dinner while we are eating here. Then complain to the landlady that you are not well and wish to sleep. Give her strict orders than no one is to disturb you unless it be Doctor Syn, for I shall call upon you later when my plans are formed. But be sure of this, I intend to best Dolgenny and spoil his game.'

Dinner having been announced, the squire moved through the room, asking his guests to follow him. With Dolgenny and Lord Noel on either side of him, he approached Doctor Syn and the Welsh lawyer, whom he addressed sympathetically.

'I am very grieved, Mr. Jones, that you have received bad news. Your friend here tells me that you wish to withdraw to the inn. You know you are welcome to stay, but I shall understand if you prefer solitude.'

'That is my wish, sir, and thank you,' replied Jones. 'I was fond
of my brother, and with the exception of a niece for whom I would
do anything, I am the last of the family. I have had a sore blow, but
your good vicar here has given me such words of comfort that I am
determined to be master of my grief for the sake of my niece.'

'I will be along to cheer you up later,' said Dolgenny largely.
'And by the way, inquire for my valet, will you? His name is Pedro.
Though Spanish, he talks good English. See that he secures for me
the best apartments, for till you are sufficiently recovered from
your shocks, and feel well enough to accompany me back to Wales,
it seems that I must stay in that ramshackle old place too.' This
order Jones ignored, and with a bow to the squire and the vicar he
left the room, crossed the hall and went out of the front door.

Dolgenny shrugged his shoulders and remarked, 'Considering
that his brother leaves him a small fortune and the best legal
practice in Carnavon, I think his grief should be tempered with
philosophy.' Throughout the dinner Dolgenny took more than his
share in the general conversation, and laid himself out to be
amusing. In this he was successful, for after Sir Antony had called
the gentlemen to their feet in honour of the Marsh slogan, and all
had repeated after him, 'Serve God, honour the King, but first
maintain the Wall', the port was circulated freely, and all were in
the mood to enjoy Dolgenny's droll stories.

Now, Doctor Syn was seated next to Sir Henry Pembury, the
squire of Lympne. This rotund old gentleman was the proud
possessor of two daughters, who, by no means getting younger
every day, persistently remained single. Sir Henry, wanting them
married, had scoured not only the countryside, but London itself
for eligible bachelors whom he entertained lavishly. But though
many of them were glad enough to accept his hospitality, not one
of them had the temerity to ask either of the daughters to accept
him in marriage. Well aware of this state of affairs, which was
common gossip in the neighbourhood, Doctor Syn saw the
possibility of using Sir Henry in order to separate Dolgenny from
Dymchurch and his good horses for the night, and so when the
whole table was on the roar at another ridiculous anecdote, and Sir
Henry was laughing that he had never met so entertaining a young
man, the vicar whispered that it was a pity that Sir Henry's young
ladies could not meet him; whereupon Sir Henry immediately
considered him as a possible son-in-law. He was a very elegant
gentleman, that was certain, and not only vastly handsome, but

accomplished.

'And very rich,' prompted Doctor Syn. 'I hear that he has everything a man could wish for, except a wife.'

'Perhaps he would like to visit Lympne Castle,' said Sir Henry. 'Is he to be long in the district?'

'I rather think,' whispered the vicar, 'that, with all respect to Mrs. Waggetts, one night at the Ship Inn will send him packing in the morning. And once in his castle in Wales, he will hardly return to poor little Dymchurch.'

'Perhaps in the face of Lympne hospitality,' suggested Sir Henry, 'he might be induced to prolong his stay.'

'He is only staying this night,' explained Doctor Syn, 'in order to rest his horses. He had driven them hard, in order to help his friend, which shows he has good feeling for man and beast.'

Sir Henry, however, grew indignant that Doctor Syn should suggest such a difficulty. 'Plague take it, Parson, but he shall rest his horses, if he is so mercifully inclined. I like him all the better for it. I am not resting mine, because they are not tired. He can leave his here and take coach with me to Lympne. I see no difficulty. As you say, the Ship Inn is not to the taste of a dandy.'

'I think he would wish to be back here tomorrow,' went on the doctor, 'in order to look after his friend.'

'I can send him back tomorrow, can't I?' exploded Sir Henry. 'You have not noticed a scarcity of horses in my stables, I trust?'

'Only on nights when the Scarecrow rides,' laughed the vicar.

'Plague take the Scarecrow and his cattle-borrowing,' snapped the old man.

'I am for persuading this gallant stranger to stay in the neighbourhood and rid us of the monster. Think he would?'

'You can but ask him,' suggested the doctor. 'He seems to be discussing the Scarecrow now with Sir Antony and the General.'

'I'll go and have a word with him,' said Sir Henry, heaving himself up out of his chair.

'Let me fill your glass first, Sir Henry,' said the vicar, suiting the action to the word.

'Thankee, parson! You're a good fellow, and I should not have spoken hastily had you not made so many difficulties.' Sir Henry drank his glass of port and carried the empty glass to the squire's end of the table.

Since another gentleman had left his chair to talk to Lord Noel, Doctor Syn politely offered him his chair and took the vacant one opposite Dolgenny, whom he hoped to hear accepting the invitation for the night to Lympne.

Sir Henry opened his campaign by pointing out the disadvantages which Dolgenny would meet with at the inn. He then painted a vivid picture of his historic castle, lighting up the gloom of the old rooms with the merry laughter of his lively young daughters.

'But you will not be alone amongst the petticoats, sir,' he went on, 'for Lady Pembury and myself have staying with us two young bucks from Town, officers in the "Blues", sir. My young girls do not take them as seriously as they would wish, and your presence will only add to their heartaches. Still, they are good fellows, and when the ladies have retired to bed, they console themselves with cards and liquor. I confess that their play is not what I term skilful, but they raise the stakes like gentlemen, and lose with a good grace.' Doctor Syn could see that the thought of plucking these officers of their guineas commended itself to Dolgenny, who outwardly confessed that he had not looked forward with much relish to a night at the Ship Inn. His one objection to the arrangement, however, came as a surprise to the vicar, for, after showing delight at the prospect of supping and sleeping at the Castle, and thanking Sir Henry for his thought about resting his horses, which he said was necessary, he added that the visit must depend upon Doctor Syn with whom it was essential that he held a conference, if the vicar would spare him half an hour of his valuable time.

'We'll take him with us,' cried Sir Henry, 'and you can talk in private as much as you like.' But Doctor Syn thought otherwise, and excused himself by saying that the inquiry, and the events which had led up to it, had so wearied his spirit that he was for obeying his physician, Doctor Pepper, and was going to have a quiet and an early night. So it was finally arranged that Sir Henry should return to Lympne alone and order preparations for his guest, for whom he would send a carriage to carry him to the Castle by supper-time. This would give Dolgenny ample time to give orders to his servant to stay at the inn, to inquire after his friend, Jones, and to transact his business, whatever it might be, with Doctor Syn. Soon after this the party broke up, and to the further excitement of the crowd, who all this while had been gaping at the General's dragoons, the great men were helped into their coaches and carriages, in which they were rumbled off to their various destinations, the dragoons escorting the General's coach to Dover.

Dolgenny shortly took leave of the squire and sauntered out towards the Ship Inn, on the understanding that he was to call at the vicarage within the hour.

Sir Antony detained the vicar for a final glass of brandy, and when they were alone he laughed. 'Old Henry Pembury thinks to snaffle Dolgenny for one of his girls! I dislike this Dolgenny wholeheartedly, but I give him credit for liking something better-looking than the Pemburys. But he's a bad man, I think.

Noel knows something of him. Says he has watched him at cards, and that those who play with him make some excuse and do not play again. Now what the devil does he want a private talk with you for?'

'I have no idea,' replied the doctor. 'It may be something to do with the Tontine, or it may be about his boast to catch our Scarecrow for us. I rather think, however, that the Scarecrow would be more than a match for him.'

'And talking of the Scarecrow, who will not take your escape lightly,' said the squire, 'I don't mind owning that I shall feel safer in my mind for you if you do go off to Edinburgh with the Welshman. You might persuade the banker to let you draw the money and go halves.'

'Jones says no to that,' replied the doctor. 'The one of us will have to die to benefit the other.'

'Then see to it that it is Jones, not you,' laughed the squire; after which the vicar took his leave, promising to take supper with the squire.

The faithful Mipps was awaiting his master in the hall, and they walked together to the vicarage.

In the study Doctor Syn told Mipps of the coming interview, and ordered the same arrangements as he had made with Jones. The pistol was placed loaded once more beneath the chair cushion. Mipps was to hide again in the alcove amongst the vicar's robes. He was to listen to everything Dolgenny said, but not to show himself unless signalled to do so by the vicar.

Dolgenny found that he was not popular at the Ship Inn. Even Jerry Jerk, the pot-boy, who was the richer by half a guinea for having given Dolgenny information about the inquiry and how to reach the Court House, ranged himself on the side of Mrs. Waggetts in her refusal to allow anyone but the vicar to disturb the Welsh lawyer. 'A sick man wants a parson in his room, but not a dandy smelling like a cottage front garden. He said no visitors but Parson Syn, and all your fine curls and scent won't make me give way. No, nor the door neither, which he's locked inside, and it's made of ship's oak.' Dolgenny was more angry with Jones than he was with Mrs. Waggetts. So used was he to bullying the little lawyer, that it hurt his pride to know that his victim was no longer afraid of him, and that he should order his door to be barred against him was galling. However, he answered the landlady casually with, 'Gad, woman, I have no desire to see him, and you may tell him so. My call was but a neighbourly courtesy, to see how he fared, and I fear that he will find the fare in this old-fashioned house poor in the extreme. You may add that as I could not stomach the look of the place, I am spending the night at Lympne Castle. My man Pedro will stay here and look after my horses. You will give him the best room in the house, and if you have no Spanish wine to his palate he will be troublesome. I shall drive down tomorrow to see if Mr. Jones is fit enough to take the road with me to London and the North.'

Now since the fat old lady always referred to herself as 'a Romney Marsh girl, through and through' she held the same view as her compatriots born and bred 'under the wall', that anyone born beyond Hythe or the Kent Ditch were foreigners, and needed watching. Therefore a real foreigner was to her quite beyond the pale of decency, and it annoyed her that this magnificent gentleman, Dolgenny, should suggest her giving up her best apartment to a swarthy Spaniard.

'I'll have you to know, sir, that my best rooms is for the allocation of the gentry. Not even for gentlemen's gentlemen, however genteel. But as for Southern cut-throats, like that there Mr. Pedro, I says no. Not even under the same roof would I sleep with him. I'm a lone widow and must look after what God has given me. He'll sleep in an attic above the stables along of the ostlers and such-like.'

'My very good woman,' urged Dolgenny, 'Pedro is my very faithful servant, and no cut-throat. Unless, of course, it amused me to point out a throat, hand him a razor, and order him to deal with it from ear to ear.' At this, Mrs. Waggetts cried out to the pot-boy, 'Jerry, my smelly salts!'

'Pedro would do it, and thoroughly,' went on Dolgenny, 'but as a creature of good taste it would revolt him. And his taste in womankind I vow is as fastidious as my own, and you can sleep in peace with the knowledge that all that God and your parents have given you is safe as far as he's concerned.

Pedro only left his native shores because he could not deal with all the se—oritas that were after him.'

'Then it don't say much for Spanish girls' tastes,' said the old lady. 'I'd not let the likes of him come near me, not if he was ever so.'

'Ever so, what?' drawled Dolgenny, eyeing her through his quizzing-glass.

'Just ever so,' replied Mrs. Waggetts. 'It's a expression.'

Dolgenny laughed and ordered her to fetch him a bottle of Spanish wine to sample.

'We keeps no fancy stuff here, sir,' she replied. 'Customs is too high, and there's no call for such nonsense.'

'Well, then, brandy will do,' ordered Dolgenny.

'I've plenty of good brandy,' said Mrs. Waggetts. 'Both squire and parson say it's of the best.'

'And you don't call it fancy stuff,' laughed Dolgenny, 'since it merely comes from France with no duty to pay.'

'There's duty to pay on all what we gets from the Frenchies,' she snapped.

'I'd pay a lot for the last bottle of cognac on which duty was paid in this house, for I wager it would be ancient.' Dolgenny laughed again at the sharp look she gave him. 'Come, come, you need have no fear of me. I have some fifty retainers in my Welsh castle. Mostly foreigners, they drink what you call "fancy stuff", for even the Spanish sailors on my boats drink the wines of their country. We find no lack of it. Vessels come, and vessels go, as they do here. What is the revenue for but to be tricked? It makes the liquor the more palatable. I confess I have never yet paid a penny piece to the customs. So I think, my good creature, you can trust me.' But Mrs. Waggetts was too old a bird to be caught and she merely answered, 'If other folk cheats the revenue it's no affair of mine. An honest woman, I pays full price for French stuff, and sells it to my patrons with the least amount of profit possible. But there's no call for fancy Spanish stuff.'

'Well, give the rascal brandy,' said Dolgenny, 'and if you want your score settled, the same room that you would have offered me. I am now going to enjoy a conversation with the Reverend Doctor Syn.' And as he sauntered out towards the vicarage, he wondered whether the vicar would enjoy it too. 'I think not,' he chuckled to himself.

It was Mipps who admitted him to the vicarage, and requested him to wait in the hall while he went to the study to see if his master could be disturbed.

'I fear I shall have to disturb him,' replied Dolgenny, and as he watched Mipps tiptoe towards the study door, he told himself that the good vicar was about to be disturbed more than he had ever been in his life. It was the vicar who came to the door and begged him to come in. Doctor Syn closed the door behind them, and invited his guest to take a seat in the same chair that Jones had occupied a few days before. It had its back to the curtained alcove. A bottle of brandy and two glasses were set out upon a table beside it.

'You will find this to your taste, I think, sir,' he said pleasantly, filling the glasses. 'A present to me from our good squire. He is a great believer in brandy, and after my wetting of the other night, advised me to put as much as I could carry into my system.' He handed a glassful to Dolgenny and was about to pick up his own, when he seemed to remember something.

'Plague take it!' he sighed. 'I knew there was something I had to tell my sexton. Well, never mind. He's gone, and left the garden door open too, and the evening air strikes me as chilly. I'll shut it.' He stepped outside to reach the door handle, and then cried out, 'Hi, Mipps. When you have done those errands will you call in at the "Ship" and leave word that I will wait upon Mr. Jones before supper? Thankee. Oh, and come back and close the garden gate, will you?' Doctor Syn smiled as he closed the garden door and walked over to the table for his brandy. 'An admirable servant is Mipps, but he has a bad habit of leaving doors and gates unfastened behind him.'

'My friend Jones is willing to receive you, it seems,' laughed Dolgenny, 'while he deliberately locks his door against me.'

'I am not altogether surprised at that,' replied the doctor, 'for his manner towards you in Sir Antony's library was something cold and distant.'

'Aye, he'll be more pompous than ever now that he inherits his brother's fortune,' said Dolgenny. 'Clever lawyers, the pair of them, but as men, so dull and obstinate that I never had much patience with them. However, since I intend to marry the niece, a certain toleration was necessary with the uncles.'

'And does this niece share your tender sentiments?' asked the doctor.

'To be honest with you, no. It seems that I have a rival—a young man who is in charge of customs. He is in consequence no friend to me or to my interests.

I think he hopes that Ann will get information out of me, which will help him to bring a case against me. He may be in love with her, or with the money she will inherit from her guardian, this

Jones. Although never encouraged by the uncles, he is for ever hanging round about her, and I fancy it is time I dealt with him.

However, at the moment he cannot hold any communication with her, as she is under my protection till her guardian returns with me to Wales. Then I shall use pressure to hasten on our wedding. Once the little vixen is my wife, I will soon stop her biting.''Then your story to Jones which I overheard,' interrupted Syn, 'was not quite true, I take it.'

'Not quite,' admitted Dolgenny. 'She was refusing my repeated offer of marriage in the drawing-room, and loading me with more scorn than usual when we heard the rock give way. She ran out to investigate, and I followed.

Providentially she fainted when she saw the crushed body of her uncle, otherwise I doubt whether I could have carried her successfully across the estuary. You will not, however, say anything of this to Jones.'

'In that I shall be guided by my own judgment,' replied Syn coldly. 'Since you are by no means penitent, I cannot view this information as a confession of a sinner to a parson. My silence, therefore, is not binding.'

'Before I have done, you will find, Doctor Syn, that your silence will be compulsory.'

'Then, sir, you had better say no more, for I submit to no compulsion against what I consider to be my duty. I will continue the task I set myself when you have gone.'

'What task, parson?' asked Dolgenny.

'I was scanning the list of my parishioners. It is here before me in this book.

I have been weighing them up name by name, and asking myself whether there is any possibility of one of them being this scoundrelly Scarecrow. So far each name has cleared itself according to my judgment of humanity.'

'A very creditable task, parson, and one that I shall help you with. I set myself the same problem in the Court House. I felt certain, as I heard the evidence, that the Scarecrow was amongst us, hidden beneath a personality that no one would suspect. I first of all weighed up the villages, and dismissed the lot. There was no brain there that could direct so vast a scheme. I searched for a clever head that could organize and lead. At the same time for one that no one would associate with crimes against the law. The magistrates, in turn, fell short of the requirements. Neither the squire nor Sir Henry Pembury possessed the figure or height of the

Scarecrow as described by Jones. Lord Noel was not the type; he is lazy. Besides, he spends more than half his days in Town. I discarded them all one by one and it left me with only one, and that one with the best disguise of all, and whose office would excuse his presence at nights upon the Marsh.'

'You don't mean Doctor Sennacherib Pepper?' asked the vicar.

'I do not,' answered Dolgenny decisively. 'I mean the parson, the Very Reverend the Dean of the Peculiars, such an apt name too, the tall, elegant, and accomplished Doctor Syn, who could play the parish priest by day, and ride the Marsh at night.'

Doctor Syn laughed merrily. 'Really, Mr. Dolgenny,' he chuckled, 'you are letting your ingenuity run riot. Perhaps you would like to inspect my Ordination Papers, and my Certificated Degree as Doctor of Divinity from the University of Oxford? I have them in this room.'

'I am quite sure you would have everything in order,' smiled Dolgenny.

'Perhaps then your inventive genius will explain how it was that, in the company of your friend Jones, I was confronted by the Scarecrow and afterwards nearly killed by him. You will own it is impossible to be in two places at once.' Dolgenny smiled again. 'I confess that puzzled me so much that I almost gave you a clean bill. Then came the evidence of the man with the bandaged head. It was obvious to me that he was speaking the truth, and that you were very anxious to put him wrong. Your faithful henchman Mipps, who of course is in the know with you, was equally anxious to support you against the man, and then the squire's irritation rescued you. Of course he did see you earlier in the night upon the Marsh, and I suggest that you rode out under the guise of visiting that sick woman, in order that you might change your clothes and pony for the Scarecrow's rags, and the fiery black horse. I suggest that you then galloped back to rescue the highwayman, that it was you who gave orders that Jones was to be set half-way to Dymchurch and dismounted on the sea-wall; that it was you who hanged the Hythe officer, and then, having given your disguise to someone else to wear for you (and I suggest it was the highwayman), you returned to the vicarage and convincingly allowed Jones to wake you from sleep. I think I may take it for granted that you will not wish me to tell my version of what happened to the squire and parish?' Doctor Syn smiled back at Dolgenny. 'And I think I may take it for granted that you will be wishing to return shortly to your castle in Wales and to the young lady you have there under lock and key? Tell your version to the squire, and he would immediately lock you in the Court House cells, for he has the authority to imprison any dangerous lunatic upon the Marsh.' Dolgenny fingered his glass and held it up against the evening light that came through the casement. 'Doctor Syn,' he said calmly, 'I have the greatest respect for any rascal of genius, and upon my soul, I think you are the most entertaining I have ever met. Far from wishing to ruin you, I am going to propose that we throw in our lot together. I think we shall come to an agreement. But first give me the private satisfaction of hearing you say that I have hit the right nail upon the head. You can deny it afterwards in public, if I should repeat what I have told you. There is no witness here to prove you have admitted it. Now, be the sportsman that I take you for, and I will gladly drink your health in this excellent Scarecrow brandy. What do you say?'

'Mr. Dolgenny,' replied Doctor Syn casually, 'I too have a knack of putting fantastic problems to my brain, which I am able very often to turn into facts. I will put a question to you before I answer yours. You may answer it truthfully and deny it afterwards, for, as you have pointed out, there is no witness here to support one or the other of us.'

'Aye,' nodded Dolgenny. 'It is one man's word against the other, and that will not cut ice beneath either of our feet. What is your question?'

'Suppose I preface it with a statement,' said the vicar. 'Hearing your story as you told it to your lady's guardian, I tried to put myself in your place, and supposing myself as unscrupulous as I think you to be, I asked myself how I should have acted. The guardian of the lady I am determined to marry has gone on a long journey. He places his ward with his brother, who is no friend of mine. If I can get the girl and get rid of the uncles, a great fortune awaits me through my wife. The uncle she is staying with has a stupid habit of perching himself upon an outjutting rock over a precipice. How can I force the rock over the precipice with him upon it? I cannot. It would take men with crowbars to lever it over, and he would turn and see them. Perhaps I cannot trust them to carry out the murder successfully. A bungle would be fatal. I must do it myself.

I must also protect myself with a convincing alibi. I must throw him over first, and then enter the house. If he screams I trust that the noise will be lost in the screeching of the sea-birds. While I am talking in the house, my men are levering up the rock. I am in the house when it crashes. I then rush out with the girl, and we find the body below, with the great rock broken on the top of it.

The girl being alone, I take her from the tragic scene to my own castle. I have her there close guarded, and seek out the other uncle with the news. The next problem will be, how can I get rid of him too, with safety to myself? That is my statement. Now for my question. When your victim fell, did he know that it was you who murdered him?' Dolgenny raised his glass and with it saluted Doctor Syn. He then said, "Pon my word, the more I see of you the better I like you. And since I am now determined that we work together, I drink to your very good health.' He emptied his glass at one gulp, and setting it on the table, proceeded to refill it.

'We are both ingenious rogues, doctor, for it seems that we both unmask the other's secret. Now listen to what I say to you alone. You are in the right of it. I did murder Ann's uncle. I did it deliberately and with premeditation. I knew when I should find him on the ledge. I knew that at the same time Ann would be in the drawing-room, and the servants' quarters were on the farther side of the house. The gardeners would be at their evening meal. I did not pass the lodge gates, but entered the grounds by way of the fields, along which, upon the sea side, runs a spinney. In this wood I hid six of my men armed with iron bars.

They all knew what was required of them. Presently along comes my victim, with a spy-glass under his arm. With no regard to danger, and no fear of dizziness, he walks straight out upon the Breast rock and halts upon the very edge of it. He then adjusts his spy-glass and begins systematically to sweep the estuary. Leaving my men, I crept along the spinney and came out behind him.

He did not hear me. You conjectured rightly, doctor, that the sea-birds would be screeching. And so they were. I stepped upon the rock. I was behind him now only about a yard and a half. In my hand I carried my cane. It was a long one with a gold snuff-box fixed like a knob on the head of it. I advanced this till within an inch of the small of his back, holding the cane firmly with both hands. Then, bracing myself, I pressed it home and pushed with all my strength. He seemed to stagger out into space, but as he went, he turned and grabbed the head of the cane. It was then for a second that our eyes met, and he knew that I had deliberately killed him. I wrenched the cane away, and down he went out of sight, but when I looked at the cane I saw to my horror that the snuff-box knob had gone. Was it in his hand? I thought not. He would drop it as he had already dropped his spy-glass. My next thought was how to hide the cane itself, for I could not carry it into the house and leave it with my hat in the hall. The servants would ask me what had happened to the knob. That cane of mine was known in the neighbourhood. Close to me I saw a marrow bed. I knew that it would not be dug until the marrows were eventually plucked, so into the soft manure on which they rested, I thrust my cane. It was a very good emergency hiding-place. I marked the spot in the heap and determined to retrieve it later. Also I knew that I must find my snuff-box on the rocks below.

Doctor Syn, I never had the opportunity to retrieve them, and that is a thing you will have to do for me. I then summoned my men to get busy, made a quick detour, and coming through the drive gates so that the lodge-keeper would see me, I strode up to the front door and inquired for the very man I had just killed.

The maidservant told me that she thought he was in the garden, but that Miss Ann was in the drawing-room. So to the drawing-room I went, and the rest you know. My men took about a quarter of an hour to heave the rock after the dead man, then they quickly made themselves scarce. That is the truth as I will admit it to you in private, so tell me also in private, am I not right about you being the Scarecrow?'

'Tell me, Mr. Dolgenny, did you ever hear of Captain Clegg?' Although looking surprised at the change of subject, Dolgenny asked, 'You mean the notorious pirate, who never made a mistake, until he was caught and hanged at Rye? I confess he was the hero of my boyhood dreams. He certainly influenced my way of life.'

'He made no mistake, Dolgenny,' replied Syn. 'Above the chimney-piece there hangs his harpoon. You may have heard that I visited the wretch in prison, and exhorted him to repentance upon the scaffold. But he made no mistake, Mr. Dolgenny, and no one on earth can bring him to life. But he rides the Marsh at night for all that, Mr. Dolgenny. And still he never makes mistakes. No canes and snuff-boxes lying about to hang him. And that is why the Scarecrow will never be caught.'

'You mean that Clegg is the Scarecrow?' asked the astounded Dolgenny.

The vicar rose, and, bowing politely, added, 'And Doctor Syn, very much at your service.' An expression of genuine admiration spread over Dolgenny's face, as he muttered, 'My God, that's clever! And it binds us together. Whether the squire would believe me or no, I take it you would not wish me to lay this information against you?'

'I told you that Clegg never makes mistakes,' replied the vicar. 'I should have two alternatives, both of which would silence you. Either I could keep you here till dark and then hand you over to be dealt with by my Night-riders, or accompany you to the Court House, and watch the squire make out the Warrant of Arrest for Tarroc Dolgenny, murderer.'

Dolgenny sneered as he asked, 'How would you detain me till after dark? I am a strong man, doctor.' As he said this he slowly got up from his chair and eyed the vicar shrewdly.

Doctor Syn, leaning over the back of his chair, suddenly threw down the cushion and covered him with his pistol. At the same time he rapped out the order, 'Sit down!' Dolgenny scowled, but obeyed. 'And now for the alternative. I dare say,' went on the vicar with a smile, 'that you are thinking, "He has no witness to prove my confession of murder, eh?" It was yourself who insisted that we could not harm each other without a witness. But I am a little more thorough in my methods than you are, Dolgenny. Mipps! Turn round, Mr. Dolgenny.' The wretched man turned to see Mipps covering him with a pistol in each hand, and he was wise enough to do the only thing possible. He shrugged his shoulders and laughed. 'I know when I am bettered.'

'Good,' replied Syn. 'Now tell me your proposition.'

'Before I saw you,' said Dolgenny, 'my object was to get you up to Edinburgh to identify yourself as Jones's rival in the Tontine. I had planned a visit to Wales for you on your homeward journey. To liven up your stay, I planned my marriage to Ann Sudden. Then an unfortunate accident occurs, and our beloved guest, Doctor Syn, is dead. Your death certificate is sent to Edinburgh, and the Tontine money belongs absolutely to Jones with my wife as his heiress. I then had a problem to set myself which would have taxed my ingenuity and given me an endless amusement. From a clue discovered, it comes out that the good Doctor Syn did not die by accident, but by murder.

Events and clues keep piling up, the guilt always pointing to the one man who had a strong motive for wishing him dead. Our friend Jones now locked up in the Ship Inn, is locked up in the cells. He is tried. He is hanged. The money goes to my wife, and so comes to me. That was in short what I had planned, sir, and I am now about to amend it, and make a bargain with you which will be to your advantage and to mine.'

'Let me hear,' said Doctor Syn.

'Although working very differently from the Scarecrow of

Romney Marsh,' went on Dolgenny, 'I have for years been building up a more than profitable business against the revenue. On my wild mountain coast, the customs are not taken seriously. Neither are they equipped to interfere with my organization.

My castle stands upon my private peninsula. It is protected by thick woods as dense and treacherous in bog land as an African jungle. It is further strengthened at high tide by the sea, and at low by a river and shifting quicksands. The narrow neck of land which joins us to the mainland is protected by great medieval walls and ramparts. I could stand siege from an army or a navy. Even under a blockade they could not stop me going and coming as I please. Neither would they ever find the wealth that I have amassed. My treasury is well hidden, and could be moved out under their noses, and they none the wiser. Doctor Syn, there is money there to fit out many a tall ship which could do business for us off the foreign coasts and on the high seas too. Collect your Tontine money, throw in what share you like, and I will equal it, and we'll see if there is money left in piracy.' It was now the sexton's turn to put in his word. 'Aye, vicar, the gentleman's in the right of it. Singing amens is all right when you wants to lie low, but give me the singing in the rigging, the chanties, and the howling of the gale.' Doctor Syn smiled and, addressing Dolgenny, explained his sexton's enthusiasm. 'Mr. Mipps was Clegg's carpenter and right-hand man.' Dolgenny once more re-filled his glass, and said, 'Gentlemen, I would not feel more honoured taking a drink with the King himself. Come, doctor, we must remove this Jones as soon as possible, collect your Tontine money, and then adventure on a large scale. We'll start for Wales tomorrow, and 'fore Gad, we'll have the wedding as soon as we arrive. No difficulty about that now, for you shall be the priest to marry us.'

'No difficulty at all, Mr. Dolgenny,' laughed Syn. 'I can draw up the licence here and take it with us. You leave me to deal with this Miss Ann. I'll talk to her to such effect that she'll sign her marriage lines with as much joy as any bridegroom could desire. But we must conform to the Rules of the Brotherhood and sign Articles. That we can do in Wales when we have formed our plans, but we can take our first pledge now, by the exchange of tokens. I see you wear a signet ring with a coat of arms upon it. A family ring like this of mine, no doubt. Is it known to your servants, I wonder, with the like respect as this is? You would not want for anything on Romney Marsh if you could show this ring.'

'And with mine on your finger,' boasted Dolgenny, 'my servants, finding you cast ashore upon my rocks, would give you the best in the castle. Without it they would as likely cut your throat.'

'It is but a sign of good faith,' went on the doctor. 'Honour even amongst thieves, eh, Dolgenny? On the signing of our pact, whatever it may be, we give them back again.' They exchanged rings, but further conversation was interrupted by a knock on the front door with the news that Sir Henry Pembury's carriage was awaiting Dolgenny in the yard of the Ship Inn.

'You will play cards till the small hours,' said Doctor Syn, 'so we will not expect you till the afternoon. Now that we understand each other, there is no immediate hurry to reach Wales. I take it that the girl is safe, and not likely to be rescued by her customs officer?'

'She's safe enough!' laughed Dolgenny. 'Young Thane will never get within a mile of her, without his throat is cut. I warrant he'd like to wear that ring of mine upon his finger!'

'There is not much chance of that,' laughed the doctor. 'Neither is there any chance of your cane being found. At least, not till the marrows are cut, and the snuff-box either fell into the sand below where it would be swept by the tide, or it may have caught in some fissure of the cliff. Did you find the spy-glass by the body?'

'I never thought of it,' admitted Dolgenny, 'till this minute. I know he dropped it as he clawed the air, but where it lies now I have no idea.'

'Well, since the tragedy appears so obviously an act of God,' said Syn, 'I hardly think that anyone will search the face of the rock for something they do not know exists. No, there is no haste as far as Wales is concerned, so if you find that you are plucking Sir Henry and his guests of their stakes, you may care to stay there for another day. Personally I shall have a lot to arrange before leaving my parish, and would be glad of more time.'

'Should I not return to the inn by three o'clock you will know that I am staying on at Lympne,' said Dolgenny. 'But urge Jones to be a little bettermannered towards me, or his presence in my carriage going north will be plaguey irksome.'

'You can leave me to deal with Mr. Jones,' replied Doctor Syn, a remark which made Dolgenny laugh as he left the study.

Mipps ushered him out of the front door, and then returned to the vicar.

'Close the door, my good Mipps. Drink a glass of brandy and then tell me what you make of all that?'

'Nothing, sir,' replied Mipps to the question. 'Why you told him all them things what we always remembers to forget, I has no idea.'

'Because, my good Mipps, I wished to get this ring upon my finger.'

Mipps scratched his head to show that the vicar's explanation meant nothing to him. 'And why you should let that scoundrel walk off with your family ring and wants to wear his instead, I shall never understand.'

'Oh yes, but you will,' returned the vicar. 'In the first place I am going to Wales on an errand of mercy. I am going to right a wrong, and in order to do that, this ring was necessary. In short, I am going to play a hand for Mr. Jones's niece, and for the customs officer. You must own it will be refreshing to be on the side of the law for a change. When I have safeguarded their interests, I shall play for Dolgenny's highest stakes, and if I cannot strip this gambler, this coldblooded murderer here, then Clegg has lost his cunning.'

'And never that, I'll swear,' chuckled Mipps. 'Queer sort of a quest we're going after, vicar! What with damsels in distress, customs officer expecting our help, and a dandy smuggler, what lives in a fortified castle! Very queer! Now if we can only find out where he keeps his treasury, it will be a quest worth doing of, that is if we relieves him of it. But can we believe what the rascal says?'

'No, Mipps, we cannot,' returned the doctor, 'but for all that I have a feeling that queer things will happen, and that our quest will be amazing. Aye, Mipps! Quite amazing!'

Chapter 8. Doctor Syn deals with Dolgenny

Doctor Syn had prophesied rightly when he had warned Dolgenny that the cards at Lympne Castle would keep him up in the small hours. Indeed it was already dawn before Sir Henry declared pleasantly that he could keep his eyes open no longer and would his good friend Dolgenny give him an arm up to bed. As for the two young officers, for the last hour they had been so gloriously drunk that they could neither count the pips upon their cards nor distinguish between a king and a knave, so that Dolgenny had been enabled to rake in a rich harvest, and since they all took it as a great favour that he should keep the scoring, his calculating brain considerably increased his winnings by taking more counters from his opponents than he was entitled to. Drunk as they were, the two officers realized that they had lost too heavily, but this did not prevent them asking Dolgenny to give them their revenge the next day, when they would be prepared to stake town property and horses.

'Good horses, Dolgenny!' cried one. 'If I lose, I can damned well walk to battle I hope!' But as his legs gave way under him as he said it, Dolgenny advised him to give any immediate battle that might come along a miss.

'My experience of battles,' he added, 'and I have fought in many in various parts of the world, is that everyone is so taken up with looking after themselves, that no one notices who else is there or isn't there.'

'That's ri', old fellar,' declared the officer, smiling up at him from the carpet. 'Then I won't patronize battle at all. Other fellars must win it for a change. Mustn't always depend on me, damn 'em.' To which Dolgenny replied that the sentiment was worthy of so great a soldier.

One by one he carried them up to their rooms, and helped them to bed to such eulogies as 'Best fellar in the world', 'Don' min' loosin' fortune to a gen'lum'. They had only praise for him, except to damn him for holding his liquor better than they. 'But no gen'lum,' declared the last to be pushed into bed, 'should go to bed stone cold sober, for 'tis a reflection on hospitality.' But Dolgenny had no mind to go cold sober, now that he had their notes of hand amounting to more than a thousand guineas in his pocket, for he retraced his steps to the card-room, and, pulling the corks from two more bottles of port, he carried them up to his own room, drank the contents at his leisure, and then flung the empties from the casement and watched them in the early sunlight roll down the steep grassy slope beneath the ramparts. As he climbed into bed he decided that Wales must wait for him till he had finished plucking such rich game, and congratulated himself that he had found such an easy huntingground. True, the Pembury women left much to be desired, and were annoying in their attentions to him, but he resolved to endure this, and even to offer them encouragement for the sake of Sir Henry's money-bags. So, vastly pleased with himself, and with the way he had handled the whole adventure since reaching Dymchurch, Dolgenny fell asleep.

He would not have been pleased had he known the swift chain of events that had been set in motion, immediately he had turned his back upon the sea-wall in Sir Henry's carriage; for Doctor Syn had hurried to the Ship Inn and urged the Welsh lawyer to be in readiness for the night mail to London. It was, he said, essential to reach Wales ahead of Dolgenny in order to rescue his niece, and to use a piece of evidence that would hang Dolgenny as a murderer. Jones was astonished at the doctor's effrontery when he announced that he intended to borrow not only Dolgenny's carriage and horses, but also his servant.

'And my excuse is to be that I am chasing you, who have given him the slip.

He will still think that I am on his side against you, until I am ready to undeceive him.' Jones was further instructed that, when he reached Portmadoc, he must wait for communication with Doctor Syn at his dead brother's house, and not go on to Tremadoc to his own home.

Next Jones at Doctor Syn's request drew a map of the principal points in Tremadoc Bay, explaining exactly the lie of Dolgenny's land in comparison with Bron y Garth. This Doctor Syn, after bidding Jones farewell and a speedy journey home, put into his pocket for further use. He then visited the squire and took supper with him, amusing him greatly by telling him that Dolgenny actually suspected both of them in turn as being the Scarecrow. Presently, however, Doctor Syn grew serious and said, 'Amuse us as it may, Tony, and I grant you it is one of the funniest conclusions I ever heard anyone reach, it is libellous, and if he utters such nonsense in public, he should be punished.'

'I'll have him in the common cell!' exclaimed the squire, 'if I hear the breath of such absurdity! You rode well, Christopher, in your youth, but if he saw you on your pony now, he would not imagine you as the hard-riding Phantom Horseman. Egad though, he's nearer the mark when he mentions me.

As magistrate and squire during the day and leader of Night-riders by night, I should have a profitable time of it. Law and disorder, eh? But as you say it is punishable talk, for men in our positions of trust must be like Caesar's wife, eh doctor?' After telling the squire no more of his plans than he thought wise, Doctor Syn promised to keep him informed of his travel and to return as soon as he had identified himself with the Tontine in Edinburgh. There was no difficulty about Doctor Syn's place being temporarily filled, as the curate of Burmarsh, under Dymchurch, had very little to do in his own little hamlet.

It then only remained to see Mipps, who was waiting at the vicarage, and had packed up such clean clothes as Mrs. Fowey had laid out, in a valise. 'I shall only take the bare necessities,' said the doctor as he added a case of pistols and his father's sword to his Bible and a volume of Vergil. 'You may pack my buckled shoes, for I shall wear riding boots, also my cloak to hide my sword, for with Dolgenny on one's heels it is as well to be prepared. And now, Mipps, unlock my old sea-chest, and bring me the tray of jewels. I wish to select two or three of the best to act as bait.' Mipps first unfastened the iron lid. Beneath it was a second lid of teak reinforced with brass, and, using the same key, the top came open in two doors, revealing many departments. One of these Mipps slipped out and held before the vicar, who uncovered a velvet pad that kept the contents tightly packed and tidy. Jewels collected from ships that were no more. 'Ah yes!' exclaimed the doctor, 'this cross, I think will be the best. Fine diamonds, and magnificent rubies! Wrap it in a 'kerchief, Mipps, and place it in the pocket of my dressinggown. Faith, if we meet highwaymen lacking the scruples of Jimmy Bone in robbing a parson, I think they'll be astounded when my sword begins to play with them. And now, Mipps, for your own part. Are you clear?'

'Got my ten Night-riders to be in Henley's Herring Hang in half an hour.

We cross Channel in Young's lugger, which I've bespoke, and transfer crew to the clipper when we gets there. Then notify Jimmie Bone, who will be in hiding aboard the French lugger Louise. Then down Channel, round Land's End up in Wales. Tremadoc Bay? I knows it.'

'Here's the chart I got from Jones,' explained the doctor, producing the map from his pocket. 'There's Port Merion, Dolgenny's land. Here's the cliff of the murder, with the house atop. Below we get here the fishing beach of Borth y Gest. Round the headland beyond you will bring the Greyhound to anchor.

Unless we get a change of wind by tomorrow, you ought to make the coast here as soon as I by road. Remember that I choose the Greyhound for her speed, and not for her storage. But she'll hold enough when the ballast is thrown overboard. Well, Mipps, a drink to our guest, and then off with you! I shall be on the road by sunrise.' Before sunrise Pedro, Dolgenny's man, found himself being shaken and ordered to get dressed immediately. It was Doctor Syn who was cloaked and booted and talking in fluent Spanish. Having studied the language originally with his good friend Captain Esnada, and having spent years after that amongst the Spanish colonists, Doctor Syn spoke like a grandee, which impressed Pedro more than the most savage threats. Dolgenny spoke a little, but badly, and therefore to Pedro's peasant mind this tall, striking figure dressed in black, who was urging him to haste for his master's sake, became of greater importance than the master himself. Besides, it was all above-board, though somewhat unexpected. As Pedro pulled on breeches and boots he gathered that Jones and given his master the slip, and had taken coach for London the night previously, and he was now being told by this distinguished friend of his master that if Pedro could not overtake Jones, it meant a hanging business for Dolgenny.

'In case of a long sojourn with your master in Merion Castle, I have strapped a valise of clothes in the boot, and since we must reach Lympne quickly to get word with Dolgenny your master, the ostlers are but now putting in the horses. I have had food and drink packed inside to suffice the three of us, for there must be little time wasted at the common coaching inns. The mission we are on is too dangerous for us to brook any interference or delay. Hurry, Pedro, my good little man!' In a few minutes Pedro was in the box with Doctor Syn beside him. 'I have not paid my master's score,' grinned the driver, as he lashed the horses into a gallop. 'My master need not return since he has taken his luggage to Lympne Castle.'

'No, Pedro, you omitted to pay the score,' said Syn, smiling, 'but I will gladly see to it on my return, that is if I do return after helping your master in this perilous adventure.' Having crossed the Marsh and climbed Lympne Hill, Syn ordered Pedro to wait with the carriage beneath the trees and not to show himself to any windows of the adjacent castle, which at this point of the bridle path was hidden by a high and fortified wall. Doctor Syn disappeared round the angle of the wall and Pedro waited for him to return with Dolgenny. Having to waste a quarter of an hour to make it seem that he had gained admittance to Dolgenny, Syn strolled round the fields out of sight and looked up to the windows above the great slope, taking care to keep under cover of the bushes. After a few minutes, when the sun was painting the seaward sky a glorious salmon pink, he saw one of the lofty casements open, and there stood a somewhat dishevelled Dolgenny, in fine clothes certainly, but with cravat undone and waistcoat unbuttoned, occupied in throwing out the empty bottles of port already mentioned. Syn smiled as he watched the bottles bump and roll, for he knew that now Dolgenny would fall upon his bed and sleep long.

Then back to the carriage, running hard, a quick climb up beside Pedro, and orders to drive on! Pedro obeyed, while Doctor Syn explained that Dolgenny dare not accompany him in his own carriage, but must follow them to London independently after making certain arrangements with Sir Henry Pembury for his safety.

'He told me to take this ring, my good Pedro, saying that if I have to go with you to Wales ahead of him, his signet will ensure you fellow-servants, and yourself of course, carrying out such orders as I know as his good friend he would approve of. It is a deep conspiracy, Pedro. I may not tell you much till we have reached the "Golden Keys" of Charing Cross. But the plot centres round your master's marriage to the lady who at the moment is an unwilling prisoner in Port Merion. Being a priest I have the power to marry them. Being also a diplomat and understanding young ladies' minds, perhaps a good deal better than your master can, I know that I can bring this girl to view her coming marriage with real joy. My friend Dolgenny will never do it. But I have confidence that I can, and so has he. Together, Pedro, we will bring this matter to a good head. But if that Jones gets to Wales before us, we are beaten. He will ruin all. For between ourselves he is a lawyer and a cunning fellow, and to get his own way he will send your master and my friend to the scaffold. Oh, and he can, the more's the pity! I'll tell you more at the "Golden Keys". I wish your master had but written his instructions as I begged him. He wasted the night at cards, and vowed he could not write a word with the wine shaking his hand. Do you think his signet proof enough that I am his friend and must be obeyed by the servants at Port Merion? If not we must use force, my good Pedro, you and I.'

'Garcia, the gaoler of the girl,' admitted Pedro, 'is but an obstinate pig, but he fears me, knowing I have my master's confidence. He will obey you when I point out the ring and explain the circumstances.'

'Then pull up the horses at this hill,' ordered Syn. 'Put on the skid while I handle the reins. Then get inside and help yourself to a piece of the cold pie and the Spanish wine I have provided for us in the hamper. I will drive as far as Ashford, and then you can let me break my fast on what you leave.' Thus, by the time the carriage rolled up before the London inn called the 'Golden Keys', Pedro was willing to stake his life that his master possessed an invaluable friend and counsellor in Doctor Syn. Leaving Pedro to look to the horses, Doctor Syn went into the inn to bespeak dinner in a private room for himself and his servant.

On inquiring whether any message had been left for him by a gentleman arriving on the Dover mail, he was given a letter, written hurriedly by the lawyer, saying that he had hired a good chaise and was proceeding immediately by post horses, hoping in this way to race the Northern mail. This note Doctor Syn destroyed, telling Pedro that by careful inquiry he found that Jones was ahead of them with a good start, and riding private post. He then called for ink and paper and wrote to Dolgenny, informing him that Jones had left London for the north, but that he and Pedro hoped to overtake him. This letter he read over to Pedro while they ate a hasty meal, and before setting off again Syn sealed it and gave instructions that it be put on the Dover mail. He smiled as he pictured Dolgenny's face as he opened this second letter at the Ship Inn, for he had left one behind him describing the danger of Jones's escape, but had told Mrs. Waggetts on no account to send it up to Lympne Castle. Therefore, the longer Dolgenny revelled at Lympne, the longer he would have in Wales to work against him.

It was a good thing that Dolgenny's horses were in fine fettle, for the doctor would hear of no delay, and instead of sleeping at inns, they both took it in turns to rest inside the comfortable carriage, while the other drove on. Pedro discovered that amongst his other accomplishments Doctor Syn had a sound horse sense. He knew exactly how much rest the animals must have, and no more would he allow them. On at full speed to the north, and at each stop the parson would oil the wheels of the carriage, and help Pedro rub down the steaming horses. So the long journey north by day and night was one longstretched-out race, with never a serious delay until they were nearing Shrewsbury.

It was a drizzly twilight and a deserted road, when Doctor Syn, whose spell of rest was almost done inside the carriage, was awakened suddenly by being jerked forward. Hearing a babble of voices, he put his head from the window and asked Pedro what was wrong.

'Highwaymen! Two!' replied Pedro in Spanish.

Doctor Syn whispered back in Spanish. 'Stay on your box. Appear to be frightened. Put your hands above your head and gibber, man, and leave the rest to me. Are they mounted? I cannot see them from here.'

'Both mounted. But one is dismounting now. He is coming to collect, I take it, se—or.' Doctor Syn then saw a tall, loutish fellow shambling towards him with a horse-pistol held before him. His expert eye detected at once that this antagonist was not very happy with firearms.

'Get out on the road!' the fellow ordered, and Doctor Syn with bent body climbed from the carriage as though it pained him to move. The highwayman called to his mate, 'Second post-chaise carriage within the hour! And another old gentleman! Hope he has a bag of guineas as heavy as the Welshman. Now stump up, old gentleman, or you'll have lead inside you.'

'I am but a poor preacher, sir, belonging to the Society of Friends thou knowest as Quakers. I have a few small silver pieces, it is true, but if thy need is greater thou art welcome.'

'What is in your baggage? Nothing of value? Let me see.'

'Although we do not set store upon the things of this world,' went on the doctor in a feeble voice, 'I am yet carrying a jewelled cross to an old lady in Shrewsbury. But thou wouldst not rob me of what is not mine, save in trust, I hope?'

'I'd rob my own mother,' laughed the fellow. 'Let's see!' Doctor Syn hobbled to the back of the carriage and began to fumble with the straps of the carrier doors.

'They are very stiff with caked mud. Perhaps thou couldst help me, friend?'

Shifting his pistol to his left hand, the fellow began to ease the strap with his right. 'Thou shouldst praise the Lord for they strong fingers, friend. See mine against thine. Very frail and white.' Doctor Syn held his right hand trembling above the pistol. Then suddenly the highwayman felt a grip of iron upon his wrist. Syn gave it a twist that made the pistol fall to the road, and then up came Syn's left with all his force beneath the jaw, and down went the fellow in the road.

The other, acting as horse-holder, could not see behind the carriage but called out to know if all was well.

'They friend is searching my luggage, but tells me to bring thee this bag of money.'

'Then bring it!' shouted the horse-holder.

Doctor Syn drew his pistol from his side pocket and hobbled round the carriage, the pistol hidden in the folds of his cloak.

'You travel in a good enough conveyance, preacher,' sneered the mounted man. 'Where's the bag?'

'I have it here, friend,' called out Syn, kicking the pistol that had fallen by the wheels into a ditch full of water by the roadside.

'I cannot walk without my crutch, and I will get it from the carriage.' Hidden by the open door, he drew his long sword and, hiding it beneath his cloak, which reached, as he stooped, to the road, he held the blade high as though it were indeed a crutch. Seeing the black figure bent almost double approaching, the horses became restless, so that the mounted man had to thrust his pistol into the holster while he steadied them, and shifted his grip on the reins. Syn hesitated as though afraid, and said, 'Pull thy friend's horse further back. I am old and have a fear of being kicked, for that would hinder me in the Lord's work.'

'Have no fear of that but of my pistol, friend,' was the curt reply.

'Come, hand over your bag. Come on! Nearer!' Syn appeared to be fumbling with the folds of his cloak as though to hand over the bag, when the highwayman felt a sharp pain in his breast bone, and a long steel blade was pressing him back in the saddle. Doctor Syn had straightened himself to his full height and in his left hand he held a far more deadly-looking pistol than the old-fashioned weapon which the rider could not reach from the holster.

'Dismount!' ordered Syn in a hard voice. The wretch obeyed, glad enough to wriggle clear of the sword-point.

'Pedro, our horses will stand still; they are tired. Unsaddle one of these, while this fellow unsaddles the other. We'll take them along. They are good enough animals, and will save our faithful ones. Now you,' went on the doctor, addressing the frightened highwayman, 'Where is the money-bag belonging to the Welsh gentleman in the post chaise? Hand it over. You took his watch too, no doubt. Hand that over too.' Doctor Syn dropped both bag and watch into his own pocket, then ordered the wretch to turn out the linings of his pockets. The results showed a few silver coins and a ring.

'Was this his property too?' The robber nodded.

'You may keep the silver. And you may fish this out of the ditch if you care to. The other one is there too, for I kicked it in when I knocked out your poor assistant.' Saying which, he threw the horse-pistol after its fellow.

'And now,' went on Syn, 'when you have let us see the lining of your friend's pockets, you may carry him until we lose sight of you. Come, Pedro, leave the saddles at the side of the road, and tie these reins to the back of our carriage.'

'My mate has nothing,' said the man. 'I always kept the swag.'

'Don't throw our saddles in the ditch, sir,' pleaded the highwayman.

'They'll fetch a little in the market.'

'We'll leave them by the roadside,' allowed Syn. 'You can return for them when we have gone. I will take your word for your fellow's pockets. You have delayed me too long. Pick him up, for I see he is reviving.' As the one helped the other to his feet, Doctor Syn added, 'And in future do not take a preacher's weakness for granted. I once knocked out a real highwayman, and he was a brave man and a fighter. The Road is not for you, my friends. You will only find a scaffold at the end of it. Now turn your backs and keep walking.' It was so woeful a sight to see them trying to hurry away, that Syn burst out laughing as he climbed on to the box seat with Pedro, who by now regarded Doctor Syn as the greatest hero.

As they clattered through Shrewsbury, they saw a post chaise waiting for fresh horses, and conjectured that it must be Jones. It was therefore not safe to change their own horses there for those they had taken from the highwaymen, as Doctor Syn did not wish Pedro to see him meeting Jones on any friendly footing. So on they went, planning to pull up well out of the town. The change over did not take long, for the horses were used to harness, and with their own pair trotting at the back the made good progress. Soon they were among the grandeur of the Welsh passes, and the inns became fewer and far between; but inns did not worry Doctor Syn as far as meals were concerned, or sleeping. All he wanted was more cold food for their hamper, more wine, fodder and grooming, and hot water for his own shaving. When Pedro heard him deploring the fact that Mipps was not available for this duty, he diffidently pointed out that he was a good hand with the razor, since he had been barber to Dolgenny for years. He was, moreover, as good as his word and the doctor was delighted, but wondered how safe his throat would be did Pedro know he had been deceived into thinking that the doctor was Dolgenny's friend instead of his worst enemy. Somehow the doctor felt that, with Pedro, he was becoming a little more important than his rightful master.

When at last Snowdon was left behind them, Pedro admitted to the doctor that he regretted that their journey was drawing to its close. He had enjoyed it and was happier serving him than his master, who was ill-tempered with servants and boastful. 'Had he dealt as you did with those robbers, he would never cease boasting of it, and the number of the robbers would increase with each telling. Besides, though Spain is not safe for me through my own faults, I love to speak the native tongue again, and your Spanish is so good.'

'Perhaps one day you will leave your master's service and let me find you work to do.' A remark which filled Pedro with delight.

And then at last Tremadoc Bay, and Doctor Syn saw for the first time in his life the mighty amphitheatre of mountain-tops, and down below, the yellow sands that are covered every tide. He pointed out the long grey stone house called Bron y Garth, and the gap on the edge of the precipice from which the Breast Rock had fallen. Although Pedro confessed that he directed the men how to heave the rock over, Doctor Syn was glad to find that they took the escapade for a piece of spite. There was no one on the rock, of course, when it was levered over, and since Dolgenny had ordered them to lie on their faces in the long grass till they were needed, they had actually seen no one but him. When they heard later of the lawyer's death, they thought it must be that he had walked upon the beach below and so had been crushed by the falling rock.

'And this, Se—or, is the neck of Port Merion. I must ring for the gates to be opened. Without Pedro you could not get those doors very wide.'

Pedro jumped down from the box seat, and persuaded Doctor Syn to sit inside the carriage for his entrance.

At last a grill was opened and Pedro shouted abuse in Spanish at the man's face behind it, which continued to stare. Pedro in desperation turned to Doctor Syn. 'He expects my master and does not know who you are. Speak to him in strong Spanish, Se—or. Tell him you are here instead of the master.' Doctor Syn stepped out of the carriage and addressed the grill.

'If you do not open these doors immediately,' he said in Spanish, 'I shall use the privilege which this ring of your master's gives me and have you flayed alive, you miserable blinking owl!' After a good deal of shouting on the other side, the doors were pulled open wide and Pedro drove the doctor into Dolgenny's closed land. Lashing the gatekeepers with his whip, Pedro drove fast, in and out of cleared bridle-paths floored with moss and flanked with impenetrable woods. At last they came into a stately avenue, and the castle came into view. Around it was the oddest collection of Spanish-looking houses, which straggled down the hillside to the sea and quayside. The inhabitants stood in knots and gaped at the strange guest whom Pedro had brought. Pedro pulled up at the castle doors and shouted for the ostlers, though they were waiting in readiness.

'Take your master's horses to the stables and see to them well!' he cried.

'They have served us well, eh, Se—or?'

'Indeed yes,' nodded Syn. 'And give equal care to the horses at the back there, for they belong to the good Pedro. We took them from some highwaymen. How many were there, Pedro?' and Doctor Syn looked sly. 'A dozen of the rascals,' replied Pedro unblushingly, 'but only two mounted, or we would have taken more horses, yes?'

'Carry my case in for me, Pedro, as I have something in it I must show to Garcia,' and Doctor Syn threw back his cloak so that all could see his sword.

Pedro led him into the great dining-hall, and placed the valise he had shouldered on the end of a heavy oak table, which ran down the centre of the room. He then shouted for food, drink and for Garcia, whom Syn found to be a great sullen giant. His looks, however, were worse than his bite, for since the wine was served at once, Doctor Syn handed the goblet which Pedro had poured out for him to the fellow and ordered him to drink. 'Drink to me, my good Garcia, for we shall be well acquainted. I am the new chaplain and overseer to your master, my friend Tarroc Dolgenny, God bless him for a jovial rogue! Your master is now on urgent and dangerous business, and we must work for him with a will. The girl Ann Sudden is safe, I trust? Good! But she'll be safer as the wife of Dolgenny. See this paper? Can you read?' Garcia nodded, and said, 'Si, Se—or.'

'Can you read English?' rapped out Syn. Again he nodded.

Syn showed him a Marriage Certificate, with the names Tarroc Dolgenny and Ann Sudden written in pencil. 'She will sign that in ink within the next few hours. Oh believe me, Garcia, I get things done. Ask Pedro! Give me some wine, Pedro, and help yourself. No, we'll eat nothing till I have got the work started, for your master

wants all in readiness when he gets to us. We'll see this chit of a
girl presently, but first to put the jewelled cross into safety.' He
unwrapped the cross and flashed the stones in the light. 'On the
authority of this ring, which of course you recognize as your
master's signet, I was told to see this invaluable relic stored in your
master's treasury. Are the keys of it on your chain there? I
promised to see this locked away directly I arrived. Take one more
glass of wine and then lead the way. Pedro will come too.' A few
minutes later Garcia led the way down a stone stairway cut out of
the solid slate, and so through a series of vaults used for storage.
These vaults were lighted by glazed windows, but in the last of
them Garcia lit a lantern and went down a broad flight of winding
steps at the bottom of which he unlocked a door. He signed for
Doctor Syn to enter, and, when Pedro had followed, Garcia locked
the door again. The place was actually a wine cellar, but there were
no bottles in the bins, only strong chests and iron boxes. Garcia
explained that this was his master's wealth. 'Jewels and gold,
Se—or! Each chest worth much! My master turns his profits into
real value. He does not trust banks. Jewels and gold!'

'Dolgenny has sense,' replied Syn. 'And now explain to me how
we move all this or part of it in order to get it away should the
castle be searched. I must tell you the truth, Garcia. Your master
is in grave danger of the law, and we shall have to be in readiness
to get him abroad and his wealth with him. Now that door there?'

'It is of iron,' explained the guide. 'But it does not open. This is
the door.' He seized the side of one of the bins and put his weight
against it. It swung slowly from the wall and disclosed another iron
door behind it. 'We unlock that and we walk through deserted
mines. Besides my master, only Pedro and myself can find the way,
though our men use it under our escort. It leads out to the Black
Rock Caves, some two miles along the northern beach.'

'Is there a safe hiding place the other end?' asked Syn.

'People who did not know would never find the mouth of the
passage from the caves. The door is of the solid rock which
opens—when you know how.'

'Tonight, or tomorrow, Garcia, an armed cutter will anchor off
the coast there. Your master has purchased her for the purpose.
How much of this he'll be able to ship I hardly know. He thought
all. Well, perhaps. We will be on the safe side. Let your men move
it all to the other end. I am rich too, Garcia, and though a parson,
I see no harm in cheating the revenue. Dolgenny says I am cleverer
than he because he never thought of being a parson whom no one

suspects. I will give you fifty guineas, Garcia, to encourage the men to work with a will. The crew is engaged to bring the cutter here, but you and Pedro and what others he wants will sail with us. The wedding festivities will be held aboard. We are going to Spain for a spell, Garcia. I have a secret retreat there where your master will be safe. A lovely spot, Garcia.'

'Ah, I thought your honour must be Spanish, the way you speak our tongue,' said Garcia. 'But for me, though I love Spain like Pedro, I should have to lie very low.'

'No one shall find you, Garcia, never fear. Besides, your master and I are planning a voyage to the West Indies. We can make more money there than in this old world. But I must visit your prisoner and then eat. But get your men to shift these chests. If plans are changed they can come back again.'

'Give me that fifty guineas, and the men will have it over there immediately.'

Doctor Syn brought the purse he had taken from the highwaymen, and counted out twenty-five spade guineas. 'Half to start work; the other half when finished, Garcia.' The man pocketed the coins with obvious delight, and to show his zeal he gave Pedro the key of the prisoner's room.

As Doctor Syn entered, Pedro had locked the door again and mounted guard outside. Ann Sudden rose from the rough stool she had been sitting on and asked the doctor who he was.

'You have never heard of Doctor Syn?' he laughed. 'Why, my dear young lady, I stand in the way of your uncle's fortune. I am afraid I am very strong.'

'Then you are my enemy too?' she asked. 'Or are you too captured by this Dolgenny?'

'My dear young lady, I cannot talk in this dreadful room,' said Syn, looking round. 'I will get Pedro to open the shutters. I see they are padlocked. Why, I can hardly see your face and since I have brought you documents to read, we must have light. Still, perhaps you had better let me see first that you deserve more comfort than all this. To be quite frank, my dear young lady, I am going to be the priest who marries you. I have the certificate here. In fact I have pencilled in where the happy pair will sign. Look, the sun through the hole in the shutter there will show you. Will you sign this willingly when the time comes?'

'Tarroc Dolgenny! Ann Sudden!' she read, and answered vehemently, 'Never!'

'Well, well, well,' sighed Doctor Syn. 'If you won't willingly, then

I dare say force can be brought to bear. Here's another one. It's the same sort of thing with a slight difference. You'd better read it.'

'It is quite useless. I refuse.'

Doctor Syn grunted. 'Your uncle said you were obstinate. I can make you sign this paper. You would not dare to refuse.'

'Has it then some threat? Is my other uncle's life to be sacrificed? Even then I cannot marry, I will not!'

'Oh, but you can and you will,' said Doctor Syn, for the first time allowing a hint of evil to creep into his voice. 'Read what you are threatened with,' and he held out the second document.

The girl took the paper in open dread, and Syn turned away as though to examine the room. A moment later he heard her gasp behind him in surprise, then he saw her arms come round his neck.

'My dear young lady! Miss Ann! Please!' he expostulated. 'You can't marry me, you know.'

'Why did you write Henry Thane?' she asked.

'Well, Miss Ann, I guessed he would not have been christened Harry, so I wrote Henry. It's usual. And I showed you the paper because I thought you might know where I could find him, for I believe he has no idea that I am going to marry you both tomorrow.'But how? And why are you so kind to me? I don't understand.'

'Leave it to me, Miss Ann,' said Doctor Syn, giving her shoulders a friendly pat. 'By my calculations Dolgenny cannot reach here till tomorrow, if then. I stole his horses, borrowed his signet ring, which seems to be working wonders, and have the good opinion of Pedro. Your attitude must be that I have persuaded you to think better of the marriage, and you needn't say which one, and that you are willing to do what I say is for your good. But have no fear of Dolgenny. By tomorrow I shall have a warrant for his arrest.'

'But how?'

'Miss Ann, I shall be able, please God, to prove what I know—that he murdered your uncle; that he plans to murder your other uncle and guardian, and then he'll try to murder me. On the other hand, he may try to murder me before your guardian. It all depends. But I shall know.' He told her briefly what had happened, though carefully concealing his plot to rob the treasury, for after all, he told himself, Ann's lover was a customs officer.

When he left her behind locked doors again, Doctor Syn asked Pedro to take him to the top of the castle tower, as he wanted to locate the Black Rock Caves.

As they reached the summit, Pedro remarked that the morning was clear and the Black Rock would not be hidden in mist. He pointed from the ramparts.

'That little ship there, riding at anchor, is opposite the Caves. There is the Black Rock.'

'It is the cutter, thank God!' muttered Syn.

'You will not think it impertinent if I tell you something for your good?' asked Pedro.

'No, my good Pedro, tell me,' answered Syn with a smile. Indeed, he felt now entirely happy because Mipps and his merry men were standing by offshore.

'It is, se—or, a waste of time to pretend,' said Pedro. 'When did we waste it on our race to Wales?'

'I think only with the highwaymen,' laughed Syn. 'But that did us more good than it did them.'

'I was thinking how you wasted one quarter of an hour, because you did not trust Pedro. I followed you, and saw you watching by the castle wall. I too saw my old master throw the bottles from the window. I told myself then that I would leave his service if I found another gentleman to serve. Our journey together has shown me that you are that gentleman, and I trust your honour thinks that I am your man?'

'Pedro, I do, and welcome!' exclaimed the doctor, delighted. 'I have many men to whom I give employment, but two of them I know would give their lives for me, as I would give mine for them. I add you, Pedro, to that list.'

'Then, since I guessed that you are in reality an enemy to Tarroc Dolgenny, I take it also that the ship out yonder is yours, not his?' Syn nodded. 'But we must let Garcia and his men think she is Dolgenny's.

To that end you and I will go aboard her at once. We then will take the poor girl away from here, on the plea that Dolgenny wants her aboard ready to sail.' As Pedro pulled Doctor Syn down river in a small fishing-boat and the doctor was getting ready to hoist sail as soon as they reached the headland, they noticed another small boat ahead of them. Pedro recognized her as customs, and on the doctor inquiring whether it would be Mr. Harry Thane managing her, Pedro said, 'Of course! He is alone the customs in these parts, and has no regular men to work with him. A lonely and dangerous business for so young a man!'

'I think that Mr. Thane will be finding a more prosperous, more delightful life tomorrow,' laughed Syn. This is a fortunate meeting we will have, and will save me time looking for him.' On reaching the deck of the cutter, Doctor Syn, who much to the admiration of Pedro had gone up the rope ladder in true sailor fashion, was much amused to see Mipps coming up from below as escort to the customs officer.

'Well, Admiral, didn't I tell you as how there was nothing in any of your line of goods?' said Mipps. 'What's the good of smuggling wines and spirits, just to be taken and drunk by the revenue men? No, there's no money in smuggling, Mister.'

'Which shows you know very little about it,' returned the officer. 'I knows nothing at all about it, so there,' retorted Mipps.

'But although I grant that your papers are all in order,' went on the officer, 'you seem to have no notion of what you are doing here or why you came.'

'Seem?' repeated Mipps. 'I tell you I have no notion. All I know is that we're here, because one always is here and can't be there.' Doctor Syn thought that it was time he made his presence known, so, coming forward with a cheery, 'Well Mipps, welcome to Wales! Crew all fit? Ah, Jimmie, glad to shake you by the hand!' (This to Mr. Bone, acting as mate under Mipps.) 'And you, sir,' he went on, addressing the good-looking customs man, 'I know to be Mr. Thane. Will you favour me with a short private conversation in the cabin?'

'I shall be glad to know, sir, why this vessel is anchored off the Black Rock,' began the officer as soon as the door was fastened. 'I should also be glad to know whether she has anything to do with one Tarroc Dolgenny.'

'Your first question, sir, is easy to answer. Although a parson, I am part owner in the little ship, and she is here to smuggle. Oh, nothing dutiable; just a girl, sir! I am to perform the marriage ceremony over her. I expect to receive her on board today.'

'Oh, you do, eh? May I ask the name of this lady?'

'Oh yes,' said Doctor Syn, 'and there was something about one Dolgenny.

Here, young sir, I will show you the document which I had drawn up,' and he handed him the certificate with the names in pencil.

The young man trembled with rage as he read. 'And you, sir!' he cried angrily, 'a servant of God by your clothes, yet willing to help a scoundrel to the purest, sweetest girl, who loathes the mere suggestion of the marriage.'

'Excuse me, sir,' corrected Doctor Syn, 'but when I left the lady an hour ago, she was so overjoyed at my helping her to a quick marriage that she threw her arms around my neck, to my embarrassment.'

'Then Dolgenny has brought her back from London, eh?'

'He never took her there, sir,' replied the Doctor. 'She has been imprisoned since the evening of the accident, and no doubt expected you to rescue her from the castle. Women are creature of whims. The least thing will make them change their minds. For instance, where nothing would persuade her to sign the paper in your hand, she is perfectly happy to sign this. Same thing, too, though worded a trifle differently. Look for yourself, Henry Thane.'

'But this has my name instead of his!' he cried. 'What does it mean?'

'It means that, in spite of your failure to rescue her, she yet prefers you. It means that where you failed because you believed the first lies you were told, I have succeeded. It means that I am an old fool of a match-maker. It means also that you are a prisoner upon this ship, in my charge till you leave her later under escort. In short, you will remain hidden in this cabin until Miss Ann comes here and marries you. Then you can take her or she can take you to Bron y Garth, where you can escape the attentions of Dolgenny on his return.'

'I shall not hide from him. I want to meet him face to face.'

'My dear young man, you will own that I am doing a good deal for you,' said Doctor Syn. 'You will therefore respect my demand to deal with Dolgenny in my own way, and without any interference.' Leaving the young man in the cabin to his own reflections, Doctor Syn found Pedro awaiting his orders on deck. These orders were to return to the peninsula, take Ann Sudden aboard, as well as Doctor Syn's baggage, and return to the cutter as soon as possible. Pedro affirmed that he could accomplish all this alone, but Doctor Syn thought it safer to go as well, in case by some unlucky miracle Dolgenny might return, in which case he would have to quarrel with him and kill him. But Dolgenny had not returned, neither had the servants had news of him. Garcia, however, was informed that the chests were to be transferred from the caves to the cutter that very night, as soon as dark. They had all been moved from the treasury already, and when Doctor Syn praised Garcia for his speed, Pedro informed him that there was a trolly rail along which the men could pull the loaded trucks with ease.

Ann was released without any questions asked by Garcia, who was glad to be rid of his responsibility, and considered that the ship was the best place for her.

The same afternoon the little Welsh lawyer, who had been delayed by lack of money stolen by the highwayman, came driving up to Bron y Garth. The servants were surprised not to see Miss Ann with him, for they had been told by a note from Dolgenny that she had asked him to escort her to join her uncle.

Jones rated them soundly for believing such lies, and determined there and then to force an entry into Dolgenny's land. With this object in mind he trotted off down the hill to Borth y Gest beach to borrow a boat. What was his joy, however, when round the bend of the headland he saw the customs boat, and determined in spite of former prejudice to enlist the help of Harry Thane. And then he saw her standing up and waving, steadying herself on the shoulder of Doctor Syn, who, as soon as the boat beached, cried out, 'Jones, my old companion in misfortune, let me be the first to introduce you to your nephew by marriage.' That night the grand old house, which had been so overclouded since the tragedy and Miss Ann's departure, once more came to life. Pedro and Mipps, who had already struck up a friendship, much to Doctor Syn's satisfaction, kept the servants' hall in fits of laughter, when they returned from the cutter at about half-past-eleven. They were allotted rooms for the night so that they could act as a bodyguard, should an enraged Dolgenny attempt any harm on his arrival.

There was a good deal of laughter against the lawyer when Doctor Syn returned his watch and ring, and the bag of money retaken from the highwaymen.

When, finally, Mipps brought a hot drink to his master's bedside, he was able to whisper the good news that every chest and box had been safely packed in the cutter's holds, and that Garcia was sleeping on one hatch and Jimmie Bone upon the other. The brass cannon were loaded and pointing towards the peninsula. Syn went to sleep with pleasant thoughts.

The next day the bridal pair announced that they were going to postpone any idea of honeymoon till after Dolgenny's return.

Dolgenny returned the following morning, in a black temper. From Dymchurch to North Wales the journey had been more than uncomfortable. In place of his own carriage he had to make the stages as best he could. With no Pedro to bully, his temper had not had full outlet, until he arrived and found no Pedro and no Garcia to bear the brunt of it. The other servants, foreigners who had got into trouble in their own land and now hiding in Dolgenny's, were fearful of being turned adrift, for though the pay for service was poor, yet there was always abundance of good food and wine. Therefore, while Dolgenny raged, their chief idea was to get away, and leave the explaining to others.

Dolgenny, therefore, could get very little satisfaction out of any except Pedro and Garcia, and these two had been in mental revolt for some time. But where these two were no one knew, or rather perhaps no one dared to say. The next person to vent his rage against was obviously his prisoner and wife to be. He hurried to her room. There was no one on guard outside as he had ordered before leaving her, but the key was in the outside lock, and this he turned. One glance showed him that the bird had flown. From the servants he learned that the tall parson in black, who wore a long sword and cloak and ordered everyone about, had taken Miss Ann out to a small ship that was anchored off the Black Rock.

He could get there quicker by horseback, but he found that the tide was up, and so had to go by boat instead. The boat he always used for crossing the estuary was the very one which Doctor Syn had borrowed and had not returned.

Everything seemed going wrong just as it had on the road. Well, he had done the journey at high speed in spite of the discomforts and delays. He had left his baggage for the mail from Shrewsbury and had ridden the passes post-horse.

But where was Ann? Where Doctor Syn? Would they be on this ship, whatever it might be, or would they go naturally to Bron y Garth for Jones to go over his brother's possessions and papers? He might go to the house first and find out. Had Doctor Syn retrieved the cane and found the snuff-box? He found a suitable boat and pushed off. Then, hoisting the sail, he steered for the beach of the tragedy.

In the dusk he saw the long figure of Doctor Syn swinging his way from crack to crack by a rope. He could make out his white shirt-sleeves and his black waistcoat and breeches against the grey slate. He was climbing down now slowly, searching the fissures of slate, obviously searching for the snuff-box.

Dolgenny hated Syn at that moment because, although so much older than he was, the parson was performing a feat which made him sick to look at or think about. The sight of the rope's end swinging not halfway down the precipice, and the parson quietly searching, when a slip meant certain death, fascinated him.

Dolgenny steered for the next little bay, secured the boat, then climbed the hill path to the terrace. Suddenly he realized why Doctor Syn did not mind heights. It was the sailor in him. The fellow had confessed he was a damned pirate.

He reached the place where the old rock had once been, and saw just beyond it the marrow bed, and his cane lying against it. Doctor Syn must have found it and had not attempted to hide it again. That meant that he had no intention of keeping faith with him.

Then a voice seemed to moan from the waters in the estuary, 'Would you keep faith with him?' Dolgenny shuddered and knew that he would not. Then he heard his name called—'Tarroc Dolgenny!' He turned towards the house, and at the open window of the library he saw Ann standing and beckoning to him. She was dressed in white, and again Dolgenny shuddered, but he pulled himself together and tried to assume his favourite attitude of superiority. He heard a creaking noise behind him. It was only the rope bearing Doctor Syn's weight. The rope was noosed over a cut tree-trunk stump. If that rope were to snap while it vibrated through the climbing, it meant certain death for the parson.

He had walked on while thinking of the rope, and was now close to Ann.

'You ran away? You were unhappy?'

'Of course I was, and very uncomfortable! The food was ill-cooked, the room was dark and dank for lack of air. Only the wine was good, and I had too little of that. And no clothes to change into! And nothing to read! And no flowers!'

'I wished to give you all those things when I came back. Well, I can now make amends. I have made a lot of money away, at cards. You shall have your share, directly we are married.'

'I have been wining, too,' said Ann. 'To make up for my misery in your house, I think. Come in, Tarroc Dolgenny, and I will show you.' He stepped through the open window, and she beckoned him towards the lighted candelabrum, and handed him the certificate of marriage.

Dolgenny read it and looked pleased. 'My name and yours in pencil. Ann, when shall we ink these over?'

'Show me,' she said, puzzled. Glancing at the paper, she moved to the door leading into the great hall, and called:

'Harry, you gave me the wrong paper.'

'So I did! Sorry, my lamb! Here!' To Dolgenny's disgust he saw Harry Thane come into the library and give her another document. This she did not pass to Dolgenny, but held it out firmly for him to read.

'So? You are married, eh? To a customs man? You poor child!

And all signed and made legal by the Reverend Doctor Syn! Very well! I shall have more to say about this. Good evening!'

'Come, Dolgenny, be a gambler in life as you are in the cards. Own you have lost! Say you are beaten and earn folk's respect.' Dolgenny sneered at the young man, and replied, 'I have not lost. I have not been beaten, and you will own this when you know what I know.' He swung round and stepped into the garden from the window, and was gone. He could still hear the rope creaking, and in the gathering darkness he could still see the rope trembling. He chuckled aloud as he remembered that when he took horse from Shrewsbury, he had travelled light, and only put his pistol, his money, and his razor in his pocket. Running swiftly along the terrace, his hand closed upon the razor. He was there. The razor was sharp. The vibrating rope was taut. A sawing noise; a hard press and cut; a snap, and the wild end of the severed rope streaking off through the rough grass and scrub, lash and then over. Dolgenny put his razor back in his pocket, and then lifted the noose of rope off the tree stump. He must destroy this, lest the evidence of the cut rope put a noose about his neck. Then he walked away towards the dark and rocky entrance of the descending path that went steeply down to the beach.

He had all but reached it, when he heard his name called in a deep voice.

'TARROC DOLGENNY!' He turned sharply. There to his horror he saw standing by the tree stump the man he thought he had murdered. The full moon which had just arisen shone clearly upon Doctor Syn, no longer in shirt sleeves, but wearing his long elegant parson's coat. The moonlight lit up his long pale face, and his eyes were hard and vivid. In his hand he held his sword, drawn. Dolgenny with a cry dropped the noose, and drew his own long sword. But at that instant his wrists were seized from behind him, the muzzle of a pistol was pressed into his side, and a hard voice said, 'Drop that!' He turned and found himself held in a firm grip by Mipps and his sometime servant, Pedro. Dolgenny's sword clattered to the paved ground of the terrace.

'I am no ghost,' said Doctor Syn. 'You thought to have killed me, but you have given me the Tontine. I might thank you for that, but I do not. I am no cold-blooded murderer, as you. Like Clegg, I would never murder; I would only execute.'

'You were on the rope,' stammered Dolgenny. 'I saw you.'

'Ann's uncle and guardian took my place but a few minutes ago. It was getting dark, and he knew the face of the precipice better than I did. He was carrying on the search for the snuff-box. He had no fear, being a mountain-born man. You are now the murderer of both brothers. Pedro, pick up that noose, and draw it round his throat. If he struggles you may jerk it, but if he is wise he will not struggle, for I am giving him a fighting death, 'sword to sword.' Pedro first untied Dolgenny's cravat, and pulled it from his throat. He then adjusted the noose, the end hanging behind his back. With Mipps holding the pistol, Dolgenny had to suffer the indignity of having his wrists tied behind him with the cravat. Then Pedro seized the end of the rope.

'Bring him into the house,' ordered Doctor Syn.

In the presence of Ann and Harry Thane, Doctor Syn told what had happened. Dolgenny was placed in a chair, with Syn and Mipps guarding him, while Thane and Pedro were sent down to the beach to recover the body of the lawyer, before the tide was at the full. Ann was ordered to go to the servants and wait, while in silence the murderer and his captors waited for the body, which was very soon carried into the room, and laid reverently upon the long oak table.

'We found this in his hand, clutched tightly,' said Thane, holding out the gold snuff-box.

Then Syn spoke.

'Mr. Thane, you will remain here, while we go to the place of execution.

We are going up the mountain behind Bron y Garth to the spot called the Ledge of Moel y Gest. It is, so Ann tells me, a large counterpart of your fatal Breast Rock. On that summit we shall stand face to face. I have something to show Dolgenny from that height. Then we shall cross swords upon that platform of rock.' Guarded by Mipps and Pedro and followed by Syn, Dolgenny was escorted from the house, Mipps carrying the latter's sword.

'It will take them a good hour to reach the Ledge,' said Thane to Ann and the servants, who, grouped upon the terrace, looked up at the mighty mountain bathed in moonlight.

At last they saw the four figures silhouetted against the sky. 'Have no fear,' whispered Thane. 'The doctor is a good man. He will win.' They saw a flash, and then from the anchored cutter a flash answered and in the still night they heard a distant cheering.

The flash was a signal given by Mipps, but the watchers below could not hear Syn telling Dolgenny that in her holds were stored his ill-gotten treasurechests, and that the cutter was now bound to the Scarecrow's retreat on the French coast.

All they could see was the moonlight dancing on two blades of liquid steel.

Now to the edge, now back towards the rock wall the clear-cut black figures moved. At last Syn drove the massive figure towards the edge. Dolgenny was fighting on the brink. They saw his arm go up to his head, as though in panic; then it dropped to his side. The moon played for a second upon the steel barrel of a pistol, then a flash of fire spurted from the little figure of Mipps.

Dolgenny's pistol flashed a split second later. Syn's blade leapt forward at Dolgenny's throat, and the great body was falling through space.

A minute later and the ledge was empty, and the watchers saw the cutter hoisting white sails.

In the morning Dolgenny's hat was found below the ledge a thousand feet. It rested on a black mountain bog patch. The bog had sucked down the heavy body.

Pedro looked at the bog and crossed himself. 'It is the Devil's Larder,' he said. 'He always dreaded it would get him. It left the estuary and climbed the hillside, master, waiting for him. The many souls he send there dragged him down.'

'Aye, he lived foully,' said Syn, 'and at the end he fouled by drawing his pistol. I am grateful, Mipps, for your quick shooting.'

'Well I'll tell you what pleases me about the fight,' grinned Mipps. 'That you remembered to change signet rings before you crossed swords.'

'Aye, Mipps, I did not want to lose the signet of my fathers.'

Two months later Mr. and Mrs. Harry Thane received a letter from the Edinburgh banker, telling them that, upon the instruction of Doctor Syn, the half of the Tontine fortune was to be paid to them, and trusting that Mr. Thane would now leave the custom work, and become a good squire to his tenants.

Two months later on the same date, a company met in the shuttered study of Dymchurch Vicarage. Doctor Syn, Jimmie Bone, Mipps, Pedro and Garcia.

'Here's to our newly enrolled lieutenants,' said the vicar, 'and you will pass the word that at the next full moon the Scarecrow rides again. With the new ships we have now purchased, we shall show bigger profits than before.' As Syn raised his glass, the others raised theirs, and in a quiet voice and with a mischievous smile spreading over his face he sang the old chanty of Captain Clegg:

'Oh, here's to the feet what have walked the plank; Yo-ho for the Dead Man's Throttle; And here's to the corpses afloat in the Tank,

And the Dead Man's teeth in the bottle.'

Printed in September 2021
by Rotomail Italia S.p.A., Vignate (MI) - Italy